BETS

CARROT QUINN

Copyright © 2024 Carrot Quinn.
All rights reserved.
No part of this book may be used or reproduced in any manner without written consent of the author, with the exception of brief quotations within critical articles and reviews.
Cover design by Alejandra Wilson
Internal design by Euan Monaghan
ISBN: 979-8-3006821-5-6

For all of us
And for the dog(s)

> *Your dress waving in the wind*
> *This*
> *Is the only flag I love*
>
> — GAROUS ABDOLMALEKIAN

CHAPTER 1

BETS

My battery is low and it's getting dark. I pull my phone from my pocket, thinking I'll check the map one last time before it dies. The screen lights up and then goes black, leaving me without direction in an unfamiliar part of the city.

The asphalt is cracked here, clumps of dry yellow grass growing up in spots. On the right are what were once storefronts, now shuttered, decades of graffiti layered on top of itself, illegible. There's a doorway that's missing a door, a pile of trash in the shadows just inside. I don't usually come to this area. While you could say that this whole city is dangerous, there are neighborhoods I've spent my whole life coming to know. When I'm in those neighborhoods I'm not afraid—I'm just home. This is not one of those neighborhoods.

I tap at the button on my phone again. Nothing.

Georgia was supposed to text tonight. I haven't heard from her in a week and I risked this outing tonight for her. We opened up another abandoned apartment building recently; if I can store up some cash, we can move a whole group in to occupy it, and it will become impossible for the city to evict.

My current situation, living in a tent in someone's back yard, had been stable enough. I've been paying the tenants in the run-down adobe house there, squatters themselves, $2400 a month for the privacy and security of camping behind their tall metal fence.

A few days ago we received a notice from the city, a sheet of paper taped to the front door, to the fence, and to all the other crumbling houses nearby—these sheets of paper fluttering in the wind, falling onto the broken sidewalk, what a waste of paper!—that the city means to demolish the entire block in order to build another workhouse for the prison.

If I can get a group of people together to move into this abandoned apartment building, not only will it give me a place to live—behind walls, even!—but I know that Georgia will move in with me too. For years I've dreamt of a place for both of us, and this is the first spark of hope I've had that it might actually be possible.

Still I wish that Georgia would text, to settle my nerves. Her absence aches, a pain I feel in my bones. How many times has she disappeared like this? The pain never lessens, the panic that wakes me at night, sends my mind cartwheeling. If we had a place together, maybe she wouldn't want to leave so much. If we had a place together, maybe she would stay.

I tap the phone again and then give up, slipping it back into my pocket and peering ahead at the darkening street. It's quiet, but I know that somewhere in these buildings are people, a family here and there that's managed to make a small, protected world—a labyrinth of flaking hallways and a series of locked doors that lead to a spray of bougainvillea in a walled garden, a grandmother hanging laundry to dry, an old man frying cricket gruel patties, maybe even a child.

There's a soft thump as an orange cat drops from a windowsill and saunters past. I think about the client I'm about to see; I've met with him before, and the vibe wasn't great. Normally I don't see anyone a second time if the vibe isn't perfect. My situation right now is much more urgent than I would like it to be.

At the intersection I squint, trying to make out the name of the street in the gloaming. There aren't any streetlights—streetlights break over time and things don't really get repaired anymore so the city has been in a long, slow slide towards darkness. I think this is the right street though? I hang a right and a few houses up there's the green door, right where he said it would be. This isn't where I met this client last time—I wonder if this is where he lives, or if he just rented the apartment to meet up.

I contemplate the green door for a time. Has Georgia ever told me that she loves me? No. Sometimes I think I wouldn't be so anxious if she did. But really, for me to not be anxious, Georgia would have to become an entirely different person. And if Georgia was a different person I probably wouldn't love her so much.

As I touch the door and think about knocking, I try to pull Georgia out of my head—but she's everywhere, like when you cut through a brush-filled alley in the morning and get covered in cobwebs. It's just... it's the way she makes me feel when I'm with her. Or rather, it's the way I *don't* feel when I'm with her—empty, lonely no matter how many people I'm around. She makes those feelings go away, and I'm whole.

Shut up! I hiss to myself. Focus!

The door opens a crack and I startle. A man peers out.

"You're not the girl I remember," he says. He's dressed like anyone you might see on the street, hustling to one of the workhouses before the sun comes up—faded shirt, the buttons at the neck undone, wrinkled pants stretched at the knees, a patchy beard. But you can tell that he's rich—the skin of his face is smooth and his posture is straight, as though he's spent his whole life looking up instead of down.

"It's me," I say, tugging down the hood of my jacket and pulling my long hair loose. He looks me up and down and swings the door wide. There's a lamp without a shade that throws a harsh light on one side of the room, the rest is cast in shadow. A mattress on a metal frame sits in the middle of the room, made up with worn sheets and a couple of fleece blankets, a few lumpy pillows. Chunks of plaster are missing near the ceiling, exposing cinderblocks. On the scratched dresser top is a small stack of bills, which I palm and fold into my pocket.

The man is staring at me, wordless. I prefer them more talkative, rambling even, but I can handle this. Unbuttoning my long jacket, I let it fall onto the bed. I'm wearing lingerie, one of two sets I own—this set is blue.

I feel powerful in this, I like the way the many straps make geometry of the planes of my body, the way my skin glows in the lamplight.

The man says nothing, just continues to stare. That's ok. I refuse to be unnerved by him. I cross the room, hold his gaze while I trace my fingers along the leg of his work slacks. He smells like cigarettes and laundry soap. The button on his pants comes undone easily, the zipper too, I tug them down and drop to my knees.

"No. The bed," he says, motioning.

"Ok," I say as I shimmy out of my thong. I'm bored already, I want this to be over. Sex work is one sure way to make an hour feel like eternity. While he fucks me, I'll think about the apartment that Georgia and I will share one day. The little garden we'll plant in an abandoned lot nearby. The basil and small tomatoes, still warm from the sun, that I'll gather for our meals.

Suddenly I realize I'm hungry. I should've eaten dinner before this. In a few minutes he'll be done, and I'll have to find a way to make the rest of the hour pass. Usually they're chatterboxes, thrilled to talk while I listen, and all I have to do is smile and nod. What to do with a guy who doesn't speak?

Suddenly his hands are around my throat and he's on top of me, pressing me into the bed with his entire weight. He's not fucking me, his clothes aren't even off. He's staring at me with an empty, fixed gaze as he tightens his grip. For a moment I forget where I am. How did I get here? I try to push him off; I hit him with my closed fists but he doesn't budge, he doesn't even blink or break eye contact.

Sounds in the room begin to move farther away, spots appear at the corners of my vision. Good god, this is not the way I want to die. I grope the blankets of the bed and find my jacket. Fumbling with it in my dazed state, I find my knife in the inside pocket and work it free from its sheath with one hand, then drive it into his neck, all the way to the hilt.

His hands move off my neck, and onto his own. Warm blood sprays me in the face. The look in his eyes shifts—from vacancy to terror. He rolls off me, making terrible shapes with his mouth, and I scramble out of the bed and try to stand up, but fall onto the floor. I wait for the sound to come back, for the spots in my vision to retreat.

When the world returns, it's still; there's no movement in the room. I close my eyes and see the sunrise on the rooftop where Georgia and I sleep sometimes, long yellow light slipping over the city. Georgia beside me, dusty quilt wrapped around her body, one leg kicked out in spite of the mosquitoes. I open my eyes to see the sticky red handprints on the floor. Oh.

I've got to think. The man's body is a jumble between the bed and the wall. Fuck.

Find his money. It's not my everyday mind talking, the one that heats corn gruel for Georgia's breakfast and seasons it with figs dried in the sun, folds our blankets and stashes them neatly in the stairwell. It's not the me who makes bouquets from the flowers that grow wild in the empty lots and knows all the dusty street cats.

It's a different mind. My survival mind. That clever, agile part that developed in me when I was a child, living in the sedan with Mother, sleeping on the cracked pleather of the backseat while the rain drummed on the metal roof and then later, on my own, wrenching parts in the junkyard to earn my keep. *Find his money. He doesn't need it now. And you do.*

Where would the money be, though? The room is empty, save for a suit jacket on a single hanger in the shallow closet. I pull open the dresser drawers—empty, empty, empty and then bingo—a black backpack in the bottom drawer. Inside are manilla file folders, stuffed with papers. Maybe his wallet is in his pants pocket? I don't want to touch the body, though. I would pay money *not* to have to touch the body.

As I rifle through the papers, the adrenaline begins wearing off and a shadowy presence seems to lurk in the corners of the room. I should get going soon. There's a document with a photo on it. It's a photo of the man, taken from the front. He's standing against a wall, unsmiling. It's some sort of identification document. For his work maybe? *Feldspar Corporation,* says the text at the top of the document. So this man works in the offices of the corporation that owns all of the prisons. He's one of many cogs in a huge, lumbering machine. Or rather, he *was*.

"Sorry dude," I say under my breath. "You shouldn't have tried to kill me." The document says that his name is Proteus Feldspar. I laugh. What a weird coincidence. There's another Proteus Feldspar—the black sheep of the Feldspar family. One of four Feldspar brothers, heirs to the family empire. But he's the brother who's never seen at public events, rarely included in family photos. It's said he disappointed his father when he was younger and so he lives a life apart, on his own. Some people don't believe that he exists at all.

As I study the document more closely, I realize there's an address. It's on Zircon Road. I know that area—the whole place is gated. It's where some of the wealthiest and most powerful people in the city live. *Could this be the real Proteus Feldspar?* If so, why would he come to a sketchy part of town and meet up with me, when he could have some high-class sex worker in his own part of town?

But then, I know why. If you want to murder sex workers, you go after the ones that no one will miss.

Anger rises in me like acid. I crumple the paper and throw it across the room. If the man wasn't already dead, I would kill him a second time.

He's probably the real Proteus Feldspar, then. Stupid evil motherfucker. He wanted to murder sex workers, so I had to kill him, and now *I'm* in trouble.

The shadows in the corners swirl. They're growing impatient. The shadows have known this whole time. The shadows knew when I woke this morning, when I made the decision to meet with this man. The shadows knew my next move before I did. They always do.

Since I haven't yet died in a shower of gunfire, it seems that our dearly departed Proteus came out here alone, without any kind of security. How much time do I have? If he rented this place, his body will be discovered when the housekeeper comes to tidy the room—I imagine a shriek, towels and cleaning products clattering to the floor.

Soon after, his father will know; there will be a manhunt. His fingernails are full of my DNA. His family owns the prisons, but I doubt I'll end up there. I'll just be dead. Deader than dead. No more sunsets with Georgia on the roof, sharing a loaf of stale bread and hearing the crickets come on. Just dead.

The panic is dancing around me in a circle now, holding hands with itself.

Find the money. I take a deep breath and send it down into the center of the earth. I do not feel, I do not have thoughts. It takes all my strength to turn the body over. What is this man made of, cement? I pat down his front, pull the square shape from his pants pocket. Remove the cash. Something glints in the overhead light—it's his wristwatch. Without thinking I unfasten the clasp and pull it free. It's the old style of wristwatch, entirely mechanical—these have been making a comeback among the elite lately, as power grids become less stable and the components that make up more modern tech become harder to find.

The watch is beautiful. The metal is heavy and cool as I slip it onto my own wrist and fasten the clasp. In the bathroom I rinse the blood from my hands, face, neck and chest. My eyes are empty in the mirror, like his were earlier. After knotting the belt of my long jacket I step out into the street, closing the door quietly behind me.

I'm almost to my neighborhood when I see the twirling lights of a cop car and get spooked. In an alleyway I grab the ladder of a fire escape and haul myself up. The metal is cool in my hands. The stairs ring out under my sneakers as I climb. The rooftop is painted white and there's a pool. The edge of the pool is strung in small, twinkling lights. It feels like a scene from an alternate world. I'd like to curl up on one of these lounge chairs and wait until dawn. But through the glowing window of the rooftop apartment I can see a young couple preparing dinner. *I can't hide here.* The fire escape on the other side of the building drops me back down into the street, where I continue moving quickly through the darkness. I run the last mile and a half to my block.

The money I make as a sex worker is the only reason I can afford my spot at all. A few days a week I put on false eyelashes and listen as terrible men boast about the fortunes they've amassed extracting labor from the working class, and then investing this money in ways that further destroy the earth.

These are often ancient men, close to their own deaths, and they are content to take the future with them when they go. They are shallow, lacking in insight, almost unbelievably dim. They consider themselves brilliant because they found a finite thing that had not yet been depleted and they depleted it. They were first at the finishing line in the race to the end of the world.

I tell these men I work cutting hair. They think that I'm respectable. A good girl. They do not know hairdressers make so little these days that they live in the camps in the abandoned lots with everybody else. The camps are free; I often wonder if I should live in the camps too and save my money. Twenty-four hundred dollars a month buys me security though. Here in this backyard, it's unlikely my shit will get stolen. It's unlikely that I'll be robbed in my sleep. For $2,400 a month I am free from that.

My breathing is labored as I stop running and stand on the dark sidewalk. I can't go home right now. I need to talk to someone about this. But who?

Of course where I'd most like to go is to wherever Georgia is. I'd like to run into her arms, let myself sink into her as if into a warm bath. Feel her fingers in my hair, press my face into her dress that smells of rosewater and the warm living animal of her body. The sound of her voice like flowing water, washing my troubles away.

But I can't go to Georgia, and there's only one other person I want to talk to right now. I enter a vast empty lot that has been repurposed as a guerilla garden—rows of corn, tomatoes, wild overgrown flowerbeds. There are trellises and shadecloth everywhere. Crouching low, I make my way among the rows. Now and then the whitewash of headlights moves over me. The light makes a shadow puppet play of tomatoes, their shapes dancing over my jacket and then away. Then darkness again.

The rows grow more ragged and wild as I near the east end of the garden. Beyond this garden is the rubble of a burnt tenement building, scooped into mounds on a stretch of broken concrete sprinkled with glass that glitters in the dark. People have set up tents here among the ruins, having towed their busted trailers onto this lot.

My phone makes a notification noise and I pull it from my pocket—*I thought the battery was dead?* The screen lights up for just a moment—no text—and then dies again. A paranoid thought pops into my head, *Is my phone tracking me?* I'm not sure it's paranoia, though. This phone is *supposed* to be safe—I paid a good deal of money to a tech guy on the black market to remove any tracking software, but the city is always coming up with new tracking software. You have to keep on top of it, which is expensive. Since I've been trying to save money, it's been a few months since I've had my phone checked out. If there is tracking software on this phone, I'm fucked. Now my phone feels warm, as though it's alive. It bleeps again and I suddenly feel very visible, as though there's a glowing target on my head. Fuck.

In the soft darkness at the end of the rubble is a tall chain-link fence, beyond which lies a junkyard. I twist the knob on a combination lock on the fence, pop it open and pull it from the large chain that holds the gate closed. As I enter the shadowy world of busted cars, their rusted bodies hulking in the tall grass, I move slowly until I find the worn path. Its shape is familiar under my feet, and I follow it as it wends through the junked vehicles. There's no movement in the lot but I can feel eyes watching me, can almost make out the whispers. At the end of the junkyard is a wooden shack, its singular window glowing with yellow light. A bit of plywood on cinderblocks serves as a step up to the wooden deck, which creaks under my weight. From within the shack comes music—fiddle tunes.

I rap on the door.

"It's me, Bets," I call out.

"Bets!" says the big man who flings the door wide, a grin splitting his face in two. We hug—he smells of engine grease and butterscotch candies. "I haven't seen you in years!" He holds me at arm's length. "Is it really you?" His words turn into a cough which rattles him, rattles the entire shack, and he releases me.

"Beryl! Are you sick?"

He shakes his head, waves his arm for me to enter the shack, and continues to cough. In the shack is a dirty couch, its cushions smashed in, a colorful quilt thrown over it. A small table is cluttered with papers, yellow receipt books, dog-eared manuals, the stubs of pencils, a calculator. There's a wood cookstove with a kettle on top and a cast iron Dutch oven crusted with the remnants of black beans. A mattress on wooden pallets. The mattress is grey, no sheets, a pile of twisted blankets at the foot like an animal's nest.

There's a bookshelf stuffed with more manuals and on one of the shelves is a tape player—the source of the music—and a shoebox of tapes. I settle into the couch, and it's so familiar to me that I feel my body relaxing, as though I could disappear here, curl up under this merry, filthy quilt and actually sleep.

"I only have unflavored tea to offer you, I'm afraid," says Beryl once he can breathe again. He ladles water from a bucket into the kettle and assembles kindling in the cookstove.

"Hot water is fine," I say, smiling. "You know I've never actually had tea, except the herbal kind my mother gathered."

"That's right," says Beryl. "There's so many things you kids don't miss, because you never had them in the first place. I suppose it's better that way."

"Beryl."

He pauses at stuffing wood into the stove and looks at me.

"I killed someone."

"You did not," he says, turning back to the stove.

"I did. He was strangling me so I shoved my knife into his neck." My consciousness is trying to float out of my body but I grab it like the string of a helium balloon and pull it down, back into me.

"My god," says Beryl. He sits back on his heels and stares into the stove as small flames lick at the wood shavings he's placed atop the kindling. "These things do happen. I just hoped that they would never happen to you."

"It's worse than that," I say. "He was Proteus Feldspar. One of the Feldspar brothers. You know, the black sheep one?"

"How in the hell were you in the same room as one of the Feldspar brothers?" says Beryl, and then he shakes his head. "You know what, don't tell me. I don't want to know."

"I didn't know it was him. And I wouldn't have stabbed him, except to save my life. But now I'm fucked. I can't go home. And you were the only person I could think to come to."

Beryl sighs. He closes the metal door of the cookstove and sits, staring at it for a time. The kettle begins to rock and then whines as it comes to a boil. There's a clean mug overturned on a dishtowel and Beryl plucks it up, pours it full of boiling water.

"Thank you," I say, as Beryl sets the mug on the stained coffee table in front of the couch. Beryl lowers himself onto the couch next to me and I feel the cushions sink under his weight. He folds his swollen, eczema-reddened hands across the big belly of his overalls. The tea is too hot to drink but I hold it close anyway, savoring the warmth.

"If this is true…then you've got to leave the city," says Beryl, finally.

"What? To where? Where will I go?"

Beryl shakes his head. "West. As far west as you can get."

I close my eyes, focusing on the feeling of the steam on my face. I'm on the rooftop with Georgia and this heat is the rising sun. It's midsummer, and in an hour it'll be too hot to be up here. I'm folding our blankets away as Georgia runs her fingers through her hair, plaits it into a long braid.

"I've never been out of the city," I tell him. "It's all I know. And besides, I can't leave Georgia. I don't know where she is right now, I'd have no way to tell her I'm going."

"Yes," says Beryl, sighing. "And if you stay they'll kill you."

I turn the mug of hot water around in my hands. There's a Christmas tree on it. "But the checkpoints. And I don't even have a map. And what's out there? Burnt-out suburbs? A thousand miles of desert? And what about the militias?"

Beryl is looking at me thoughtfully, his eyes wet and rimmed in red.

The skin of his face is pocked and scarred, and he looks about a thousand years old. Has he always been this old?

"You know I always heard," says Beryl, "that the farther you get from the city, the less militias and feds there are. The state doesn't have much resources left. Very little gasoline, ammunition, grid power. It uses what it has in the cities, to police us. The countryside has been totally abandoned. And the militias can't stand to be without their trucks and their guns. You won't have access to much manufactured goods or electricity out there but if you can find a way to scrape out a life, you can be free. I've always heard that there are people out there, doing just that."

"That's insane," I say. "I don't know the first thing about that. I'd definitely die."

"If you stay here you'll die," says Beryl. He pauses for a long moment. "And you know, it's not just me who thinks you should go west." He pushes himself up from the couch slowly. "It's your mother too."

"My mother?" I frown in confusion. My mother's been gone for years. Beryl shuffles past the bed and ducks behind a curtain into a closet, reappearing a few minutes later.

"I've been saving this for you," he says. He hands me an envelope, soft at the corners and smudged with dirt. Inside is a sheet of notebook paper folded into thirds.

Dear Bets,

Once you're grown, come to Nevada where the wild burros are. We can make a life there.

"How long have you had this?" I say, stunned.

"Years. Your mother said not to give it to you until you were grown. I suppose you're grown now. You're what, twenty?"

"But I told you that she disappeared when I was a kid, and you know I've always wondered where she went," I say. "Why didn't you tell me about this letter? All these years without a word from her." My eyes are filling with tears.

"It's dangerous beyond the city," says Beryl. "Like you said. Your mother wanted me to wait to give you this note. I imagine she thought if I gave it to you when you were still just a kid you would try and find her, and you wouldn't make it out there. You're older now, you're more likely to survive."

"How did she get this note to you?"

Beryl shrugs. "The same way everything gets past the checkpoints. I imagine it was smuggled. The guy I get carburetors from, one day he just had it for me."

I cannot speak. Again, I grab the balloon string of my consciousness and yank it down, back into my body.

"I wondered where she was for all these years," I say, so quiet that I'm not sure I've even spoken aloud.

Beryl is silent. Then, a fire grows in my chest, like an engine finally turning over.

"Why didn't she come back for me, then? Why didn't she come back?"

"I imagine it was too dangerous for her to return. What good is she to you if she dies trying to get to you? Better for her to wait in Nevada until you're old enough to make the journey to join her."

"No seriously, if she's been out there waiting for me this whole time, fuck her. Why should I go all the way to Nevada, through the deserts and god knows what, just to find her. Can't you help me Beryl? Please? You must know some other place I can go. Somewhere not as far. You must have connections. I don't want to leave this place that I know. And I can't leave Georgia. She's all I have. She's my whole world."

"I'm sorry peanut. All my connections are junkyard people. And I've never gone outside the city myself. You're tough. I don't know what's out there but it's got to be better than this, and if you can survive this then you can survive that too."

"Do you know where Nevada is, at least? I don't even have a map."

Beryl shakes his head. "What about your buddy Malachite who gets things on the black market, used to find me parts when you lived at the junkyard?"

"If it's so great out beyond the cities, why don't you go there, Beryl?" I'm crying now. "Why have you stayed?"

"I was born in this junkyard, and I mean to die here, Bets."

"You're not gonna die."

"Well. Maybe I don't want to live."

CHAPTER 2

I run out of the junkyard and through the rubble of the last block of the garden, darting around piles of crumbled bricks, then duck through a hole in the fence. The dark of the streets is unbroken at this late hour; the entire city has gone to sleep. My street, when I reach it, is quiet. I punch the code into the gate in the metal wall and enter the backyard where my tent is. There's a note stuck in the zipper—it's from the tenants in the house.

Police were here, they want to talk to you.

And then a scrawled phone number. Damn. That was fast.

Ducking into my tent, I kneel on my sleeping bag, rifling through my things. *How much time do I have?* I don't own very much. There's a suitcase of work things: heels, cheap lingerie, makeup. Then I have a backpack with everything else: a few changes of clothes, a good knife, a small cookstove made out of an aluminum can—which I fill with twigs for fuel—and a metal pot.

And my phone, of course. I need a phone to do sex work safely—to screen clients, to set up appointments. Without one I'd be in danger. Thinking of my phone makes me pull it out instinctively but as I stare at the dead screen, I remember my worries about being tracked and a wave of fear washes over me.

I'll have to leave the phone behind.

No. My fingers close around it more tightly. Fuck! I force myself to drop the dead phone and shove it into the corner of my tent.

Then I think about the note from my mother. I remember nights alone as a child, sleeping on the cracked pleather of the backseat of our sedan while rain fell on the metal roof. A few years later, when I was nine, Mother disappeared. She never returned from her second job, the details of which I did not know, and I was forced to fend for myself, moving into Beryl's junkyard. He took in street children and let them live there in the abandoned vehicles in exchange for spending our days wrenching parts for him. I never heard from my mother again. And now this.

Is she really out there, waiting for me? Or am I just exhausted and afraid, wanting so badly to believe. And yet, if I stay, I die. If I leave, I'll also likely die. But what if I don't die, out there in the lands beyond the city, alone?

I sit on my sleeping bag for a few minutes, letting my thoughts spin. Every so often I reach for my phone again, like I'm reaching for a part of my own body, and then draw my hand back. I can't take the phone with me; it's just not worth the risk. I don't want to get disappeared. It's happened to several people that I know. Every time someone new gets disappeared, I downplay my relationship to them in my head. A *friend* becomes *someone that I know*. I distance myself from them emotionally. Otherwise, the loss would destroy me.

It's time for me to go.

My backpack is small and light, even packed with everything that I need. I leave the suitcase of sex work things, and the tent—although I bring the tarp that I've strung over it to protect it from the sun and rain, as well as the sleeping bag. I leave the extra clothes behind to keep the backpack small; I don't want to look like someone on the run.

I wish I could let my friends know that I'm going but I don't know how to reach them quickly without my phone, and I don't have the time to try and track them down. There's only one place I want to visit. Walking quickly along the street, trying not to glance over my shoulder, I pretend I'm just a worker, on my way to the night shift at the neighborhood's distribution warehouse. I push my way through the rosebushes along the south side of Georgia's grandmother's house and rap softly at the window. A lamp comes on and I press my hand to the glass.

"It's me, Bets," I hiss.

The window slides open an inch.

"You frightened me," whispers an old woman. She peers out into the darkness. Her skin is pale, almost translucent. "Who are you?"

"I'm going away," I say. "But I'm safe. I promise. I just wanted to let you know. And will you tell Georgia, when she returns?"

"Who is Georgia?" she says. "And where are you going?" She reaches her hand out the window, and I grasp it in mine. Her palm is papery and warm. I can't risk telling her my plan—likely she won't remember, but if she does, the feds could find out. I push the folded note from my mother into her hand.

"Will you give this to Georgia," I say, "next time you see her?"

"I don't know a Georgia," she says, her brow knit.

"It's ok," I say. "Just give her that note when you see her. And will you tell her that I love her?"

Georgia's grandmother stares at me, her mouth turned down. And then her face softens. "Ok," she says. "I've got to close this window, there's a chill. Please be safe in your journeys." She withdraws her hand from mine and the window slides shut. The lace curtains fall and a moment later the light switches off, and I'm alone again.

As I walk the dark streets, I consider the checkpoints. There's a checkpoint on every major road that leaves the city. You have to have some sort of reason to be let in or out—official business, work, something like that. And of course, if you're on any of their lists, they won't let you through the checkpoints at all. That's their opportunity to apprehend you.

If I wasn't on their lists before, I definitely am now.

And what will I do if I get past the checkpoints, anyway? Where the fuck is Nevada? I've never been out of this city, in all my life. I've watched old movies when I could find them, seen photos and heard stories about the land beyond this place. But I've never seen it for myself. And I'm not sure how to get where I'm going. I wish I had a map, at the very least.

Fuck! Where can I find a map?

The sound of my fist pounding on the door to Malachite's apartment is too loud and I startle, peering into the black of the parking lot, expecting floodlights to come alive, pinning me there on the landing. But nothing moves, not even the door. I knock again. *Boom boom boom.* There's a feeling of movement, but no answer. I try the doorknob—it's unlocked. Inside, the grey-black of the stairwell melts into the darker black of the entryway.

"Malachite?" I call out.

"Sabrina?" says a voice from the bedroom. I touch the cool wall with my hand, using it to guide me.

"It's Bets," I say. In Malachite's room is a small lamp illuminating him where he lies, tangled in a dirty comforter on a mattress on the floor. He lifts his head to look at me and his face is slick with sweat. There's a smell in the room—vomit, or something worse.

"Are you ok?"

"Sabrina was supposed to bring me antibiotics. I've had this abscessed tooth."

"Antibiotics are hard to find right now."

"I know," says Malachite. "I'm supposed to be the guy who finds stuff for people. And here I am, sick because I can't find some stupid antibiotics."

"How long have you been like this?"

"Sabrina was supposed to come a few days ago."

I take in the room with its yellowed walls, the wall register ticking out heat. There's trash on the floor next to the bed—discarded soda bottles, a crumpled paper bag. And then I see the dog, curled in the concave space formed by Malachite's torso where he lies on his side. It's a brown dog, short hair, very small. It's looking at me with its ears back and a face that looks like it wants to bite me very much.

"How are you managing the pain?" I ask.

"Fentanyl," says Malachite. "Easier to find than antibiotics." He laughs.

"You need be careful with that stuff," I say, uselessly. I wonder if I have the capacity to add Malachite to the list of people that I worry about. You can't worry about everyone. If you worry about everyone you'll break, and become an additional person that people have to worry about.

"Speaking of things that are hard to find," I say. "Do you have a map you're willing to sell me? I'm trying to go to Nevada. I don't really know where that is."

"Nevada, huh," says Malachite. He closes his eyes, and I think he's asleep.

"Malachite?"

"Check the closet," he whispers.

The minute I take a step towards the bed, a low growl comes from the little dog. Another step and the dog lunges like a snake. I jump back, circling around the other side of the bed to the closet at the far end of the room. A pull chain illuminates the books that fill the small space. They're piled in stacks, not organized in any way.

I squat on my heels and touch their spines. Horror novels, old westerns, a few dozen copies of *National Geographic*. Cookbooks, self-help books, encyclopedias. I read the titles of each stack several times, but there aren't any maps. I pull out *An RVer's Guide to the American West*.

"How much for this?" I ask, holding out the book. The dog pulls its lips back and shows its small yellow teeth.

"Two hundred," says Malachite, without opening his eyes. I unfold the bills in my pocket and peel off a handful, laying them on the hardwood in front of the closet.

"Hey Malachite," I say. "You think you're gonna be ok?"

"Sabrina's supposed to come," he mumbles after a moment.

"You got a phone?" I ask. "You want me to text Sabrina for you?"

"I texted her earlier today. Not much I can do now."

Malachite pulls the blanket up to his ears. I can't tell for certain, but it looks like he's shivering.

"Ok," I say. "You think I can sleep on your couch for a few hours? The cops were out earlier, and I want to let it cool down a bit before I try to get out of the city."

"Sure," he says, quietly.

I can't sleep. Curled up on the loveseat outside Malachite's room, staring into the dark, all I can do is worry about Malachite. Maybe on my way out of the city I can find Sabrina, whoever that is. There's just enough light from the street filtering into the hallway to make out the other objects in Malachite's apartment—a refrigerator, a box fan, a metal table and chair that look like they once belonged to a patio set. And Malachite's bicycle, leaning against the wall.

Malachite works as an official courier for the city—since gasoline is scarce these days, many deliveries are done via bicycle. During the day the streets are filled with hundreds of these couriers, dipping in and out of traffic, delivering everything from mail to food to drugs. It's the reason that Malachite is so good at getting things that are hard to find, like books.

Antibiotics, I realize, must be even more scarce than I had thought, if not even Malachite can find them to treat his own infected tooth. How long until antibiotics are gone for good? It's a terrifying idea, and I add it to the list of things a person shouldn't think about.

The next time I open my eyes, warm diffuse light fills the apartment. It's morning. For a moment, I can't recall where I am. Then my eyes focus on a small brown shape facing the loveseat, looking up at me. The dog. Fuck! I'd only intended to sleep a few hours.

"Malachite?" I call. "I'm still here. I overslept. I'm sorry." Rubbing my face with my hands, I take a moment and try to get my thoughts in order. The dog sits on the hardwood floor and watches me as I pick up *An RVer's Guide to the American West* and stuff it into my backpack. "Malachite?"

Malachite is in his bed, on his side, still tangled in the blanket. He's very still, and his mouth is open. He looks dead. He's not though, right? I move towards the bed as the little dog sits in the doorway, watching me. He doesn't growl this time. Is Malachite's chest rising and falling? It's so hard to tell. I move closer. The smell is bad. *Please don't be dead, Malachite,* I think.

He's dead.

Fuck. This is not what I need right now. Pacing helps, and I move back and forth in the little room, kicking the trash out of the way.

What I need is to think, but my mind is a tangle. A rushing river.

Have I ever seen a rushing river? Do they have rushing rivers in Nevada? I should get out of this apartment. Soon. And then out of the city. And how exactly will I do that? I gather the money off the bedroom floor, the money I left for the book, and stuff it into my pocket.

"I'm sorry Malachite," I say. "I'm really fucking sorry."

His kitchenette consists of a counter with a hotplate and a microwave, and a couple of cabinets. In the cabinets I find canned beans, bricks of top ramen, and a jar of peanut butter. I put the peanut butter in my backpack but the ramen won't fit. Wrenching open the tap, I fill a plastic cup with water and it shakes as I drink from it. The tap water tastes like metal.

Sitting on the loveseat with my backpack in my lap, I stare at the wall. The light in the room is growing brighter, less diffuse. Soon the whole city will be awake. The streets will be crowded with traffic, the sounds of honking, the haze of trash fires. Vendors will be selling fry bread, motorcycles and bicycles will dart between the trucks and cars.

Bicycles. Malachite has a bicycle.

The courier uniform almost, but not quite, fits. I'm standing in the small bathroom, just big enough for my upright body, and peering at myself in the mirror. The khaki button-up shirt and trousers were on the bedroom floor and I'm not sure how long it's been since they were washed. The uniform doesn't smell like vomit, though—just like a regular human, sweating in the sun, trying to make deliveries on time. It's a little loose on me, and I imagine it was big on Malachite too since we're about the same size. New clothing that fits is hard to come by—this uniform was likely passed down from another courier.

"I'm a courier for the city," I practice saying in the mirror. "I have some packages to take outside the city limits."

The bike has panniers with some flat packages to deliver—courier things. Since I have the storage now, I add all the food from Malachite's cabinets as well as a few plastic bottles of water. I rummage through the drawers of his dresser and find a wool sweater. Arranging the undelivered packages on top of Malachite's things, I close the panniers carefully. Everything else is still in my backpack, which I'll carry on my back.

Four blocks away, I remember the dog.

I want to scream, but I don't. I just turn my bike around, pedaling back up the street towards Malachite's apartment.

Surprisingly, the dog lets me lift him. He's warm and solid in my arms, like a burrito fresh from the taco cart on the corner.

"Are you hungry?" He accepts a spoonful of peanut butter. "Now we're friends, yeah?" I put a bowl of water on the floor and he drinks for a long time, and then pads over to the corner of the room and lifts his leg, peeing on the molding.

If I put the sweater on top of the packages and sit him in there, then cinch the pannier around his shoulders, there's just room enough for him to ride with his little head sticking out. He doesn't resist this arrangement.

"Don't get me in trouble, ok?"

The bike feels good as the tires move smoothly over the pavement. I grip the handlebars tight and maneuver in and out of traffic, focusing on what's ahead of me, letting the cacophony of the city flow over me like water. Shouting, honking, pedestrians, lights. I glance back at the dog—he's sitting calmly in the pannier, turning his head to sniff the passing world; he's chill like he does this every day. Maybe he does?

I wonder if he smells the sewers and the fast-food grease. The burning plastic scent of a trash fire in the alley. I've been told that when I was a baby, they scooped up the trash in huge trucks and took it out of the city, dumping it in piles in the countryside. Imagine a city doing that for its people!

Beryl said that the city is hemorrhaging the last of its resources on a war against its own people. That there isn't any money left for anything else. Is this what always happens, in the end? I imagine that someday the last of the gasoline and ammunition will run out, and the city won't have resources at all. And then what? What happens after that?

I wish I could run all these questions by Georgia. For now, I add them to the list of things not to think about.

By mid-morning I see the checkpoint on the western edge of the city, where the knot of development loosens into suburban sprawl. A huge domed grey roof stretches across the road, a cluster of law enforcement vehicles underneath. I look down at the embroidered name tag on my shirt. *Stranger.*

My last name is now Stranger. I am an official courier for the city. I have some packages to deliver to the suburbs…

The uniformed man doesn't even wait for me to reach his little booth before stepping out and waving his arm, gesturing for me to go… where? I try to follow the motions he's making but I'm too freaked out to think clearly, there's static at the edge of my vision. Why does he want me to get off the road? My heart is doing things in my chest, and I try and still it. Nothing bad has happened yet. It's important not to get worked up before the bad thing has actually happened.

I get off the bike and walk it into the shaded area under the domed grey roof. The man nods his head at me and disappears inside the booth again. Sitting on the concrete curb, I absently stroke the head of the dog, who is resting, eyes closed, in the pannier. I wonder what I'll do next, if I make it past this checkpoint. I haven't studied the *RVer's Guide to the American West* yet so I'm not sure if it even covers the area immediately outside the city.

Where will I sleep tonight? How far can I get before dark?

The man has reappeared and he's waving his arm for me to approach. I walk the bike up to the booth, trying to keep the static from overtaking me.

"Sorry for the delay," he says. He's bent over a tablet, jabbing at it with his finger. "Our systems were down." He looks up at me, his brow knit with alarm. "They've gone down before, but never for three hours like this morning. I'm not sure what's going on."

"Oh," I say. Never has a law enforcement officer been this forthcoming with me. He must believe all of it—the uniform, the name tag. That I work for the city, like him.

"Stranger." He reads the tag on my shirt, then takes in the panniers and the dog. "We don't get many couriers going outside the city." He looks at his tablet again. "I can't get the logs to load. Seems like we're still having issues. I'll have to enter your information manually, later. Sorry again about the delay. Be careful on the road ahead." He turns away from me and goes inside the little booth.

I don't speak. I command my leg to swing over my bike, command my feet to start pedaling. Command myself to look forward. The blacktop unspools under my tires. The air is clearer here at the edge of the city, less immediately cloying, although the horizon is still shrouded in haze.

My anxiety dissipates as the checkpoint recedes behind me. I've made it through the first obstacle! Now, in the absence of my fear around the checkpoint, a new darkness enters my mind—I imagine Georgia, returning to the city to find me gone. My eyes tear up and I wipe the water away angrily.

"I'm sorry," I say aloud. "I'm sorry Georgia. I never in a million years would have left you. I had no choice."

The sun is higher in the sky now and I wonder if the systems have come back online at the checkpoint, if the law enforcement officer is entering my information and discovering that there are no deliveries through this checkpoint scheduled under my name. I'm tempted to turn and look back, but I don't.

You never, ever look back. That's another way you survive.

CHAPTER 3

When I was six years old my family moved into what would be our final apartment. I don't remember much about that early time, mostly just a few scenes, and a feeling—the safety of being behind four walls. And the luxury of having a car, the sedan we parked outside. I lost my father first, and then we lost the apartment, and my mother and I moved into the sedan. Eventually I lost the car too, and her.

Groups of humans, when left to their own devices, will create their own social structures, however imperfect; when I was thrust into the city as a newly orphaned child, a series of interactions led me to Beryl. Beryl was kind to me, although he didn't have to be.

Beryl's junkyard is a sprawling property in the heart of the city, where he puts orphaned children to work stripping things that can be melted down, salvaging parts that are still good—and in exchange he feeds the children simple meals, and gives them blankets to make nests in the cars for sleeping.

The Beryl of my childhood was always wearing his stained overalls and fishing butterscotches from the deep pockets for me and the other children, and he never tried to put his hands on us. When I grew older and saw more of the world, I often asked myself what horrible, horrible thing he had done that had turned him so kind.

Sucking dick paid a lot better than salvaging parts in a junkyard, and by and by I turned to that sort of work as I grew up, even though I knew Beryl wouldn't approve. You had to reach your quota of parts wrenched each day to earn your nest of blankets in an old cargo van or under a camper shell on the grass, so I'd work as quick as I could and then sneak out of the junkyard for the night, not returning until just before dawn.

If Beryl had caught on to what I was doing I knew I'd be kicked out of there, and that would be the end of me. I hid my money in a coffee can buried in the ground, and then eventually I needed a second coffee can. Soon I was able to buy a phone to screen my clients; your chances of getting murdered or abducted go way down when you can do that.

It was only luck that I survived that window of time between beginning sex work and getting a phone. Not everyone does. Two years ago I was able to move into the tent in the nice backyard with the high privacy fence, and I really started to feel like I was making something of myself in the city.

Beryl once told me that stability is a made-up concept. It keeps us disappointed that we never actually arrive anywhere, keeps us from experiencing the joy of existing in this one insane fucking moment.

Since passing the checkpoint I've been biking west on a frontage road below the freeway. Occasionally a car thrums by on the pavement above me. Compared to the din of the city it's eerily still out here. I've passed a few abandoned motels, their doorways gaping. I've passed a burned-out fast-food burger joint and a boarded-up strip mall. Now there's the rumble of a truck's muffler on the freeway above me, and then the rumble stills. I hear doors slam.

"Hey!" a voice shouts, and I stop the bike and look up. Two huge men lean against the railing and look down at me. Their bald heads shine in the hazy sunlight, and they've got rifles slung across their backs. Fear slinkies down my spine, making my arms tingle.

"I haven't seen you before," one of the men shouts. "You got a permit to be in this neighborhood?"

"Yeah," I say, forcing confidence into my voice. "I have a permit."

"No, you don't have a permit," the man says. "Because we give out the permits. And I've never seen you before."

"What are you delivering?" says the other man. "Maybe if you give some of it to us we'll give you a permit."

The men disappear from the railing, then the rumble starts up again and the tires squeal as the truck turns around. They're driving the wrong way. On the freeway. To get back to the last exit. To come find me.

Fuck.

How fast can I go on this bike? I'm pedaling as hard as I can as I hang a left and see more boarded-up strip malls. Turning onto a side street, I come to a residential area where the houses all seem abandoned—broken window glass, weeds so high you can't see the front doorsteps. Some of the roofs are caved in. I duck into an overgrown alley and see a footpath—or maybe it's a path made by coyotes, deer, and feral cats—and I push my bike, plowing through the weeds. Stickers gather in my shirt and on my shoelaces. Looking back to check on the dog, I can see he's got his eyes shut, letting the tall plants brush against his face. I can hear the rumble of the truck a few streets away.

The weeds open a bit and there's a backyard to my left. The yard is enclosed in a chain-link fence and I can see that it's entirely overgrown with blackberry brambles—it's like one huge bramble bush, taller than I am, from the gate to the back wall of the house. The vines are in full leaf, and their ends are heavy with clusters of fruit. The smell of this ripe fruit hangs in the still, warm air. I open the gate and observe the bramble. Down low to the ground there's open space, a dim sort of cavern made for a much shorter animal than I am, but I think I might be able to get in there if I crawl. As I take the dog out of the pannier and set him on the ground, he just stands there, looking at me.

"Do what I do, ok?" I say. I take the panniers off the bike and lay it on its side, and then I crawl into the cavern. I drag the bike and the panniers after me. The dog follows, hopping lightly around obstacles. It's cool in this tunnel of blackberry canes, and a little dappled sunlight patterns the soft ground. I scoot further inside, and the roof of the tunnel is higher now, making it easier to move.

By the time I reach the back wall of the house, the dim space is high enough to nearly stand in, a sort of bramble cave. There's smashed cardboard on the ground, some dirty clothing and a single shoe, the laces missing.

"I think someone stayed here," I say quietly to the dog. He circles the perimeter, lifts his tiny leg, and lets loose a stream of urine on a branch. I rest my bike against the back wall of the house and sit on the cardboard, willing myself to relax despite my racing thoughts.

I wish I had my phone. If I had my phone I could figure out where I am and where I'm going. I could find out how my friends are doing. I could leave another voicemail for Georgia.

My phone connected me to the world. Now I've cut the cord and set myself loose… into what, exactly? I listen for the truck—I can still hear it, but I'm not sure what direction the sound is coming from, or how far away it is. And then, after another few tense moments, the sound is gone. I close my eyes and the stillness of the blackberry cave is all around me, a stillness that's soft like goose down.

It's gonna take me a while to get used to how quiet the world outside the city is. In this stillness, this absence of danger, ache blossoms in my chest. When I open my eyes there's an ant, making its way across the dirt. Does this ant know what happens in the human world? Does this ant care about our dramas? The dog is curled on the old clothing, his nose on his tail.

"I bet you're hungry and thirsty," I say. I pull one of my water bottles from my pannier and pour a little into the jar lid I brought to be the dog's water dish. The dog lays into it, biting happily at the water. I find a brick of top ramen, break off a hunk, and spread it with peanut butter. I give that to the dog too. He crunches it, drops it into the dirt, picks up the now-filthy snack and crunches it again. I spread the rest of the ramen brick with peanut butter for myself.

My appetite is absent, though, and the noodles are difficult to eat. It feels insane to be biking away from Georgia and the city. Absolutely insane. I feel like I'm turning inside out. Maybe I should go back. To die would be better than this.

No.

I bite a mouthful of dry noodles and peanut butter, forcing myself to chew. An intense drowsiness overcomes me after eating. These brambles are holding me. What wealth, to have a fortress such as this. I wish I could stay here forever. But I can't. And where, again, am I even going?

I open one of the panniers and rifle around until I find *An RVer's Guide to the American West*. Its heft is comforting; so many words and images inside, so much potentially helpful information. I flip through it, looking for maps. An overview map of the U.S. shows me the major arteries of the interstates, not much else. I put my finger where my city is on this map and drag it west. When I reach an icon for a listing, I flip to that page in the book. The listing is for something called a KOA in a town called Hamiston.

Water, WIFI, Pool, says the listing. *A gravel road leads to this peaceful campground, which is surrounded by fields.* I close my eyes and imagine the campground now. The gravel road is barricaded. The pool holds ten inches of water and twelve years of rotting leaves. The water still runs. There is no WIFI.

I'm not sure how much use this book is going to be for me. It has potential water sources, at least. And maps with a little detail are better than no maps at all. Frustrated and wishing I could talk to Georgia, I fish a pencil from the pannier and flip through the book to a page with a good amount of white space.

I'm curled up in a secret cave inside some blackberry brambles, missing you, I write in the margins. *I have a dog now, he's the size of a burrito...* I tell Georgia all about my day, about everything that's happened since I met with Proteus Feldspar last night. Once all my thoughts are down I put the pencil and book away, cinch the pannier shut. I feel better now. Emptier.

The wool sweater makes a decent pillow, and from my position lying down I can watch the light move through the blackberry canes. The dog approaches me, sniffs my sweater, and plops down against my side. *I should gather some of these blackberries and get on the road again,* I think, and then I fall asleep.

///

When I wake the light is golden; late afternoons are always this color, the light gone long and then filtered through the haze of the city. The dog is curled in the dirt at the opening of the cavern, guarding us. For a moment I do not know where I am and then the day coalesces around me, my memory becoming solid again. Nevada. I'm biking west, to Nevada.

At dusk I am back on my bike, my hands and teeth stained purple, a plastic sack of berries in one of my panniers. Presently a half moon rises. That's only half as much light as a full moon, but then again I'm only half as exposed. The dog is tucked down into the pannier, top cinched closed so he can sleep. I'm going to ride for as long as I can tonight. It seems safest to ride in the dark.

Taking smaller side streets seems like it would be safer, but I'm afraid of getting lost, so I decide to stay on the frontage road. This freeway is on my map, so as long as I follow it I'll know where I am. There's very little traffic, and every time I see headlights in the distance I dismount and drop down into the culvert next to the road, make my bike and myself small in the brush there.

As I pedal, I sing softly to myself, afraid of making too much noise but also feeling smothered by the heavy quiet, needing to beat it back with the sound of my own voice. I think of Georgia. I think of my parents, when we still had our apartment. The wallpaper that was made to look like wood paneling, and the way it was peeling. The stained ceiling panels that leaked when it rained. The carpet that smelled of mildew. My parents, gone for most of my waking hours.

My mother, a shadowy figure sitting on the edge of my bed when I would wake in the night. Stroking the hair off my forehead with her hand. The smell of cigarettes and fryer grease, the stained apron knotted around her waist. Early in the morning I would find my father sitting at the kitchen table drinking roasted barley tea. Red eyes and his fingers curled in, hands cramped from factory work. Looking ahead at the wall. Not seeing me.

A little grey has just begun to wash the night sky when I turn off the frontage road and into a neighborhood. All night I've been passing the silent shapes of abandoned houses and shopping centers. There's been the occasional car on the freeway, which I've hidden from, and the rustlings of night animals, but I haven't seen a single sign of human life in any of these buildings. Are there people living here, somewhere? Hiding?

The houses in this neighborhood are bigger than the others, and on larger plots of land. Farms and what were once the summer homes of the rich. They have long driveways, horse pastures now overgrown. I follow one of these driveways in the early dim, to a large country house. The house is dark, the front steps overgrown with weeds, the windows gaping like eye sockets. I stand for a time in front of the house, holding my bike, waiting for movement or sound.

There is nothing.

Still, I won't go in the house right now. I need a place to sleep and the house, although probably unoccupied, will be full of mold and broken glass and mouse shit. I follow the dirt drive to a small barn at the back end of the property. The barn is intact—drafty, dirt floored, swept clean and still smelling of hay. The dog, after I release him from his nest in the pannier, stretches and urinates on a post. I don't have any cardboard so I spread my sleeping bag directly on the packed earth.

My legs feel shaky—my muscles are exhausted. I pour a little water in the dog's dish and then eye the bottle—just half a liter left. I'll have to find some more soon. In the bottom of the pannier is a can of beans and I heft it, then realize that I don't have a can opener. Laughing quietly to myself in the dark I realize dinner will be peanut butter on dry ramen again… Or is it breakfast? As has become custom, a quarter of the ramen goes to the dog.

The dog is not sleepy. He's sitting on the dirt next to me, facing the door to the barn, which I've closed and barricaded with a wooden table that was in a part of the barn that seems to have been a workshop.

"It's good you're lookin out," I say. "Just don't draw attention to us while we're here." The dog glances over his shoulder at me. His eyes are huge and wet in his small face. He's some kind of mutt, a little brown being of indeterminate ancestry. All the dogs are mutts these days. Mutts were what existed long ago, and in recent decades mutts have returned. Now they're waiting patiently for their chance to inherit the earth.

I wish again that I had my phone. I open the RVer's guide and write another letter to Georgia.

I left a note with your grandmother. If you go find Beryl he can tell you what it means. I miss you so much. I was just thinking that I almost had enough money to move us into that apartment. That's why I was seeing that client, even though I knew he was sketchy. I shouldn't have done that.

My eyes are welling up. In this moment my aloneness is as vast as outer space, and there's nothing between me and it. I'm a little kid again, an orphan sleeping under a truck topper in a junkyard. I start to shake, and reality skips a beat. My consciousness is echoing, bouncing around in the void. Cold terror in the pit of my stomach. Without my connection to Georgia, how do I know that I exist? I hold my hand in front of my face, turn it back and forth.

"Do I exist?" I say aloud, to the dog. He's nosing at my sleeping bag, and I open it so that he can crawl inside. He thumps down against me and I feel his warmth, radiating like a hot water bottle. "Maybe you are proof that I exist," I say to him. "A little bit of proof." Reality stills, settles back into its groove. I feel the fatigue in my body.

What time is it?

I remember the watch and squint at it in the dark, but the hands are all wrong. I press it to my ear; there's no ticking sound—the watch has stopped. I unclasp it from my wrist and drop it in my pannier. Maybe at some point in the journey I'll find someone who knows how to make a watch like this work, or I can trade it for something useful. And anyway, the delineations of numbered time hardly matter right now. All I know is that night is becoming day and the birds are welcoming the dawn. I've never been so physically exhausted in my life. The hard ground is like the softest feather bed. I close my eyes.

CHAPTER 4

When I step outside the barn to pee in the afternoon there is a deer, browsing in the fallen apples of an abandoned orchard. A pang of regret—I wish I had a rifle. Although guns are popular with some of my friends, I've only ever chosen to arm myself with a knife. I want the freedom to move quickly and I don't want to draw attention to myself. I want to be liquid, able to flow around obstacles as they appear. A rifle would make me clumsy. One would be really useful right now, though.

"What would we even do with a whole deer?" I say to the dog, as I gather bruised apples in my shirt. The dog pads around behind me, sniffing the fruit. The apples are crawling with wasps, and I shoo them away. My legs feel rested and I'm antsy to get back on my bike. First, though, this house.

The back door to the house is locked but the window is busted out and I brush away the broken glass and pull myself through, lifting the dog up after me. Inside it's dim and smells of rotten wood. Trapezoids of sunlight gather on the dirty linoleum in the kitchen, and beyond that is a carpeted living room where the furniture hulks like dusty, sleeping beasts.

It's amazing how quickly a person's cozy home, after being abandoned, will turn into this—an eerie, sickly place where you don't want to stay for more than a few minutes. Is it the dust? The mold? Or is a house itself a living being, animated from within by its inhabitants, and when they leave the house becomes a corpse and begins to rot?

There's a staircase, stained with water from the roof, and I climb it to a landing with three closed white doors. The brass knob of the middle door is cool in my hand. The room is a bedroom—there's a bed, the quilt and sheets pulled back exposing the bare mattress, a bookcase cluttered with books, and a closet tangled with clothes. The dust motes drift, unbothered, in the light from the window. Then a small rustling—it's the dog, he's padded up the stairs after me.

I sit on the bed and look out the window at the apple orchard and let the sadness spread out from my heart like a fog. It spills out the doorway and onto the landing. It seeps under the doors of the other two rooms and then I'm there, back in my dream. The dream I have often at night, that I've been having since I was a small child.

In the dream I'm in a large house, and I'm searching for something. I wander through rooms that open into other rooms. The rooms hold antiques from another time, junk, furniture from the apartment I shared with my parents. The rooms hold people I love who've been disappeared. The rooms hold people who I haven't yet met. The people welcome me, or they do not know me.

Sometimes I take up residence in one of these rooms but always their true occupants appear after a while and tell me that I have to leave. None of the rooms hold what I am searching for and so I push on, deeper and deeper into the house. I sink down into the bowels of the house, or up into its castle spires. The house's corridors are a maze and I cannot find my way out.

The light is getting longer in the apple orchard.

"Long light o'clock," I say to the dog, who has curled up on the carpet at my feet. "That's what time it is. We're making a new system of time, out here beyond the city. Long light o'clock is what comes before Time to Ride my Bike."

The closet is full of useful things but I'm not sure what to take—my panniers are pretty stuffed right now. Do I need more warm layers? Clothes to trade if I meet people on my journey? What sorts of people are out here beyond the city, besides the militia? I haven't seen anyone yet. Maybe there will be people at the KOA, my first destination, chosen arbitrarily from the RVer's guide.

The fabrics of the clothes in the closet feel good under my fingers and there's a human scent here, someone's lingering laundry detergent. Should I take another sweater? A canvas jacket? My fingers pause on a dress, its fabric smooth and light. A simple, airy dress printed all over with flowers, a few buttons at the throat, an elastic waist. I pull the dress off its hanger and fold it carefully.

That smell rises up again; what is it? A smell from another time. A smell that's supposed to invoke a shared cultural memory of something but that something doesn't exist anymore.

///

The lid of a rain barrel connected to the house's gutters comes off with some effort and inside I find good, clear water, yellow from the tannins of fallen leaves and dancing with mosquito larvae but otherwise untainted. In the kitchen cupboards there are a few plastic bottles and I fill these, as well as my own. There's a can opener and some canned goods too, rusted and missing their labels. Likely too old to be edible and I don't want to risk botulism, so I leave them, but take the can opener.

"Goodbye," I say to the house, as I push my bike down the dirt drive and back towards the road. I feel like I'm leaving a mausoleum. When will humans once again walk through those halls and bedrooms? In a hundred years? Longer?

The air is different tonight as I cycle away from the house, the dog curled up in one of my panniers. The city is the brown smell of trash and industry but out here there's something else. A cold, clean smell that is somehow familiar. But from what?

When have I experienced this before?

Maybe it's a memory that's stored in my cells from previous generations. A smell from an old world that is also, for me, the smell of a new world. The world to which I'm headed. I shiver. It's not just the air that's different tonight; my mind feels clearer too. I'm rested. This is my second day surrounded by silence, with little to occupy my thoughts.

I'm at the fringed edge of the suburbs, the houses far apart and on large tracts of land. The fields are overgrown with brambles and weeds. The cars that pass are fewer and farther between; I spend less time in the culvert, crouched next to my bicycle, waiting for their headlights to sweep over me and away. My legs pump rhythmically. My mind is an empty vessel and into this vessel comes the mirage of memory, the details so sharp I can almost smell them.

Georgia and I are opening up an abandoned apartment building in the city. The building is locked, plywood nailed over the windows, "no trespassing" signs everywhere. We've got a few hours to work before the security guard on this block passes by on his shift and sees our headlamps. If we can get enough of the apartments open, we can move in folks we know from one of the encampments.

We make quick work of the plywood over the first broken window and climb inside. There's debris everywhere: busted furniture, clothing, wind-blown trash. The toilet in the bathroom has an ancient turd in it, but no water. We do a sweep to make sure no-one's already living here and that it seems safe enough—no collapsing ceilings or floorboards rotted enough to fall through—and we move on to the next apartment, which is nearly identical.

The window beneath the plywood on the third apartment is intact, and we don't want to break it if we don't have to, so Georgia uses the tools in her bag to force the door. Inside, our headlamps reveal something surprising—everything in this apartment is in order, untouched.

A sofa with a velour blanket tossed over the back, a low coffee table with a splay of magazines, a rag rug, a bookshelf. A small rack next to the door holds a couple pairs of shoes. It's as though the tenants have just stepped out and will return at any moment. At first I think someone might be living here, but then I see the thick dust on the bookshelf, run my finger through it.

"You've gotta see this," says Georgia, from the kitchen.

An avocado-green stove and refrigerator. Glass fronted cabinets. Georgia is pulling canned goods and boxes out of the cabinets one by one and inspecting them; macaroni and sardines perfectly preserved, as though they've been in a museum. There's a row of silver tins on the countertop, lined up by size. The first contains recipes, written in tidy cursive on index cards. The second holds sugar, hardened but still useable. The contents of the third makes me jump.

"There's fucking coffee in here!" I say. "Coffee!" Coffee's been nearly impossible to come by the past few years. It's worth so much money on the black market.

"Fuck," says Georgia. She grabs the tin from my hands and holds it up to her face, breathes deeply. "We can sell this, make a security fund for the new tenants. That'll be a huge help to them." She digs a plastic bag from one of the drawers and dumps the coffee inside. The tin falls onto the ground and I pick it up, put it back in its spot with the others, brush the stray coffee grounds off the countertop with my hand. "Don't open the fridge," says Georgia.

"I know," I say. "You don't have to keep reminding me." The first rule of Entering Abandoned Buildings Club is *never open the fridge.*

In the bedroom the circle of my headlamp illuminates a bed with a striped bedspread pulled taut. Not all the way taut, though. There's a lump in the middle, as though a couple of pillows are stashed under there. I step into the silence of the room. It's a tomb. This room is a tomb, and that lump in the bed is a body.

"Georgia?" I whisper. I can't seem to raise my voice. I can hear her rustling around in the kitchen. The sides of the quilt are tucked into the mattress, and I tug a corner free. Under the quilt is the body of a little old man, curled into the fetal position and perfectly still. The skin of his face and hands are shriveled, like the mummified cats we sometimes find in these buildings. He's wearing pajamas and he's drawn up into himself, as though he was cold when he died. I arrange the quilt back over him.

"You're lucky you got out when you did," I say, before closing the door of the bedroom.

I find Georgia sitting on the floor in front of the bookshelf in the living room, sifting through photographs and stacks of mail. There are cut glass figurines on the bookshelf—a horse, an elephant, a bear.

"I found a pistol in his dresser drawer," I say. "No ammunition though."

"*His* dresser drawer?" says Georgia.

"What if we boarded this apartment back up?" I say. "Kept it like it is. We could say that it's too wrecked to be livable. Paint a warning on the door."

Georgia shrugs.

"Sure." I sit next to her on the carpet and she puts down the mail, wraps one of my hands in her own. "Another body?" she says.

"Yeah."

Her dark eyes are clear. The skin around them is lined from all the time she spends in the sun in the guerrilla garden, digging in the dirt there. I've offered to try and find her a big hat but she says no, she likes the way the sun feels on her face. I told her that I'm worried about her getting skin cancer and she said that she doesn't care and besides, she doesn't think she'll live long enough for that. *It's still possible to live a long time,* I said. *But why would I want to,* she answered back.

She reaches a cool hand into my hair and leans in, kissing me. Her breath smells like citrus and her lips are soft. For a moment I melt into the kiss, forgetting everything. Then I remember that Georgia will never be mine; each time I try to know her better she disappears, only returning when I've ceased looking for her. She's like a feral cat that will only slink close and let you pet it when you're looking away. Every kiss she gives me feels like a parting gift.

"Let's open up the other apartments," I say, pulling away.

The wind changes and I'm back in my body, back on the bike. The darkness is vast, my bicycle a ship that slices cleanly through the cool sea of the night. I don't know what time it is but last night I noticed that the moon rose just before dawn, so tonight I'm waiting for that; the light of the silver half moon will signify that it's time to find a place to hunker down and sleep. I'm beginning to enjoy being unstuck from time like this, unfettered by the tyranny of minutes. The hours are liquid, they rush by and then slow to a trickle and sometimes stop entirely, forming a deep, clear pool in which I am suspended.

I should eat.

My legs shake as I climb off the bike and guide it to the shoulder of the road. Not bothering to move to the culvert, I just uncinch the pannier and lift out the warm, sleepy dog, and then lay the bike down on its side. I haven't seen a car for hours. Have I reached the edge of all human existence? Is it just me now in this wild frontier, alone forever?

No, that can't be. There are other people somewhere out here and I'm going to find them.

My new can opener slices easily into one of my cans of beans. Half a brick of dry ramen completes the meal. The dog disappears into the wide darkness and then returns, shakes himself and pushes his way under my arm, onto my lap. He eats his ramen ration from my fingers and then circles once and curls up with a sigh.

"Do you love me or just my body heat?" I ask the dog. "And my ramen?" Speaking of ramen, I'm going to have to find some more food. A brick of ramen each day with some peanut butter or beans is not enough. Hunger has been following me as I pedal west, like an alarm bell I can't shut off. I'm really banking on there being people at the KOA—and not just any people, but good people. And not just good people but good people who have food they're willing to share with me. That's a whole lot of unknowns that could determine my survival. And what if the KOA is abandoned, or occupied by militia?

Another thing not to think about.

There was a sign for a small town in the last of the light and I used that to place myself on the map in the RVer's guide. I started off the night about an inch and a half from the KOA, and I've been traveling a few inches on the map each night. I'm worried that I'll miss the exit in the dark with no headlamp but there's not really anything to be done except continue pedaling and trust that things will work out somehow.

I can feel the aloneness, lurking a stone's throw away in the dark. Better get back on my bike before it catches me. As I pedal, the sound of my own voice floats above me; I'm singing to remind myself that I exist. The dog is curled in the pannier, asleep. He dreams of past lives, his small belly full of ramen. It feels as though I'm hurtling forward now, the night soft and yielding. Like I could ride a thousand miles. Like I could make it all the way to Nevada in one go. Fatigue is a stranger, someone I can't remember knowing.

The surface of the road jostles violently, startling me out of my reverie, and I tense on the brakes and roll to a stop. There's a hissing noise, and I press my tires. My front tire is deflating. *Fuck!*

Straddling my bike, eyes unfocused on the road, I realize I don't have a patch kit or an extra tube. I wait for inspiration to strike but there's nothing. There's just a little food and water left, and there hasn't been a car all night. Who knows where I am, or how far it is to the next thing. Or even if there *is* a next thing. There's a pressure in my head. I'm starting to panic.

I must not panic.

My legs are shaking again when a little silver of light crests the horizon. The half moon! It's time to camp—this busted tire will be a problem for tomorrow me. Along the roadside is a forest, and I push my bike into these trees. The ground is yielding underfoot.

I've been in ragged forests in abandoned lots in the city, full of trash and danger, but this feels different. There's a soft, welcoming feeling to this forest. A warmth that tells me this will be a safe place to rest. Relief floods my body as I unfurl my sleeping bag onto the fallen leaves. The dog drinks from his jar lid of water and then crawls inside the bag with me, his nose pressed into my armpit.

I miss you so badly, Georgia, I whisper into the forest before I fall asleep.

CHAPTER 5

The sound of footsteps makes its way into my consciousness. My head is resting on the damp fallen leaves that carpet the forest floor. The dog is curled against my stomach in the sleeping bag, quiet. I focus on the bands of morning light that I can see between the trees. Crunch. Crunch. Crunch. The dog surfaces, pops his little face out of the sleeping bag and listens. Somehow, he knows not to bark.

There's a gentle kick to my lower back.

"Are you alive?" says a voice. "Get up."

///

The pavement is cracked and potholed, but the road to the KOA is tidy, clear of debris and fallen trees. I'm pushing my bike over this rutted pavement, the dog bouncing in my pannier, while two women in loose tunics and blousy pants with rifles slung across their backs walk beside me.

On one hand, it was incredibly lucky that I got a flat tire and stopped to camp right before the turn off to the KOA, which I definitely would've missed if I'd continued biking in the dark. On the other hand, I have no idea who these people are. They won't answer my questions and so I push my bike in silence as the warm sun climbs above the dense fir forest. Are these people going to shoot me?

The air this morning is even clearer than when I set out last night and I inhale deeply, appreciating the simple, sensual pleasure of the fragrant pines on this, what may be my last day on planet earth.

Ahead are some small cabins—they must be the original cabins of the KOA. But they're glittering in the sunlight, and as we draw closer I gasp at how they've been redone. Their wooden outsides are tiled over with squares of aluminum cut from soda cans, turning each dull brown house into a shimmering, multi-colored disco ball that flashes in the light.

In the space around the cabins are huge sculptures built from trash; animals, snakes and horses and wolves, made from rusted car parts and hunks of broken appliances. Neon wind socks, affixed to these sculptures via tall poles, flutter in the breeze.

Chickens congregate around the bases of these sculptures, pecking at the earth. Between the cabins are mosaic walkways of stones and broken tiles. There's a large building, what I imagine was once the KOA's office, and the outside walls are painted over entirely with bright geometric shapes and swirling, psychedelic patterns. Beyond the cabins are gardens, hemmed in with fences made of more colorful trash, much of it glinting in the sun.

My captors march me and my bike into one of these cabins. At first I can't make anything out, but after a moment my eyes adjust and I see a woman reclining on a purple velvet sofa. She has a smooth, dark bob and red lipstick, and she's not wearing a shirt; or rather, she's wearing a shirt made out of chunky jewel necklaces all draped on top of each other; whether the jewels are real or fake I can't tell.

Around her waist is a knotted sarong; her legs are crossed and the sarong rides up, exposing her thigh. Her legs are smooth and her small bare feet are clean. Her eyes, lined heavily in black, stand out in the dim cabin, which smells of roses. Incense smoke curls in the light from the single window.

When I imagined that a group of people might be living at this KOA I pictured chickens, maybe sheep or horses, concrete parking areas torn up to make gardens. Humble people in clothing fashioned from rags working the land, children with dirt-smeared faces. Not this.

The woman gazes at me, unspeaking, while I clutch the dog in my arms and size up the objects in the cabin, ranking them in my head as more or less difficult to acquire, at least according to my understanding of things.

Velvet sofa: not that hard to get. She could've snagged it from an abandoned house. Incense: very difficult to find, as international supply chains no longer exist, and this particular incense probably isn't made in the US. Sarong: like the couch, she could've scavenged it. The necklaces too. Roses: maybe she grows those herself.

Red lipstick: incredibly difficult to acquire. Makeup hasn't been in production in the US for a decade, and whatever lipstick you might find lying around is likely old enough that it's crumbled and no longer useable. Maybe she makes her own, from her roses? I've heard of this. You can make good money fashioning DIY cosmetics and selling them.

"You've traveled a long way," she says, interrupting my thoughts. Her voice is forceful, and she speaks with an accent I can't place.

"All the way from the city," I say.

"My name is Lisle," says the woman. "And you're a courier? Your name is Stranger?"

Confused at first, I then remember my uniform, now rumpled, stained and smelling of sweat and the earth.

"No," I say. "I stole this. To get through the checkpoints. To escape."

"Why would you want to escape?" she says with a small smile. "They have everything in the city. Food. Clean water. Safety."

"I wasn't safe there," I say. "Only the very wealthy are safe. People are being disappeared all the time."

"Yes," she says. She gives me a fierce look. Her bright red mouth is turned down now. "I don't know if you are telling the truth. Maybe you are escaping the city. Or maybe you are an infiltrator, here to tear our peaceful village apart."

"I can try and prove—"

"Shht! You cannot prove anything to me." She touches the jewels around her neck. "You yourself do not even know who you are." She lifts a string of rubies (or fake rubies?) and runs her fingers along them.

"I'm looking for my mother," I say. Her fingers pause.

"Your mother?"

"I got a note from her. Well, it was an old note. She disappeared when

I was nine. I've wondered my whole life where she went. Then recently this friend gave me an old note from her, saying I should meet her in Nevada. So I'm trying to get to Nevada."

Lisle is staring at me. The eye contact grows uncomfortable and I look away, at the incense smoke curling in the window. I rock on my feet, cradling the dog.

"What time were you born?" says Lisle, finally. I tell her and she lifts a stack of cards off the table in front of her, begins to shuffle them. "I am going to help you find your mother," she says. "I am going to speak to the oracle."

"The oracle?"

"We have an empty cabin for you," continues Lisle. "You will stay and rest awhile. We'll talk again in five days, on the new moon."

The floor creaks behind me, and a warm hand grasps my elbow. I startle.

"Let's go."

On my fourth morning in the village I am not disoriented when I wake. Instead of grasping around for my bicycle, thinking I've overslept in a culvert alongside the highway, I simply lie comfortably on my back on the soft vinyl mattress of the narrow cabin bunk, warm under a pile of blankets, and watch the light from the window move on the honey-colored logs, the dog still asleep in my arms.

Hunger finally compels me to rise and I slip on the dress I found in the abandoned farm house—I turned in my courier uniform to be hand laundered in the river that runs behind the village, although to be honest I won't be bothered if I never get it back. Then I pull the wool sweater on over the dress and walk barefoot to the kitchen pavilion where soft-spoken people in loose, flowing clothing are gathered, eating millet gruel from pottery bowls.

"You're up!" says the man serving the gruel. He's old, with just a few strands of silver hair on his head, which is shiny and covered in spots from the sun. He dips his wooden ladle into the huge steel pot and then tips the ladle into my bowl. With a shaking hand he adds a hunk of fried pork skin and then a raw egg, cracked on the edge of the pot. He smiles at me—he's missing one of his front teeth, and the rest are brown.

"Hi David," I say, my voice still groggy with sleep.

"New moon in Taurus today," he says. "And with Jupiter in retrograde too."

"What does that mean?" I drop a few spoonfuls of gruel onto the dirt for the dog, plus a bite of the pork skin, and he greedily horks it up.

David's eyes widen.

"You don't know? It's the most powerful new moon we've had in ages." He shakes his head. "And today is the day of your ceremony."

The ceremony! I almost forgot. I've been so busy resting in this pleasant place, spending my days watching people make pottery, mill grain and sew loose garments on treadle sewing machines and chanting in the outdoor amphitheater with the others.

The chants happen after breakfast, with everyone seated in the dirt, their drapery pooled about them, hands clasped in their laps. The chants aren't led by any one figure but seem to rise up spontaneously after a period of silence; quietly in one corner and then spreading like water until the clearing vibrates with sound.

"The ceremony will have something to do with my astrological chart, yes?" I ask. "And some mumbo-jumbo about talking to the oracle about my mother."

"But it's not mumbo-jumbo," says David. He's smiling at me indulgently, as if I were a child. "The oracle knows. And through the oracle, Lisle knows too. And your chart will also reveal information about you. *Important* information."

"And then my bike will be returned to me?" This forced rest has been heavenly, but I'm also getting antsy. I'm not that far from the city. What if the feds are still looking, and they find me here? David smiles again, but says nothing. Other people are working their way through the breakfast line, their eyes downcast, and David plops gruel into their bowls. Yesterday I saw him walking with Lisle, in the golden hour when the day was cooling. They were arm in arm on the path along the river, their bare feet sending up small plumes of dust.

David has been chatty with me since that first morning, unlike the other villagers who smile at me but seem uninterested in talking, and a few days ago I tried to ask him how this place came about. But he launched into a long story about the oracle's creation of the world, and Pluto transits, and soon I'd lost the plot and was bored. I remind myself to try and ask him again, in a different way. Maybe after the ceremony.

Lisle is on the small stage in the outdoor amphitheater when I arrive. The amphitheater is made of mismatched boards arranged in geometric patterns that radiate outwards, like a star, and Lisle paces along this. She's wearing a green cloak, open at the front—her chest is covered in the heavy, layered necklaces again and below that she is naked. The cloak glides open and shut as she walks back and forth on the stage, and there are mesmerizing flashes of skin. There's an open area on the bare earth among the people gathered and I take a seat here.

I've left the dog behind in my cabin, worried that he would cause a distraction, and I can feel his absence, like a limb that's been removed. I picture him sleeping in a sunbeam on my blankets, well fed and grateful for the rest we've been getting, and that makes me feel better.

"Bets." Lisle has stopped pacing. She's standing in the center of the stage, facing the crowd. Her arm is raised, and she's pointing at me. "Bets," she says again. "Come up here with me."

I rise. I feel cold, even though it's sunny in this clearing. The quiet people with their downcast eyes move aside as I make my way to the stage. Being close to Lisle again is intoxicating—there's the smell of roses, her bright mouth, her jewels glinting in the light.

Lisle kneels on the worn wood of the stage and gestures for me to kneel across from her. She reaches out and takes my hands in hers. Her grip is strong and warm and sends a tingle up my arms.

"I talked with the oracle," she says. She's speaking loudly, projecting for everyone to hear. "And the oracle gifted me with a vision." She closes her eyes, as if traveling backwards, into her memories. "I see your mother, in prison." She opens her eyes and looks at me. Her gaze is intense, but I will myself not to look away. "There's a fire. After that… I couldn't see."

"You saw my mother in prison?" I say, my voice unsteady.

"Yes," says Lisle.

"And then a fire?"

"Yes."

I don't know what to say. I'm confused, my mind whirling, trying to make sense of this. The oracle says Mother isn't roaming free in Nevada—she's in prison somewhere. And there's going to be a fire. Is this true? And if so, what am I supposed to do? Am I supposed to find this prison and save her, before the fire happens? But how can I do that?

"I also looked deeply at your chart." Lisle is speaking and I try and re-focus on the sound of her voice, follow it over the rush of noise in my head. "I wanted to know your heart. I wanted to know what lives inside of you. The things that even you do not know about yourself."

I don't say anything, just breathe slowly, inhaling the ghosts of roses.

"I won't tell you the details of what I saw," she says. Now she turns and faces the gathered crowd. "But I will tell you all that I saw a darkness in Bets' heart. A darkness that, if unchecked, will spread like an infectious disease, dirtying us all. Our community is a safe and righteous place, full of people who live clean lives. There is no place for darkness here, and until Bets has atoned for the harms she has caused and the harms she will cause in the future, and the harms she causes in her dreams and the harms she causes in all the parallel realities of the multiverse, there is no place for her here either."

A quiet murmuring comes from the crowd. I'm fully in my body now, shocked.

"You think I'm bad?" I feel like crying.

Lisle is almost shouting now. Her heavy accent clips her words. "If you are going to walk this earth, you must atone for all the harms you have caused and will ever cause. You must be made clean again."

The guard who found me in the woods is mounting the steps to the stage. Presently she rests her rough hand on my shoulder.

"Come with me," says the guard. I look out at the crowd, searching it for a kind face. I see David, standing in the front row. His hands are clasped behind his back and he's staring up at me, his expression unreadable.

"But what about the dog?" I stutter, to Lisle. "I left him in my cabin."

Lisle looks at me and says nothing. Her black eyes have gone dark. Have her eyes always been this way? Did I imagine a warmth before? The guard grips my shoulder hard, and I cry out in pain. She lifts me to my feet. I turn back to the crowd but they're all looking down now, at their clasped hands, even David.

"The dog!" I say again. "You have to take care of the dog!" I'm crying now. I don't care where they take me, really, or what they do with me— but I want the dog to be ok.

What if they forget about him in the cabin? What if they drive him away, into the woods, and he's eaten by a larger animal? He trusted me! He trusted me all this time, and now I'm abandoning him! I struggle against the guard and another rushes forward, grabs my other arm. Now the two of them are dragging me off the stage. I wish I had my knife with me.

The dog! my mind screams. *What about the dog!*

CHAPTER 6

The cabin I'm trapped in is one room, each wall the length of twelve of my strides, no light switches, and the door is locked. I know this because I've walked its perimeter, moving my hands over the smooth logs, trying to "see" everything that I can. There's a single window, too high for me to reach, that's been boarded over; the smallest bit of light escapes from one edge of the board, washing part of the wall in grey. There are no bunks or benches in this cabin, nothing but a four-gallon bucket of water in one corner with a metal cup floating inside and a second bucket, this one empty—to use as a toilet, I suppose.

I sit on the dusty concrete floor and think about Georgia. I let my eyes unfocus and make shapes of the dark, which softens and splits and wriggles until I become dizzy and disoriented and have to run my hands along the wall again to remind myself that I am upright, that I am a physical body on earth.

"I wish that you were here," I whisper. That feeling of total aloneness is back, has found me here where I can't run away—in this dark cabin with the window boarded over.

"Georgia," I whisper. "Do I exist? Please tell me that I exist." I think about the dog, am overcome with terror on his behalf, and begin to cry. The terror engulfs me like an incoming tide. This powerlessness shakes me to my core. It reminds me of the first time I ever felt this powerless and alone, when my father disappeared and later, when my mother was permanently gone too. I gaze at the fractured darkness and become unstuck from space-time, my memories carrying me back.

CHAPTER 7

My father disappeared while we still had the apartment. One day he simply didn't come home. My mother stood at the window, anxious eyes scanning the street. If a car rattled past she'd snap the blinds shut. She sat me down and told me that his job at the factory hadn't paid very well, so he'd been moving some products on the side.

Most goods were scarce, and there was money to be made in finding things for people. But selling things on the sly was illegal. Getting caught could get you disappeared.

"We won't be able to afford this apartment much longer, now that your father's gone," my mother said. Her face was vacant in a way it often got, when she was thinking and her thoughts were overwhelming her.

We were able to squat the place for a few months after we found the eviction notice taped to our door; the landlords lived far away and the courts were overwhelmed, so there was some slack between when we were supposed to be out and when the city came and locked us out. By then we'd moved some bags of essentials into the sedan, and when the locks appeared the car became our new home.

We parked on a quiet block—this was back when there were still quiet blocks, when you could sleep outside without needing protection from a gang. Our life in the sedan wasn't bad, actually; my mother had lost her second job and so she spent much of the day with me.

We would sit in the park and she would help me with my schoolwork—history workbooks, much of it propaganda, that each child was required to complete and turn in weekly at the local school offices.

When you turned in your workbook you were given a box of food; bread, spaghetti, cricket gruel, corn oil. The families of children who didn't complete their workbooks were fined. If you couldn't pay the fines, the whole family could be sent to prison.

It was late summer, and the heat was waning. Since we weren't paying rent we had money for things like dried apples and soy meat. We gathered chickweed in the alleys and made salads from it, picking the small round leaves from the tough stems.

Mother showed me how to make a small stove from a tin can and we broke dry twigs for it and cooked our cricket gruel in a pot over that. In the afternoons we lay in the grass and Mother told me stories about the way things used to be.

At nightfall she walked to work, leaving me in the sedan, where I would lock the doors and climb into the backseat and pull a blanket over myself so that I was hidden. I'd sleep with my face pressed to the cracked pleather, inhaling the scent of her cigarettes.

One day when I was alone in the park I met a young girl. My mother had decided that, at nine years old, I was old enough to look after myself during the day and so she'd picked up another gig. Doing what, she wouldn't tell me.

That morning the sun was gentle and my workbooks were open on the picnic table and I was listening to the birds in the bare winter trees. "This second job could help us get an apartment again," my mother had said as she filled my backpack with my workbooks.

She spread peanut butter on a few cold corn tortillas, folded the sandwich into a plastic grocery bag, and handed it to me. I stood on the frosty grass, shivering in my jacket. The sun had yet to crest the tall buildings that surrounded the park. The car rumbled to life, spitting blue exhaust. "Remember what I said. Don't talk to anyone, and don't leave this park. I'll be back later."

The peanut butter on corn tortillas was the only food I had for the day. Yesterday my ration was the same. It was afternoon now and I was dizzy. The words in my workbook blurred.

"Hey."

She was pretty, with straight white teeth and tidy, shining blonde hair. Her coat, scarf, and gloves were three different shades of pink. She was standing close enough for me to smell her strawberry shampoo.

"I've seen you here before. I come most days with my nanny to have a picnic. My mom said I could ask you to eat with me. We packed extra food."

My mother had told me not to speak to anyone. At the other end of the park a red checked blanket was spread on the grass. A young woman arranged glass containers, pulled plates from a tote bag. Silverware glinted in the sun. Hunger was a small animal that paced back and forth inside of me.

"Ok," I said.

Most of the foods were unfamiliar to me. I ate quickly, the salt and fat and other flavors exploding in my mouth. How much could I get in before they noticed how dirty and undeserving I was and kicked me off their crisp, bright picnic blanket?

The picnic blanket was the cleanest thing I'd seen in ages, and they had it spread right on the muddy grass. The nanny was beautiful, her dark hair smooth, her cheeks rosy from the cold, silver bracelets around her wrist. On the curb idled a long, dark car; their security.

"My name's Brittania," the girl was saying. "And my nanny is Kayleigh."

"I'm Bets," I said. I inhaled the last few bites of a soft, salty vinegary food, rolled into cylinders and wrapped in leaves. "Can I have a slice of cake?"

Kayleigh the beautiful nanny carefully placed a square of vanilla cake on my plate. The pure white frosting had rainbow sprinkles. I'd never had cake like this, not even on my birthday. I felt as though I'd fallen into a dream world.

"My mom says we should help the less fortunate," Brittania was saying. "I bet you want to see my house? I could show you all my toys."

"Ok," I said. There was nothing I would say no to in that moment.

Five blocks from the park where I spent my days doing my workbooks alone and my nights sleeping curled in the backseat of our sedan was the gated community where Brittania lived. The high metal gates slid open for her black sedan and we glided into a spotless world of big houses with green, square lawns. The backseat of the car smelled of leather and the heater put me into a stupor. I hadn't realized that I'd been cold all day, tensed at that picnic table, and now my body melted into the soft seats.

Brittania's house was so big inside it felt spooky, like birds would explode from the rafters. Chandeliers hung from the high ceilings and the furniture was ugly and stiff. Brittania's room was better; deep pink carpet, pale pink walls, piles of plush stuffed animals.

"Let me show you my dolls," Brittania was saying. We'd left her nanny in the kitchen, where she was washing the picnic things. I lay on the carpet and rested my head on a pink stuffed bear. I couldn't shake my stupor. The warmth, the belly full of food, and the fact that I didn't need to keep a vigilant eye on my surroundings lest someone try and steal my backpack had me more relaxed than I'd felt in months. "This is Judy." Brittania was straightening the skirt of a doll with long blonde hair. "She rides a horse. Have you ever ridden a horse?"

"No."

"I didn't think so. This is Dorothy. She's Judy's best friend."

"Ok."

"Do you want to be my best friend?"

"What?" I asked.

"You can be my best friend," Brittania was saying. "You can come over to my house every day and I can show you my dolls."

I didn't know what to say. There was a flash of pain as the Dorothy doll hit my legs.

"You're not even listening! Pay better attention!"

"I'm sorry," I said, sitting up. I was out of my stupor now.

"It's ok," said Brittania sweetly. "I forgive you. Here, let me show you some of my dresses."

It was evening when the long black car dropped me back at the park. My mother hadn't returned yet, and I climbed onto the playground equipment, to the tunnel where I hid after dark while I waited for her.

My head was dancing with the smell of bubblegum and strawberries, with the softness of carpets so clean they made me sneeze, with cupcake frosting and shining crumpled candy wrappers. The kind, beautiful nanny and her gentle hands pulling the snarls from my hair. I curled around my backpack and closed my eyes to shut out the night. There was the rumble of the sedan as it pulled into the park. The slam of a car door.

"Were you ok today?" said Mother. She was opening my workbooks and checking to make sure I'd completed the worksheets. We needed the box of food provided by the city each week, and we couldn't afford the fine.

I stared at her. She left me alone every day with hardly any food, and then she had the nerve to ask if I was ok?

"I was fine," I said.

"You didn't finish your worksheets." She tore the cellophane from a pack of cigarettes, shook one out and lit it. From her purse she produced a pencil, began writing in the workbook.

"Whatever they ask you, just give the answer they want, ok?" she said. "Like here, where it states that abortion is wrong because it deprives the economy of workers, and asks you if this is true or false. Just say true. Don't try to be smart."

"I know."

Mother finished the pages and returned the workbooks to my backpack. I was in the backseat of the sedan, a blanket wrapped around my shoulders. We could afford to run the car heater for a little while, now that mother had this second job.

The smell of gasoline and the gentle vibration of the engine comforted me. Mother drew on her cigarette, cracked the window, blew the smoke out the window and rolled it back up. In a few hours she would leave again for her night job, and I would sleep.

"I don't like leaving you alone," she said. "Just a little while longer and we'll be able to get our own place." She shut off the engine and I felt the cold pressing its hands against the car windows, eager to get in.

Mother shook another cigarette from the pack. I wondered how she was able to buy cigarettes, when we barely had money for food. I remembered the warmth of Brittania's room, tried to draw that memory around me against the encroaching night.

After that first delirious afternoon at Brittania's house, warm in her pink bedroom and full of food, I started spending most of my days there. She showed me all her dolls and stuffed animals and then she showed me her doll houses and tea sets, her dresses, her hats and wigs and tiaras, her purses, her makeup kits, her nail polish, her bicycle, her rollerskates, her shoes.

She explained her belongings to me one by one while I lay on the plush deep pink carpet, stupefied from cupcakes and cookies and candy, from macadamia butter on water crackers and fistfuls of grapes and delicate little salmon roe sandwiches.

The parade of her belongings and the sing-song of her voice was like a pleasant, if meaningless fever dream I experienced while reclined in the pile of her teddy bears, twisting an iridescent taffy wrapper in my fingers, watching the way it winked in the pink light of her bedroom lamps.

If I went too long without making a sound of understanding, a muttered "cool" or "that's really pretty," she would throw whatever she was describing directly at me—which hurt if it was a shoe, but just made her look stupid if it was, say, a feather boa.

I tried not to laugh—laughing was a sure way to upset her more, after which I would be driven into the hallway and she would slam her door and I would hear her wailing, the sound like a wounded animal being burned with hot coals. The only thing to do when this happened was leave, head down, and hope I would see her at the park again soon.

The next day I wouldn't see her, and neither the day after that, but eventually she would reappear, and sweetly take my hand. I'd learned from this experience what not to say or do, and I was getting better at not getting kicked out of her house. Just before sunset each day I'd excuse myself and run back to the park, backpack full of workbooks bouncing against my back, and I'd hide in the tunnel on the playground equipment and wait for my mother.

When she arrived a few hours later she'd light a cigarette, punch the dome light in the sedan to turn it on, pull the workbooks from my backpack and finish my homework without speaking. We were talking less and less these days. She seemed tired from her second job, like a vitality was being drained from her.

I watched her finish my homework and light a second cigarette off the dying ember of the first. Bitterness rose up in me as I wondered again how she could afford cigarettes when, according to her, we had no money for additional food.

Tomorrow she'd make me another sandwich of peanut butter on cold corn tortillas, and I'd throw it in the trash again on my way to Brittania's. Was there some way I could stay at Brittania's forever? How good it would feel to sleep curled in that plush pink carpet at the foot of Brittania's bed like a dog.

One day we were in Brittania's kitchen, her showing me all her play cookware while the nanny smashed pie crust with a rolling pin, when there was a great commotion. The housekeeper rushed around picking up dropped toys and hanging up coats and straightening pillows, and a heavy creak sounded as the front doors swung open and in walked a couple that I guessed to be Brittania's parents.

Her mother was short, plump, blonde, and frowning, wearing a checked wool dress and a white beret, and her father wore a dark suit and had the tight, shining cheeks of someone so wealthy that his face didn't show his true age. Brittania had frozen in her play, a bright enamel pot in each fist, and the nanny looked stunned for a moment and then rearranged her mouth into a smile.

"You two are back a week early," she said cheerily.

"What's that supposed to mean," snapped the mother. The nanny looked down at her pie crust and continued rolling but slowly, stiffly. "Brittania," the mother said. "Come here." Brittania stood and shuffled over to her mother, wrapped her arms around her mother's waist and buried her face in her mother's wool dress. Her mother stroked her hair. "My darling. It's been so hard to be away from you." She looked up at me, sitting cross-legged on the smooth white tile of the kitchen.

"You must be Bets, the poor girl from the park? The nanny told me about you. I hope you've felt welcomed and well taken care of at this house."

"I have," I said.

"And you'll be staying for dinner tonight? It's a special occasion—Father's company has a new acquisition!"

Usually we ate in Brittania's room or at the heavy wooden table in the kitchen where the nanny kneaded bread dough in a dusting of flour, but tonight the French doors of the dining room were opened and the long dark table within was set with white plates, white platters, white tureens, gleaming silverware and a feast so opulent that I was intoxicated just looking at it.

A dozen taper candles dripped onto the linen table runner and fresh bouquets made the room smell like springtime, even though outside it was still midwinter. I stared at the flowers, thinking about how there were food shortages everywhere and so many things were nearly impossible to get, and yet somewhere there was a farm that existed solely to grow… these flowers.

"You like the bouquets?" I startled. It was Brittania's father, leaning in the doorway of the dining room. I'd been drawn inside like a moth to a flame, and I realized how strange I must look in my dirty, faded clothes, pressed close to this table with its glittering spread.

"Those flowers were grown by the inmates in workhouse A-7," he said. "Inmates have few opportunities. They appreciate the chance to work, even for free. To participate in something as wonderful as flower growing. Because of this we have fragrant bouquets in the dead of winter, something that would be impossible otherwise. It's beautiful, isn't it?"

"Prisoners grew these?" I asked.

"Of course," said Brittania's father. "Prisoners produced almost everything in this room. In this house. The dishes, cutlery, furniture. They raised the farm animals and grew the vegetables. They tailored the suit I'm wearing and they built my car. They sewed your clothes, too. And made your shoes."

I looked down at my shoes, which were scuffed and too small. Each night I sighed in relief when I removed them in the back of the sedan and my cramped toes were finally able to uncurl.

"If prisoners are making clothes and shoes and food and stuff," I said, "why are those things still so hard to get?"

"The demand is still higher than what the prisoners can produce," he said. "In the past, we imported those things from other countries, where the people making the goods were paid so little that they were nearly working for free. We don't buy anything from overseas anymore, we have to make it here. But there aren't nearly enough prisoners to make as much as we used to have."

I stared at him. He was repeating the propaganda from my school workbooks. Or at least, my mother had said it was propaganda, while she filled out the answers in the workbook for me, cigarette dangling from the corner of her mouth, the slug of ashes growing longer until it fell onto her dirty jeans.

"There are plenty of people in the city who are criminals," continued Brittania's father. "People who move goods on the black market, who steal and cheat and lie. These people have no future, and contribute nothing to society. In prison, these people are given an opportunity to help rebuild this great nation—that opportunity is a gift. We only need to know who these people are so that we can put them to work, and of course we need more prisons to house them. It's an elegant solution to this country's current economic problems."

Brittania's father uncorked a bottle of wine on the table and poured himself a glass, raised it into the air. "And that's why we're celebrating today—because my company has acquired another tract of land, full of decommissioned apartment buildings, that will be rebuilt as a new prison!"

Brittania's mother entered the dining room with a steaming pot and set it on the table with the others.

"It's good that you're here," she said to me. "We know how hard it is out there. You're just a child. However you've suffered—you don't deserve it. You deserve to be well fed, to be housed and cared for. I'm glad that we can give you a little of that care. I hope it shows you what's possible. What sort of life you might make for yourself one day."

"It's been very nice to spend time here," I said quietly. I was watching the nanny use tongs to transfer fresh rolls from their baking sheet into a basket lined with white cloth. She finished and folded the cloth over the rolls, as though tucking them into bed. I imagined how I would tear open one of those rolls and spread butter on the inside, how the butter would melt and run down my arm while I ate it.

I returned to the park much later than usual that night. Our car was there, sitting in our spot, the driver's side window cracked, a curl of cigarette smoke drifting out.

"Where were you?" Mother hissed angrily when I pulled open the back door and slid inside, onto the cracked pleather. The engine was running and the air in the car was warm and stale.

"At a friend's house," I said.

"Friend? What friend? You don't have any friends." She yanked my backpack from me and pulled out my workbooks. A peanut butter sandwich fell out, onto the passenger seat. Fuck! I'd forgotten to throw it away. She held it up and shook it. "You find another place to eat today? Huh? Who have you been hanging out with?"

"What?" I said, shocked. "Just a friend I met here in the park. I go to her house."

"A friend with a house?" Mother's eyes were narrow slits, her lips pulled back in a scowl. "Who have you been hanging out with?"

"No one, mom! It doesn't matter!"

She dropped the sandwich.

"Whoever it is, you'd better stop hanging out with them. Nothing is free in this world. You hear me? *Nothing*. If someone's giving you something, it means they want something from you. Tell me you won't hang out with this friend again."

"I was so hungry," I said, quietly. Mother turned and faced the front of the car. There was the flick of her lighter as she lit another cigarette. The cherry glowed red in the dim.

"I'll try and get us some more food," she said. "Just no more going to this friend's house, ok?"

"Ok," I said.

I was more careful after that. I waited in the mornings for an hour after my mother left before making my way to Brittania's neighborhood, and I always returned to the park well before dark. The one time mother came back early and caught me gone, I told her that I'd been scavenging in the trash piles in the alley, and I showed her a box of worn down, broken crayons and some colored paper that I had found. I'd stolen these things from Brittania's house, broken the crayons and rubbed the paper in the dirt a little, keeping them in my backpack in case I needed to use this excuse. Mother looked at me sideways but said nothing.

She'd started giving me two peanut butter sandwiches a day and cooking me cricket gruel in the morning. I choked down the unsweetened gruel, which was nearly inedible without the spice of hunger, and, no longer trusting the trash can, I threw the sandwiches into a dirt yard full of barking dogs on the way to Brittania's, watching the dogs snarl and huff as they shred the meager rations.

I'd stopped waiting for mother to announce that our life on the streets was over—that she'd found us an apartment. I knew that no apartment was forthcoming. Whatever mother did for her second job—move goods on the black market, most likely—it seemed to pay only enough to cover the two packs of cigarettes she smoked each day.

There was no future for us. And that's why I had a new plan. My new plan was to convince Brittania's family to adopt me. Why not? They had a huge house and plenty of money. I was their daughter's best friend.

Brittania's mother was home most days now, and one morning while we were playing with her pink plastic horses Brittania told me that her father would be home that weekend, on a break from overseeing the construction of his new prison.

I decided that was the weekend I would propose that they adopt me. I would borrow a dress from Brittania, and let the nanny braid my hair. Brittania's parents would be overjoyed at the idea—of course they would be! And I would never have to spend another night in the sedan, curled on my side under a too-thin blanket, shivering from the cold.

I felt light that afternoon as I ran back to the park, knowing that my new life was just a few days away. The haze over the city had been particularly thick lately, but today the winter sun was gentle, almost springlike, and the future felt like a warm place. I was a block from the park when our sedan pulled up alongside me and jostled to a stop.

"Where do you think you're going," said Mother.

"I…" I was too startled to think of what to say. "I was just out looking—"

"Bullshit," said Mother. "I know you've been up to something. I followed you this morning. I saw you enter that gated community. I waited for you all day. What were you doing in there?"

"That's where my friend lives, ok?" I said.

"You're friend lives in *there*?" cried my mother, jabbing her finger in the direction of Brittania's neighborhood.

"Yeah," I said. "So what? My friend's name is Brittania, and her family has been feeding me. They have lots of food. LOTS of it. It's been great." I was crying now. Mother opened the door of the sedan, stepped out, and slammed it behind her.

"Do you have any idea what those people do?" She was screaming. I looked around to see if anyone was watching but we were alone on the trash-strewn street. "To get all that money? Do you have *any* idea?"

She grabbed me by my shoulders and shook me. Her face was blurry through my tears. "I've been using our money to feed you extra when I should be saving it for our future, and this whole time you've been *lying* to me? And what? Throwing the food away?"

My mother was gone. She'd disappeared, and a monster had taken her place. She hit me in the face—hard. I fell over onto the dirt street and felt the pointed toe of her boot in my back. More kicks—on my legs, in my ass, in my shoulders. I curled into a ball, but the kicks kept coming. I shut my eyes, closed my mouth, locked the doors, and descended a narrow staircase deep into the root cellar of my body.

There was a small, windowless room there with a heavy, wooden door. I pushed the door shut with great effort and latched it with a thick iron latch. I lit a single candle and crouched in the corner of the room. Far away I could hear shouting and noises, but in here it was safe. Here in the cellar I felt nothing.

I waited for a long time after the noises stopped before climbing out of the cellar. When I opened my eyes the sedan was gone. I was in pain—great, throbbing pain, but I also knew that this was only the beginning of pain, that the worse pain would come later, in more ways than one, and that I had a short window of time in which to move my broken body to safety. I pulled myself up with great difficulty and limped back the way I had come, towards Brittania's house.

Sitting in warm, fragrant water in the clawfoot tub, I winced as the nanny moved a washcloth gently over my bruises.

"I'm so sorry this happened to you," she said. Brittania was at her horse riding lessons, and her mother was out. The house was quiet. It felt good to have the nanny's attention so focused on me, to have the enchanted world of this house all to myself. It felt special. I wondered if this was what it would be like sometimes, after they adopted me. I closed my eyes, tried to make the moment last forever.

There was the sound of the front doors opening downstairs. Then the clack of heels on tile.

"Kayleigh?" Brittania's mother called out.

"I'm upstairs," responded the nanny in her calm, even voice. I could hear Brittania's mother sigh in frustration as she mounted the steps to the second floor. In the doorway she stopped, her eyes wide in surprise.

"Bets!" she said. "What happened to you?"

"My mother…" I trailed off. I looked at the nanny and she nodded, her eyes full of warmth. "My mother found out that I was coming here and she beat me, left me in the street."

Brittania's mother gasped and covered her mouth with her hand.

"Why, that's horrible," she said. "Why wouldn't your mother want you coming here? We feed you and care for you, when she so obviously won't!"

I was crying now, the tears running down my face, dripping off my chin into the bathwater.

"Well, Bets, I'm glad that Kayleigh was here to tend to your injuries. You're welcome to stay for dinner this evening if you'd like."

"I better not," I said. "If I'm late getting back again mother will be even angrier." I wasn't ready to mention my proposition. Not now, naked in this tub, my bruises on display. I still wanted to wait until the weekend, when I could wear a nice dress. I didn't want them to see me as a pathetic street kid, begging to be adopted. I wanted them to see my potential—everything that I could be. That was the only way it was going to work.

"I just don't understand these parents," continued Brittania's mother. "Why they don't look after their own children. Why they squander their money instead of saving and investing. Many of them have been given every opportunity, and they just keep making terrible choices!"

"I know," I said. "That's how I feel too. But she says that you all are terrible people! And you're not! I know you're not!"

"Why would your mother say that about us?" Brittania's mother was silent a moment, her eyes thoughtful. She pulled out her phone and tapped at the screen. "What does your mother do for work?" she asked.

Mother was sitting on the hood of the car when I returned to the park, watching the last of the light fade, smoking a cigarette. When she saw me she leapt up and gathered her jacket around me, and began to cry.

"I'm so sorry," she said. "I'm so, so sorry. I don't know what came over me. I've been so stressed lately from these long hours at work. I haven't been myself. I just snapped. I'm so sorry. This is not who I am. I want to do better."

I inhaled the warm scent of her, tried not to wince in pain. Her tears wet the top of my head. I was far away, candle in hand, halfway down the cellar stairs. Her words came from a great distance. I felt nothing.

That night it rained, and I focused on the sound of the water drumming on the metal roof as I lay curled in the backseat of the sedan. I couldn't sleep. Just a few more days until I left this life behind forever and moved into that warm house full of love and care. Just a few more days.

CHAPTER 8

The morning after my mother beat me in the street, the gate to Brittania's neighborhood didn't open when I punched in the code. I stood staring at the gate, waiting for it to swing inward but it only sat, silent and unmoving. It was the same code I'd used every day to enter Brittania's neighborhood—but this morning the gate wouldn't let me pass.

I entered the code again, more slowly this time, thinking that I'd maybe gotten a number wrong. Again, the gate did not move. I banged my fists against it, this tall soulless object that separated my two worlds. I must've made a mistake. That had to be it. I entered the code again, and again after another moment. The gate made no sound. Not even the wind stirred.

Mother had been extra kind to me that morning. She'd kissed the top of my head, brushed my hair roughly, slipped dried fruit into my backpack alongside the peanut butter sandwiches.

"I'm so sorry I haven't been taking good care of you," she'd said. "I'm going to do better. Things are going to change." She opened her pack of cigarettes, showed me that it was empty. "I've decided to quit smoking! See? I want to get us out of this hell that we're in. I've just been so checked out, but I know what's important. You're all that I have in the world. I don't want to lose you."

Her words had floated in the air around me, declined to settle on my heart. I was thinking about breakfast at Brittania's, wondering if they were making blackberry waffles. Soon I wouldn't have to go back and forth every day—maybe, once they adopted me, I'd even have a bedroom in their house of my very own!

I punched in the code again, my fingers stiff from the cold, and a long, sharp sound came from the box on the wall. A red light switched on. I froze, confused, and after a moment heard the sound of tires on gravel behind me.

"We've got an attempted entry," I heard a voice say, and then the crackle of a CB radio. A large man stepped out of a golf cart. "You know you can't go in there," he said.

"My friend lives here," I said. "Brittania. I know her parents too. I'm at their house every day!" The security guard looked me up and down—my faded clothes, my school backpack, my too-small shoes.

"What are your friend's parents' names?" he asked.

"I—I don't know," I mumbled.

"Right," he said. He pressed the button on his CB radio. "Jim, can you come over here?"

I ran. The crunch of gravel sounded as the man stumbled back to his golf cart, the rumble of the engine starting. I was fast, though. And I knew this neighborhood. One turn into an alleyway, another turn into an empty lot. Duck behind the row of dumpsters. The tips of my shoes fit easily in the holes in the chain-link. Over the top and down the other side, onto the dirt. Stars of pain as I landed on my hands and knees. This road would take me back to the park.

Was I hidden enough in the park, though? Mother wouldn't return until later. There was an abandoned warehouse next to a loading dock and I made my way there, clambered up a metal staircase sprinkled with broken glass, darted along the dim hallway to a room with busted out windows, rotten drywall, the floor covered in fallen ceiling tiles.

I didn't come here usually because it wasn't safe—I'd heard lots of sketchy things went down here. But I knew the security guard wouldn't follow me here. That was the only safe I needed right now.

Clearing a spot with my foot, I sat and hugged my knees to my chest. What had happened? Had I gotten the code wrong somehow? Or had Brittania's family changed it, and forgotten to tell me? It must be a mistake. In a few days I'd see Brittania in the park again when she came to picnic, and we'd clear this up.

I was hungry. I wished I hadn't thrown my food to the dogs that morning. Even the dried fruit! There was no way to get more food until later, when mother returned. I curled on my side on the floor, using my backpack as a pillow, and gazed out the empty window at the rooftops, the drooping powerlines, the gunmetal sky. By evening, I imagined, the security guard would grow tired of looking for me and give up his search, and then I would go.

It was black in the tunnel when I woke that evening. I'd returned to the park, and when it had started to rain I'd crawled into my tunnel. What time was it? I didn't know. I peered out, into the wet dim. The spot where the sedan usually sat was empty. Where was Mother? I felt strange from hunger—light and clear, a little dizzy. A bit of worry was gnawing at my heart.

When I woke again it was truly late, the deepest part of the night, and still Mother was not there. I knew, beyond all reason, that something was wrong. Mother had never just not come back. Never. I tried to think of where I could go, who I could ask for help. But there was only Brittania and her family. They were all the friends I had in the world. And if I went back to that gated neighborhood I might be arrested. And then disappeared. I was cold in the tunnel, and very hungry.

Eventually morning would come, and the day would warm a little. Maybe I would see Brittania in the park today. She'd be wearing her pink dress with the bows and carrying a box of cupcakes. The sun would be out. She'd run towards me, laughing, and explain that they'd forgotten to give me the new gate code. I'd be stiff from my long night in the tunnel and so glad to see her.

The cupcakes would be vanilla with rainbow sprinkles and I'd eat three of them, one after the other, and then we'd go back to her house, where I'd take a hot bath and then wrap myself in a fluffy robe and the nanny would braid my hair.

A little water was leaking into the tunnel. The rain was heavier now, drumming loudly on the plastic. Lying down there was no way to stay out of the puddle that was forming but if I sat up, I could scrunch myself against the tunnel wall and stay more or less dry. No more sleep for me tonight, I guess. I just had to wait until dawn and everything would be ok. Everything was going to be ok.

On the third morning I knew that it was time to leave the park. Mother had not returned. Brittania had not returned. The rain had stopped, and a deep chill had settled over the city. Winter's last hurrah. I'd scavenged cardboard and some plastic grocery bags from a dumpster nearby and used these to cover myself in the tunnel at night. The only food I'd had was half an onion bagel, found in a puddle on the ground behind the dumpster. I wished I had some way to start a fire.

I didn't think about the future—I didn't have any thoughts at all. My heart was a dead bird inside my chest. Presently the bird began to stink and crawl with maggots. Shouldering my backpack I began to walk, lightheaded with hunger, unsure of where I was going.

My feet took me to the abandoned warehouse next to the loading dock. It wasn't safe here, but what was the worst that could happen? Death? Death wouldn't be so bad. At least I wouldn't be hungry or cold anymore if I was dead.

The broken glass crunched under my feet as I explored the different levels of the building. The walls of the empty rooms were covered in graffiti—militia tags, propaganda, crude drawings of sex. Some rooms had moldering mattresses on the floor. I stepped carefully over used syringes, crumpled trash, bottles of urine.

At last I found what I was seeking—another human being. A woman was curled on one of these mattresses. Her thin hair was splayed around her, and she was underdressed for the weather, in white clothes turned the color of dirt.

"What the fuck do you think you're doing?" she said when I entered the room. She sat up, and I saw that her face was old, as though she'd been alive for a thousand years.

"I don't know actually," I said. "My mom disappeared. I don't have anyone in the world."

She looked me up and down.

"You shouldn't be here. You're just a kid."

"Do you have any food?"

"Fuck no I don't have any food. Who do you think I am? Now get lost."

I took off my backpack and sat on the floor.

"I'm sorry," I said. "It's just that I don't have anywhere to go. There's literally nowhere. If it's time for me to die, that's ok. I accept that."

"Die?" she said. She began to cough, and spat yellow into her hands, wiped her hands on the mattress. "You won't die if you stay here." She laughed. Her laugh was hoarse. "You're young, you'll live a long time. But you'll wake up every day and wish you were dead!" There was the sound of boots on the metal stairwell.

"Shit!" she said. "You've got to go. Look. Go to Beryl's junkyard. He takes care of kids like you. Ask on the street until you find someone who knows where that is. Now get the fuck out of here!"

I ran from the room. My life, it seemed, had become a series of running. I was tired of running. I was tired in general. But still, I ran.

CHAPTER 9

When I wake on the concrete floor of the KOA cabin the bit of light coming from the window is absent. It must be night. The floor is cool, but not too bad—I've slept in colder places. For an indeterminate amount of time I've been lying here, unsure if my eyes are open or closed, if the dark I see is the dark of the cabin or the dark of my own mind.

I drifted off and then startled awake again and again, from one terrible imagining into the next. Lisle on the stage, telling me that my heart is full of blackness. That there is no place for me.

My mother, spitting rage, slamming the door of the sedan and driving away as I lay in the dirt street on my side. The gentle scrape of the nanny's acrylic nails on my scalp as she braids my hair in the warm kitchen with its smell of baking bread.

The years I lived at Beryl's junkyard, wrenching parts alongside the other children, Beryl's kindness and stale butterscotches, retreating at night to the truck campershell in the weeds. The ache of missing my mother those first years on my own.

The first time I met Georgia was at a rally against skyrocketing food prices. She and her friends were giving out dumpstered bread. I joined her in the wee hours that night, gathering the day-old bread from the trash compactors behind the bakeries on the wealthy side of town—it was risky work, but she had a stolen key and if you timed it right you could get as much bread as you could possibly carry.

We finished just before dawn and she let me crash on the floor of her bedroom, in an apartment she shared with eight other people. I remember waking beside her bed and watching her sleep, her wild hair splayed across the rumpled pillow. The blanket, a quilt with squares missing and torn, bunched around her feet, the warm animal smell of her already knitting itself inside of me, fusing with some deep understanding of home.

Georgia's friends became my friends, and I felt as though I had found my people. But organizing in the city is incredibly dangerous. My new friends and I trusted each other with our lives. It was worth it because we knew that if we just tried hard enough, we could change things. We could halt all this suffering, this darkness and death.

I learned later on that believing a thing doesn't make it true. The disillusionment came slow at first and then fast, like a broken dam whose waters, once rushing, cannot be stopped. For a long time I didn't want to acknowledge how the dam was cracked. How no matter what successes we had, there were never any real gains; power only shifted, and after the dust settled the monster was still there, only a slightly different shape. Our hearts broke, and over time the group fractured, and many friends disappeared.

We were insane for the light, and the light burned us up.

The cabin is silent the next time I wake; the grey light on the upper part of the wall means that it's day. My mind feels mixed up. There's too much in there, layers of sediment and right now it's all swirling around, like snow in a shaken snow globe. I rub my face with my hands—my cheeks are puffy and hot.

What is the point of this imprisonment? Is it supposed to kill me? If so, by what means? Starvation? And if not, if death is not the point, will I be let out eventually? Or tortured in some other way?

My memory wanders back to my mother and I think of her talking to me about the second job she'd just gotten while we sat on the picnic table in the empty park, sharing a pot of cricket gruel. The pay was decent, she was saying, and in time she would be able to make more. I wasn't paying much attention; I was watching the aluminum pot, counting the number of bites we'd each taken, guessing how many bites were left.

It was three days until Friday, when I could turn in my workbooks for another box of food. Maybe this week there'd be unlabeled cans. Those were exciting, because you never knew what was inside. Sometimes it was meat, or fruit.

In the years since that conversation, I'd tried to puzzle out what her second job had actually been; I'd replayed her words that day again and again, looking for clues but finding nothing. No-one knew for sure where people were taken when they were disappeared, but most likely they were simply imprisoned and made to work for free producing consumer goods. The one thing I knew for sure was that when people were disappeared from the city, they rarely came back.

I watch the grey light as it shifts on the cabin wall. I'm going to be trapped here forever, lost in the halls of my memories. Counting my losses with both hands. Honestly, I cannot think of any worse fate.

CHAPTER 10

The hunger is gone. Food has become an abstract concept, the thought of chewing and swallowing almost barbaric. My head feels light, buzzy; it's harder, now, to track the passing days. Has it been a week that I've been locked up in this cabin? Longer? I'm not sure.

Mostly what I feel is cold; the chill has gotten into my bones, and I can't stop shivering. I think I've come to understand why I am here. Lisle saw the black spot inside of me, the inherent badness. The reason that the world had rejected me, spit me out like a piece of rotten food.

A slow starvation death in this cold cabin prison is what I deserve.

It's night, and I'm wandering the house in my dreams again. A door opens onto an abandoned apartment like the ones that Georgia and I liberated for the people of the city, and the sadness contained inside drifts around me like ghosts. One room in the apartment is the backseat of my mother's sedan; she's sitting in the driver's seat and I call her name, but she won't turn around and look at me.

Other rooms hold only objects, and a feeling that the occupants have just stepped out; I examine the dirty dishes in the sink, the clothing tossed carelessly on beds, the contents of the bathroom drawers. I feel most alone when I am in these rooms, as though I am intimate with the human world the way one can be intimate with the set of a play, but that I'll never be one of the actors, never be written into the script.

Then there's a warm room with a crackling fireplace, a couch piled with blankets. The dog is curled in a tight donut in the blankets. He sees me, lifts his head and wriggles his whole body.

"Dog!" I say. I lower myself onto the couch, curl my body around his. The blankets are soft, and I pull them over both of us. The dog licks my nose. His mouth smells like trash and his fur is dusty. "Can dogs see into souls?" I ask him. He lays his ears back on his small round head, stares at me with his dark wet eyes. Licks my face again. He tucks his nose under his tail, goes to sleep.

Under the blankets with the dog is safe. He and I are joined, two beings in the same world. He trusts me. It may not count for much among humans, but here is a being who I have done right by. The dog thinks that I am good. Who knows the true measure of my soul, Lisle or the dog? What is the true measure of my soul?

The wooden floor creaks under footsteps, and then the couch springs shift as someone settles themselves down. They smell of butterscotch candy. I pull the blanket from my face. The man's big overalls are stained with grease. His hands are pink with eczema, and he rubs them together.

"Beryl?" The dog shifts, pops out from the blanket like a cork from underwater. He bounds to Beryl and sits on his lap. Beryl scratches behind the dog's ears. "What are you doing here?" I ask.

"I live here," says Beryl. He digs in the bib pocket of his overalls with one large, red hand, extracts a butterscotch candy and hands it to me. "Among other places. What are *you* doing here?"

"I like to visit this place sometimes," I say.

"I know you do," says Beryl. I hold the butterscotch tightly in my fist but I cannot imagine eating.

"I was just thinking," I say to Beryl, "that I'm probably bad? That there's a black spot inside of me. A black spot that can never be cut out. Except it's confusing, because the dog thinks that I am good. So I was wondering, who is the more accurate judge of these things? How do I know for sure if I'm bad or good?"

Beryl crunches his butterscotch thoughtfully. "Listen kid," he says to me. "There's no black spot inside of you."

"What?" The fire crackles. Its warmth is soft on my face. "But I feel the black spot there. Sometimes it grows, gets big enough to swallow me. I got my mom disappeared. When Brittania's parents asked me what she did for work I told them that I didn't know, but that one of her jobs might be moving goods on the black market. I never saw her again after that day. I'm the reason she's gone." I'm crying now. It feels like throwing up. Snot is running down my face and my eyes are blurred with tears. Beryl waits for me to finish.

"You know," he says. "I have a few burdens of my own. They're heavy on my shoulders." He pats my feet under the blanket. "The thing is to not shrug it off. You've got to let it settle into the deepest parts of you, into all the cracks. Until there's no separation left. I know you're strong enough to carry it."

I'm crying again, turning inside out. It comes in waves. I'm no longer on the couch with Beryl, in the warm room with the fire. I'm in the sea, being tossed around in a storm. I'm inhaling lungfuls of water, sinking to the bottom of the ocean. I've died, and my body is being consumed by the things that live in the sea. As my body fragments I become formless. I contain nothing.

When I wake I'm empty. The dusty concrete floor is back, cold underneath my body. The cabin is dark, the boarded-up window is dark. After a few moments I sit up and rub my legs, my body incredibly stiff from lying on the hard floor. I decide I should try and move around a bit and the wall holds me up as I walk along it, tracing my fingers over its surface.

When I reach the door I press my ear to the heavy wood. The village after dark is so quiet. This silence is not something that, as a child growing up in the chaos of the city, I could have ever imagined. This collective rest. The earth, closing its eyes. I picture the villagers at home in their beds. The chickens in their coops. The gardens quiet under the moon. What phase of the moon is it now?

The doorknob is cold in my hand. I've tried to pick the lock with every item I could find in the cabin—which, granted, is not very many items—a sliver of wood, a loose nail worked from the wall with my fingers. And anyway, I have many skills, but lock picking is not one of them. I'm much handier with a crowbar. If only there was a little more light. And Georgia. Georgia knows how to pick locks. I jiggle the doorknob. It turns.

The door is unlocked.

I freeze with the doorknob in my hand, waiting for the rigid stillness of the night to shatter like a sheet of glass. There'll be an explosion of guards. I'll be beaten. That's it! This is when the beating will begin.

Nothing happens. After a moment I turn the knob again, and pull it towards me. The door opens easily. Outside, the wholeness of the night is unbroken. The air is soft. I can smell the forest.

When I step onto the deck, I almost trip over my bike, which is propped against the doorframe. My eyes are adjusting to the light of the half moon in the cloudless sky and I can see the panniers, strapped to the rear rack. Still full with my things. My backpack rests on the deck next to the bike. I squeeze the flat tire—it's been repaired. No dog, though. My heart sinks.

Suddenly I realize that there's someone standing there, in the shadows, and I startle.

"I don't mean to scare you," says David. His blousy clothing glows softly in the moonlight. "The feds are here. You've got to get going. I brought you your bike. There's food in the panniers."

"You're setting me free?" My brow knits in confusion.

"Bets," he says, his voice tight with urgency. "You need to leave." He steps closer. I can see the whites of his eyes in the dark. He reaches out, grasps one of my hands in his. His hand is bony and warm, and his nails bite into my palm.

"I won't live long enough to see what happens after the Pluto return," he says. "But you will. Now go. You don't have much time."

Adrenaline wins out over my fatigue and I climb onto the bike and pedal as noiselessly as I can through the village, past the cabins and then alongside a series of dark vehicles parked near the main office building. I force my shaking legs to pedal faster. The village recedes behind me and I am swallowed by the dark again. The cracked asphalt carries me to the highway and the wide interstate is empty, its concrete glowing softly in the moonlight.

As I pedal, heart racing, the wind lifting my hair around my face, the continued loneliness of this journey envelops me. Without the dog I feel vulnerable and exposed. Without that one small friend, I feel as though a single gust of this wind could knock me over. I know I should get as far as I can before the sun rises, but I'm dizzy with hunger and my vision feels strange—the road blurs and then clears, spots dance at the corners of my eyes, it's hard to make sense of the textures of the night.

I've made it just a few miles down the highway, by my guess, when I drag my bike off the road and deep into the trees, crashing through the undergrowth until I know I'm not visible from the road. I heft my bike over logs and through the fallen leaves to a clearing. The sky is just beginning to pale when I smooth my sleeping bag onto the loamy ground.

When I open my panniers, I find my leftover ramen and peanut butter as well as a sack of millet. My water bottles are full. It's warm inside my sleeping bag and I have a brick of dry ramen in there with me, that I break into small pieces and make myself chew and swallow.

My head is an abandoned building, full of birds. The birds are knocking around, the sounds of their wings echoing off the high stone walls. I don't understand anything, but I think I may be safe now. I close my eyes.

It's midday when I wake. I stare at the sky through the leaves while the previous nights' events coalesce around me. Once my mind clears I sit up, careful with my aching body. As I'm removing things from my panniers, a slip of paper falls out and I hold it up to the light.

Go towards your shadow, not away from it. Love, Lisle.

What the fuck?

I drop the note onto the leaves and stare at it as if it's a scorpion with its tail curled, ready to sting. What does that even mean? I sit motionless for a moment, paralyzed by fear and then shake my head, trying to clear it. It doesn't matter what the note means. I'm free now and my bike is fixed. That's what's important.

Eat, commands some exhausted executive part of me. I snap twigs off the lower limbs of the pine trees for my tin can cookstove and pour millet and water into my pot. The grain, when ready, is thick and comforting in its blandness, and I eat the entire pot, even scraping up the burnt bits stuck to the bottom. Afterwards fatigue overwhelms me, and instead of packing up my sleeping bag like I'd planned, I lie back on the ground and watch the light move in the trees. Letting my eyes unfocus on the bits of blue sky between the branches is its own sort of food.

Something in the soft, dark night wakes me, and it takes me a moment to remember where I am. Then the fear dissipates somewhat—I'm in the forest. I am safe here. I have no idea what time it is but the moon is out, casting the trees in silver. There's the rustling again—is it a racoon? A coyote? An animal that I'm not familiar with? I reach for the pot and lift it, ready to smack anything that would try and take my millet.

A small round creature wriggles at me in the moonlight.

"Dog!" I gasp. He dances onto my sleeping bag and jostles up against me. Putting his paws on my chest, he licks frantically at my face. I run my hands over his thin frame, his fur sticky with pitch. Now I'm crying. "Dog! How did you find me?" I sob as I hold him against me. He smells of the earth. "Oh dog!" He's warm and alive. His fur is wet with my tears.

I make another small fire and put the pot on. Some water, a handful of millet, a spoonful of peanut butter. "I'm going to make you a feast," I say. The jar lid is still in my pannier, and I pour some water for him and he drinks. "Oh dog," I say, stroking his fur. "I never want to lose you again."

After the dog is fed we both curl in my sleeping bag, my large body around his small one. The moon sets, and the wind sings a lullaby in the boughs of the trees. Maybe it's stupid, but for a moment, before drifting off, I am the happiest that I've ever been.

In the morning, I admit to myself that I have no idea what to do next.

Sitting on the ground with the sleeping bag wrapped around me, the dog sleeps on my lap while I read *An RVer's Guide to the American West*. There's a chill in the air today. I wonder what the date is, when the leaves will fall, how long I have until the nights freeze.

Growing up, I learned the cycles of nature in the city; watching the weather, the trash-choked ditches, the brush of neglected lots and the copses of trees in industrial neighborhoods. I studied the feral creatures, who were just trying to survive as they went about their business. I was a feral creature, just trying to survive, going about my business. Out here is not so different from the streets; there's less to eat, maybe, or at least I'm not sure where the food comes from. Otherwise, it's familiar. Stay warm. Stay dry. Stay moving.

The maps in my book are little help. They tell me that Nevada is still to the west, and there are entries for campgrounds between here and there, but I have no idea the current state of these campgrounds. They could be abandoned, all the infrastructure broken and destroyed. Or some of their infrastructure could still be intact—they could be useful as places to refill my water. Or they could be occupied by cults or militia.

What I need is more current information. I should've asked people at the village for intel on the road ahead. The days before I was locked up had passed in a daze—I assumed I would have more time there. I wish I'd asked David more questions. Now I'm on my own again, with limited food, and still no plan.

And what about what Lisle said, that my mother is in prison and soon there will be a fire? Where are the prisons, and which one would she be in? Do I try and find her and save her before the fire or do I just stick to my original plan and head west to Nevada, assuming Lisle's info is bullshit and my mother will be in Nevada like she wrote in her note?

The most important thing right now, I decide, is to get farther away from the city. Farther from the feds—far enough that I never have to think about them again. Other decisions will have to come later. So I'll pack up my panniers and continue west. But first, I need to clear my head. I whittle the tip of the pencil with my knife and heft the RVer's guide, flipping through until I find a page with lots of white space. In the cabin I'd missed being able to journal, to get everything I was thinking down on paper. So now, sitting in the dappled light of morning with the dog curled next to me, I begin to write.

CHAPTER 11

JANE

I should have slit his fucking throat.

I knew who he was the moment I saw him coming towards me on the sidewalk that cold winter morning as I walked to my first appointment of the day, but I hesitated. I hesitated because I'd grown comfortable, because I didn't want to believe it was true—that this moment had, in fact, come, the moment I had always imagined. The knife was in my pocket, the same place it always was when I went to my appointments. I'd used the knife before—I was no stranger to this knife—and yet I hesitated. That hesitation cost me everything—my freedom, the possibilities of my future, and especially, Bets.

That scene played in my head again and again as I rode in the back of the windowless transport van, listening as the sounds of the city lessened and were replaced with the heavy quiet of the countryside. It continued playing in the months that followed; when I was stripped at the prison and handed my work coveralls, when I was given an aptitude test and placed in a managerial position in one of the workhouses.

The man walking towards me, my knife in my pocket. I should've slit his throat. Everything would've turned out different.

Focusing on my work helped me avoid thinking about Bets. She had been nine years old when I was arrested, and she was street smart. She would have found a way to survive. I told myself that I'd protected her in this world for as long as I could. We'd been walking a thin line since

Jacob, her father, had been disappeared. I was amazed that we were able to make it in the sedan for as long as we did.

My work as an abortion provider that I took on to supplement my night job in the warehouse provided a glimmer of hope for a different kind of future; if I was careful and fastidious, I might be able to make the connections needed to secure us another apartment.

Rents in the city had risen to astronomical heights; there was no way I could pay outright, even with my two jobs, but if one worked at it long enough it was possible to find an in; it was all about who you knew. Providing underground abortions took me into both the shacks of the very poor and the mansions of the wealthy.

In those mansions I was meeting a great deal of influential people; people whose families owned entire city blocks. In time, I imagined that one of the apartments on one of those blocks owned by one of those families might be mine and Bets'.

That's not how things played out, though. That man, walking towards me on the sidewalk that cold winter morning. I knew exactly what was happening. I could've run back to the sedan, driven to the park and picked up Bets, and we could've fled the city using the forged documents I had that allowed me to move about freely to see my clients.

The money I'd hidden in the cracked upholstery of the car would've bought us enough gasoline to get beyond the reaches of the city and its enforcers; we could've made it to one of the safehouses in the remote countryside where I had connections through my abortion network.

From there we could've made a plan to flee even further, to one of the communities I'd heard about that was capable of hiding people, of erasing people's pasts. By the time the city found our trail we would've been gone.

I hesitated, though. And that hesitation cost me years of work, and everything I had built. On the rough ride to the prison in the back of the transport van I was so disappointed in myself that I couldn't even cry. I never did allow myself to cry about that day.

Fortunately, my position at the prison overseeing workhouse #4 wasn't intolerable; I was able to align myself with the guards, my managerial position got me extra rations at mealtime, and the long hours kept my mind off everything I had lost.

Ten years passed in this way, with hard work and a growing intimacy with the inner workings of the prison. I was able to curry favor further and further up the chain of command, until I was one of the most trusted and well-connected inmates in the entire place.

Which brings me to today. It's morning. A Tuesday. I was awake all night, staring at the white-painted brick of the wall of my cell, which is illuminated by the florescent lights of the hallway.

All night I was running my eyes along the grooves between the bricks, following them as I went over the details of my plan. Although I've had ten years inside these walls to work out these details, to make sure they're as foolproof as they can be, there's still a chance that one small thing will go wrong and fuck everything up.

While making the plan, I associated each step with a corner of the brickwork in my wall and I often lay awake at night, going over it in this way. It's helped me commit to memory the tools, the characters and their roles, and the timeline in which everything must happen. I've practically worn these bricks down with my eyes, going over the details of my plan, which, after all these years, is beautiful; like a line of dominoes set to gracefully fall. The plan is a work of art, and today is the Tuesday morning in which I find out if it goes as planned. With luck, I'll never have to see this brickwork again.

The idea for the first step in this plan came to me a decade ago, during my intake at the prison; I was in the medical ward, sitting on a metal chair in a paper gown, waiting to be inspected for contagious disease.

It was quiet in the medical ward. There were fewer guards than in the main part of the prison. Nurses, on account of the ammunition shortage, carried only tasers and pepper spray. I realized that if I faked illness, I could gain access to the medical ward. That would be the first step in my plan.

Of course, life is long and full of irony. So much irony, it feels as though god is sometimes laughing at me. At all of us. One year into my stay in the prison, I did become ill. Not fake ill, but actually ill.

My symptoms were sporadic at first—hives over my entire body, night sweats, bouts of intense fatigue. They came and went, and then they began to return with regularity, and there was vomiting too, and my vision would get wonky. I was terrified at first, and then I found the rhythm of my illness, began to ride it the way one rides a bicycle on a rough road.

I learned to mask my symptoms when I needed to get work done, and play them up when I wanted to visit, and become more familiar with, the medical ward. Of course there was nothing the nurses could actually *do* for me. The nurses had few resources to test for diseases, much less treat them.

They at least granted me a checkup every three months, where my blood would be drawn, a few tests would be run, and I would be told that my illness was a mystery. They'd give me a few vitamins, allow me to rest for twenty-four hours in the ward, in a room crowded with other hospital beds, and then I would be sent back to my cell.

Today, Tuesday, is checkup day.

I feel like I'm floating on the long walk to the medical ward. My body is so tense that it's lifting itself off the ground; my feet barely brush the linoleum. The old linoleum that peels up where it meets the wall; the linoleum under which it's easy to hide small things. Small things like keys.

A guard walks ahead of me this morning, unlocking the doors. For years I have watched him do this. I've watched the shape of the keys against his hip, tried to commit them to memory, sketched what I remember on scraps of paper. I've given this paper to Darcy, who works in the metal shop. After many failed attempts, Darcy was able to create a key that works for each lock—most of the time. These keys are now tucked under the linoleum near the doors.

The nurse on shift today, Susan, is in a good mood. Susan has been examining me for a long time, and as she presses the cold stethoscope into my back, I list the usual symptoms, but play up the vomiting, visual disturbances and lack of appetite. With luck, she'll allow me to rest here for forty-eight hours this time, instead of the usual twenty-four.

"Are there any private rooms today?" I ask her. "I have the beginnings of a migraine, and I'd like to be where it's quiet."

"I'd give you painkillers for your migraine," she says, flipping through my chart, "but we're still waiting on those. The delivery truck is delayed again, it seems like. I'll see what I can do about the room."

The door shuts softly behind her as she leaves. She's bluffing about the painkillers. There hasn't been a consistent source of those for years. Right now, I know, there's a bottle or two stashed somewhere in the medical ward, but they're given in only the most urgent of cases—broken bones, stab wounds, and to ease the passage of death.

When I close my eyes, I can see the map of the medical ward's corridors in my head—if I were to walk out this door, take a right, pass through another door, walk down a flight of stairs and take a left, there'd be a series of doors that led outside, to a side parking lot. I could've found a way through these locked doors years ago. I could've arranged a pickup with someone on the outside, so that there was a car waiting for me. I could've bribed the underpaid guards to wait an hour before sounding the alarm—that would've given me the head start I needed.

These work prisons are minimum security, understaffed, and the interruption in the tech supply chains have set their surveillance and record keeping technologies back decades. One individual successfully escaping is not unheard of. In fact, it happens more than the people who run the prisons like to admit. If I wanted to, I could've freed myself long ago.

But this is not that sort of plan.

I let the nurse lead me by the arm to my private room, wincing as though I'm in pain, covering my eyes with my other hand.

"Would it be possible to turn out the light?" I ask her as she folds down the sheet on the narrow hospital bed. "My migraine…"

She looks past my shoulder, considering, and writes something on her chart.

"Alright. And I've got this room for you for forty-eight hours, Jane. Since it's the only thing we can offer you, I wanted to do my best."

"Thank you," I say. I curl on my side under the covers and she punches a code into a small box next to the wall. The light fades away and the door closes behind her as she leaves. A wave of nausea works its way through me, settles in the back of my skull, and finally dissipates. I apologize to the gods of chronic illness for pretending to have a migraine on a day when I'm actually feeling pretty good. I hope they don't punish me for that.

Under the blankets I make a little cave and wriggle carefully out of my coveralls. Although the overhead lights are off, a bit of light seeps in under the door and I'm worried that the camera in the room will still be able to see my movements. This is one of the things I couldn't test – so I have no idea what the cameras can or can't see when the lights are off. There were several things I couldn't test.

Is this plan a beautiful line of dominoes, set to fall smoothly, or is it a chaotic clusterfuck of pure chance? There's only one way to find out.

In the legs of my baggy coveralls is a set of nurse's scrubs, as well as a surgical mask, folded and stitched to the fabric, and two pouches holding wads of small trash bags. The scrubs were swiped for me by Rebecca in laundry.

It was hard to get the things I wanted—the homemade keys, the uniform—while keeping the entirety of my plan from the inmates whose help I needed. I told them that the items would assist me in smuggling things for the guards, and I did smuggle in a handful of items for both women, as payment and as proof.

Once I've changed into the scrubs, I lay the coverall flat and begin inflating the trash bags with my mouth and tying off their ends. I stuff the inflated bags inside the coverall, and it begins to take shape. I just need something that looks convincing enough, when the nurse peers into this dark room on her rounds. Although the illusion will likely last only a few hours, with luck it'll be forty-eight hours before they know I'm gone.

When the nurse led me into this room I stumbled, grabbing the doorway for support. What the nurse didn't see was the wad of mashed up bread I stuffed into the hole where the door lock engages with the doorframe. I worried that the keypad would beep or otherwise alert the nurse when the door shut and the lock failed to engage, but it did not. The technology still left in this prison is failing. There will be nothing to replace it with when it's gone.

The door opens easily, much to my pleasure and surprise, and I slip into the hallway. The surgical mask is on my face and I keep my head lowered. Left turn, right turn, follow the hallway to the end. Bend down to "tie my shoe" and grab the key from under the linoleum. The key sticks at first, it won't turn, but I jiggle it a little and it goes.

A series of doors, their plate-glass windows crisscrossed with metal wire. Each door with its own key. I drop the keys into the pocket of my scrubs as I collect them. Now I'm in the administrative wing of the prison, where a nurse might appear out of place. I'm not worried about running into anyone here, though. A waterline conveniently burst in the bathroom a few minutes ago and is currently flooding a few offices. All the staff will be there, trying to stop the water and mitigate the damage. I have Deborah, who works as a janitor in this wing, to thank for that. Her help cost me a cellphone, which took a full year to acquire.

The records room is quiet, its single window letting in hazy yellow light. There are grey metal filing cabinets stacked six feet high. The lack of tech resources means that instead of each inmate existing as an entry in a computer they're here, in these filing cabinets. Each inmate has a folder with their photo, name, SSN, legal records, etc.

If you escape the prison and your folder is still here, then you can be recaptured and brought back, with years added onto your time. But if your file disappears, it will become as if you never existed at all. Bribing someone to trash your file and then escaping—that's how to become truly free. Another thing I could've orchestrated for myself years ago, if that was all I wanted.

But this is not that sort of plan.

Patting the pocket of my scrubs and finding only keys, I laugh out loud. I forgot one of the most crucial items. I fucking forgot! Turning, I survey the contents of the room. A long, heavy wooden desk, a dusty swivel chair. Wood paneling on the walls. A couple of lamps.

My fingers shake as I unscrew the nut that holds the lampshade on the lamp. The light from the bulb sears itself onto my eyeballs as I press the edge of a folded piece of paper to its surface. There are sounds of shouting at the end of the hallway, where the flooding is.

Come on, come on!

Presently the paper begins to smoke, and there's a small flame. The filing cabinets are locked but I found the key in the top drawer of the desk and I unlock the first drawer, holding my paper torch to its contents. Then I open the other drawers quickly while the first one catches flame. Entire identities ignite, their folders curling as they turn to ash.

The fire moves up the column of cabinets, and I use paper to help it along. The smoke alarm from the ceiling lies on the floor, its batteries pulled out by me. More shouting in the hallway. The door to the records room rattles—I locked it behind me—then a key is inserted into the lock. The door opens a crack but is stopped against the heavy wooden desk that I wedged between the filing cabinets and the door.

The fire is spreading quickly now, smoke is filling the room. That desk should hold the door long enough for all the records to catch. I slide the window open and shove out the screen. The records room is on the second floor of the administrative wing. There's the parking lot, and the double razor-wire fence beyond. Directly below me is a lot of shrubbery. I jump.

The sound of breaking branches. My shirt rips. Bright pain as something sharp runs itself along my torso. Then stillness. Above me I can hear the shouting, the alarms. I pull myself upright, drop to the sidewalk. I've lost the mask. It takes a minute to untangle the sticks from my hair. An inspection of my side—a little blood, but nothing that requires immediate care. Nothing that will stop me from carrying out the rest of my plan.

Slow, steady steps across the parking lot, towards the wing of the prison that holds the kitchen and the dining hall, my shirt held carefully closed. I want badly to look up towards the records room, to watch the fire spreading through that wing, but I do not. I imagine it, hold that vision in my mind, let it fill me up with the energy of a thousand suns. May this burning propel me through these next hours and days. May I never forget how powerful I feel in this moment.

Today is delivery day for the kitchen, and the food supply truck is there, backed up to the loading dock. The delivery driver, Marcos, is a good guy—smart, generous, down to work with you to smuggle little things in and out of the prison. He's also strong and heavily armed.

Your gun can't do much for you, though, when you're in the throes of passion—and that's why he's currently tied up with duct tape in the kitchen's walk-in pantry, where he's been meeting Sandy, the cook, for about a month now.

Sandy needed drugs, and I've been getting her these drugs, in exchange for her building this relationship with Marcos. And this one final act from her—tying him up in the pantry for an hour—was in exchange for a phone I'm supposed to bring her next week, so that she can call her son. She won't be needing that phone, though.

Oh, and I asked her for one other thing. Normally, different inmate work crews take their meals in the cafeteria at different times, which staggers lunch over a two-hour period. I asked her to mess up the schedule, so that all the inmates were in the cafeteria—or nearby, milling around, confused—at noon.

Noon was ten minutes ago.

The sliding metal door on the loading dock is unlocked, and with some effort I am able to lift it. Inside are the boxes of food—cricket meal and corn gruel, mostly—that are used to make our meals. I wander through the kitchen and push through the swinging doors to the cafeteria to find chaos—shouting, people standing on tables, trash cans upended, a few women hitting each other with red plastic trays, either in seriousness or for fun I'm not sure.

When this happens reinforcements are brought in from other parts of the prison, and the women are beaten and tazed into submission. A few are slapped with charges of inciting a riot, as an example to the others. Years are added to their sentences. Not today, though. Everyone is in the other wing of the prison, busy with the fire.

There's a cracking sound as two women are successful in ripping the cafeteria door off its hinges, and I smile. It's been a while since we've had some good ol' fashioned pandemonium in the prison, and getting everyone together in a crowded space was apparently the only spark that was needed to light the fuse.

This particular chaos was not part of my plan, but it doesn't surprise me, either—with the food rations getting smaller, and the increasing shortages of the few goods we have access to in here, things have been feeling extra tense.

"Jane!" A woman in a grey coverall shuffles up to me. She looks at my nurse's scrubs in surprise. She's got short, blunt hair, dyed magenta. Courtney. I know her from workhouse #4, where I'm the manager. Unlike me, who keeps mostly to myself, Courtney is popular here. She runs with a large group of women; she's likely tangled up in various dramas and hierarchies, knows who to talk to in order to organize the others.

"Courtney," I say, grabbing her hand and squeezing it. "I need you to do something for me." She looks confused. There's a crash behind us as the large water dispenser is pushed off a table and empties itself onto the floor. "I need you to get everyone outside, through the loading dock door. Every single prisoner. Now."

The keys are in the delivery truck. I settle into the driver's seat and click the seatbelt into place. It's been so long since I drove a vehicle—my mind wants to take me back to the sedan, with Bets, but I don't let it.

The fire. Think about the fire.

Smoke is billowing into the sky, now. How long until the fire grows strong enough to make its way to this wing of the prison? Out of sight, on the other side of the building, the staff and guards are likely pouring from the ground floor like ants from an anthill that's been doused with bleach. I don't have much time. None of us have much time.

The truck starts on the first turn of the key, and its rumble shakes me gently. On the other end of the wide, mostly empty parking lot is the tall, double razor-wire fence. And beyond the fence, a perimeter field of bare dirt and then the road, past which is empty desert.

How far can the inmates get before the federal law enforcement arrives from the city? It's a long drive for the feds, over roads that are barely maintained. And anyway, it doesn't matter. The records are gone. Burned up. These inmates don't exist anymore.

I wonder what the impact of the fence will feel like. If the truck will make it through unscathed. If I will.

I shift the truck into drive and slam the gas pedal down.

CHAPTER 12

BETS

The wind whips my hair around my face as I stare out over the desert. I'm stopped on a rise, straddling my bike, the dog deep in the pannier, hiding from the wind that knocks us around like a hand.

It's been four days since I left the KOA, and in those days I've traveled down, out of the mountains. I've left the pine forest behind and entered this flat nowhere place, with dirt and some sort of fragrant, oily brush and this wind and light—so much light.

In the forest there were streams every day—I hardly needed to fill all my water containers between sources. Here, though, there is very little to drink, or if there is more water, I don't know where to find it. The road has changed, too. The empty highway is rougher, riddled with fissures, brush sprouts out of it in clumps. Sometimes there are piles of debris, both manmade and thrown by floods.

This comforts me—the feds can't follow me on these roads, and I've relaxed quite a bit, taken to biking during the day instead of at night—but the broken roads make the going slower as well.

The exit signs, faded and peeling, that still remain on the highway seem more and more absurd. They point to burnt-out gas stations whose storefronts gape like empty mouths. I don't stop at these places. I pedal on, bracing myself when I ride over a patch of busted concrete, dismounting to lift my bike when there's a huge crack in the road.

Now I think again about my empty water bottles—I finished the last of my water this morning—and run my tongue over my cracked lips. And that's when I see the clump of shapes on the far horizon. It's impossible to tell what the shapes are from this distance—wrecked vehicles? Slow moving animals? People? It's a risk, I know, to bike in the direction of something unknown, but right now the unknown is a risk I have to take.

"Who do you think they are?" I say to the dog, and my words echo a bit before being carried away on the wind. I pedal as fast as I can down the hill, trying to gain on the group. Throughout the day I inch closer, watch the figures morph, shift, and reform, until I can clearly make out a cluster of bicycles pulling trailers. They're traveling slowly but persistently, and even though I'm biking as fast as I can it still takes me all day to catch them, because they never stop to take a break.

By evening I am almost upon them, my legs aching from the effort. Thirst is like a wad of dry paper in my mouth. When I've almost reached them, the cluster of bicycles and trailers slows to a stop. The people dismount, shake out their limbs, drink from shiny metal canteens.

I'm close enough to see that the people are hunched, their clothing the color of dirt. I dismount my bicycle and we stare at each other for a few moments. There are five of them. Their faces are rough from the sun. I cannot tell their ages.

"We seen you in the distance," says an older man, and I startle. In the four days since leaving the KOA my mind has gone a bit strange from the solitude, and now this man's voice makes reality skip a beat, like a video where the audio isn't in sync with the visuals.

"I've been riding from the city," I say. My words reach them and float away, leaving quiet in their wake. We both listen to the wind whipping the oily brush. The trailers are made of scrap wood and pieces of plastic. I wonder if they function as tiny shelters, to get out of the weather. I lick my cracked lips again. "Where are you all from?"

"We come from the east," says the man. The others look from him to me, and then back to him. "We had a little village in the mountains. Then disease come and took most everyone away."

"Disease?"

"It was terrible, and we were the only ones left," says a woman. She's got a shawl draped over her head, shading her face. She looks to be about sixty, although I can't know for sure.

I wonder if I should be afraid of these people, but I'm too thirsty in this moment to care. And besides, death by some quick disease wouldn't be the worst way to go.

"Do you have any water you could spare?" I say, after a moment. "Or know where I could find some?"

The man and the woman look at each other.

"You got anything you could trade?" says the woman.

"I have some millet," I say reluctantly, thinking of the few handfuls that make up the last of my food.

"Nah," says the man. "We got grain. You have anything else?"

My mind is empty—and then I remember the courier packages, unopened, that I stuffed into the panniers in Malachite's apartment. I've been saving them for… I don't know. Maybe this moment.

After spreading my sweater on the hot asphalt of the road, I lift the dog from the pannier and set him onto it. He shakes himself and then sits, eyeing the strangers warily. There are three padded envelopes of various sizes.

"I have these packages," I say. "I stole them in the city so I could pretend I was a courier. To get past the checkpoints. They've never been opened, and I don't know what's in them. I'll give you all of them for a few liters of water, if you have it."

The woman's eyes shine from within her dirty shawl, and the man smiles.

"I knew you'd have something good," says the woman. She steps forward and reaches out a small hand, the palm lined with dirt. I give her the envelopes and she touches each one thoughtfully, studies the addresses, shakes them.

"Let's open them tonight, by the fire," she says. Her eyes are wet with excitement. She presses one envelope to her face, inhales deeply. "It smells like… other worlds." The man undoes a rope and pulls a canvas tarp back on one of the trailers, revealing a large plastic barrel.

"Take as much water as you can carry," he says. "We'll come to a river around sundown, can fill up again there."

"Oh my god thank you," I say. The water is warm and odorous but it is wet, and I drink an entire liter, forcing my dry throat to swallow. I fill the jar lid for the dog and he drinks and drinks. Afterwards I am dizzy but I can feel the life percolating back into me.

"You're welcome to join us tonight," says the man. "We'll camp at the river, you can't miss it. We've got some javelina we can share."

I do not hesitate. "Ok," I say. "Thank you." What other choice do I have? If these people mean to murder me, then at least I'll spend my last day hydrated, and with company.

An hour later there's a sudden change in the air—I can feel the moisture on the skin of my forearms. The wind cools. Then the sounds of insects, and maybe frogs? The smell of muck. The nights have been so silent, so warm and open and dry, I've spread my sleeping bag on the bare dirt and slept under stars brighter than anything I could've imagined. Now there are sounds again, the natural world rustling about. All because of water. Water!

The river is brown, slow, wide. At first glance its banks seem unattainable, choked with brush and trees. But the group finds an animal trail and I follow them down, to a stretch of muddy beach. The deep water mesmerizes me—this water that has travelled far from some mysterious place and which goes... who knows where.

Presently the group unpacks the trailer holding their water jug and one of them, a young woman, lifts it to the dirt, walks to the water's edge and dips an aluminum bucket. The water, when sloshed in the bucket, is a pale yellow. The young woman is wearing robe-like garments sewn from homespun cloth—all of these people look as though they've come from a place where they didn't have access to salvaged fabric.

The young woman has removed her sandals, which appear to be fashioned from the rubber of car tires, and she tucks the ends of her robes into her belt before stepping into the mud and bending at the waist to fill her bucket with the river.

Her face, where it peeks from her robes, is calm in a way that startles me. Something stirs inside me as I watch her hands, brown from the sun, lift the bucket from the river. She turns and catches my eye but she doesn't smile. Her expression doesn't change at all, and we watch each other as she makes her way back to the blue water jug.

"Hey." I jump. It's the older man, who I spoke with earlier—he's standing right next to me. "That's Opal. She's about your age, seems like. Maybe you two could be friends. Would be good for her to have a friend." He's smiling, his cracked lips stretched over his yellow teeth.

"Opal?" I say. I'm nervous now. All day I rode behind this group, observing them from a distance. They often sang while they biked, strange low songs lacking in music, more like chanting but no chanting I could make sense of. Now the blue jug is full, and Opal has disappeared, moved on to other tasks. The light is dimming and I watch the group unpack the other wagons.

The older woman I gave the packages to drops an armload of branches on the ground and then squats on their heels and digs a shallow firepit in the sand. The others are spreading blankets on the earth and pulling cooking pots from fabric sacks. The dog wanders over, having completed his rounds. I've left my bike leaning against a tree and now I push it down the bank, to a spot somewhat removed. My shoes are off and the cool sand feels incredible on the soles of my feet.

The sky is clear again tonight, I figure it likely won't rain and so I smooth my sleeping bag right on the earth. This sand will be nice to sleep on, much softer than some of my recent campsites. I fill my own water bottles, the dog's dish, and dump my last few handfuls of millet into my pot.

When I woke this morning I was so worried about where I'd find my next water that I didn't consider where I'd find my next food. Now the urgency of thirst is gone and hunger has taken its place. I break a few dead sticks from a tree next to my camp and then pause, look over at my neighbor's fire, already crackling, and feel my feet, almost of their own volition, turn in that direction. I do not know these people or their intentions but my body knows deep in every cell that survival, right now, is other people and so I walk to the fire.

Opal is adjusting some blackened aluminum pots in the flames, pinching logs at their ends to reposition them in the glowing coals. She's squatting on her heels, soles planted firmly in the sand. Her face is lined with dust, her robes are striped with it. In the pots a gruel is bubbling. It smells like cinnamon. She brushes a strand of hair off her forehead and a streak of soot takes its place.

"I was wondering if I could cook my millet on your fire," I say. It feels awkward to string words together for another person. What if I say too much? Or not enough? I feel that my naked hunger for the company of other humans, written too plainly on my face, makes me repulsive.

"Sure you can," says Opal. She smiles at me, her face softening. "Fire's big enough."

Squatting next to Opal and adjusting my own pot on the coals is a pleasure so acute that I start to cry. I grimace, turn my face away.

"How have you found the road so far?" Opal is speaking. I try out a few responses in my mind. What can I say that will make the conversation last longest?

"It's been lonely. Aside from a few days at the KOA before I was imprisoned and I had to escape, I haven't had anyone to talk to except the dog." *God dammit!* I admonish myself. *That was too much!*

"The KOA just west of the city? I've been there," says Opal. She's gazing thoughtfully at the fire, and I can see the flames reflected in her dark eyes. "We did some trades with Lisle when we were in those parts."

"You do trades with Lisle? What sorts of things do you trade?"

Opal looks at me, surprised. "Plants," she says. "We gather and trade medicinal plants. It's how we make a living. The trailers are full of them." Making eye contact with Opal feels like staring directly at the sun. I fight the urge to turn away.

"That... that seems very useful," I say.

"It is. So many people have lost everything. They have no medicines of their own. Or medicinal practices. We stop in villages and share our herbs with people. Tend to their ill. In exchange we accept food, supplies, information on the road ahead. We're providing something that everyone wants. As a result, everyone is our friend."

"That's really lovely," I say, and I mean it. Opal snatches a pot out of the fire, sets it in the sand. I stir my own millet with a spoon—it's burnt to the bottom of the pot, which means that it's done.

"You're welcome to our gruel," says Opal, "we have plenty." I wonder if she can smell my burned millet, and I feel embarrassed. I'm not sure what's in her pot, but it looks better than what's in mine.

She's sitting on the sand now, cross-legged, and she pushes the pot towards me and dips a spoon into the gruel, places the spoon in her mouth while gazing at the river, which has faded in the gloaming to a thing that is felt more than seen.

I dip my own spoon into her gruel. It's wonderful in my mouth, full of bright flavors that bring memories flooding back—could that be cinnamon? Real cinnamon? If anyone can get spices, I suppose it would be this group. The dog is beside me, watching me patiently. I place my own small pot of burnt millet in front of him.

"Eat up," I say, and he does.

There's a shape in the shadows thrown by the fire—it's the older woman. She tells me her name is Charlotte and then holds something aloft—it's the packages I gave her to open. I almost forgot about them!

Now she grins and rips the first envelope lustily, digs around inside. She extracts sheets of paper that shine in the fire—the sheets are colored foil. Stickers! They're colored foil stars. Charlotte laughs, delighted. The next envelope contains a book, and Charlotte squints at the cover in the firelight.

"Windows 95 Manual," she reads. She frowns, turns the book over in her hands, and then laughs. She looks at me as she returns the book to its envelope. "The paper is useful at least. I'll open the last envelope another time," she says. "I like the suspense of it! Thank you Bets, for these gifts. I hope you'll stay with us awhile." She looks from me to Opal, and back to me. I say nothing, worried that whatever words come out of my mouth will ruin the moment, break it forever.

The next morning the sky is just beginning to lighten and I'm lying on my back in my sleeping bag, the dog against my side, his small head resting in my armpit. I was awake for hours in the night, watching the stars, the only sounds the soft shush of the river moving in the dark. When I have too many thoughts like this it's almost impossible to sleep.

I know that suffering comes from wanting things. I have tried so hard not to want things. But I'm just a little animal. I can no more control my longings that I can control the moon.

That ache, that frantic, fearful ache. It would be easier to make sense of it if my injury was visible—missing half the fingers on my left hand. Blind in one eye. A terrible limp. I roll onto my side and watch the sleeping forms of the others slowly take shape in the dawning light. The dog is unaware of my inner turmoil. He considers himself warm and safe, which I suppose he is. I too am safe at this moment. Then why can't I feel it, all the way down to my bones, like he can?

His small doggy stink, like a trash can filled with corn chips, wafts out of the sleeping bag. I can smell myself too. The sweat from biking all day in the heat gone cold, and then warmed over again. The grease of my hair. This dress, its flowers already fading, the fabric stiff with salt. The smell of my dog and myself comforts me. We're just two mammals curled against each together, keeping each other warm. In the city, the human smell in close spaces took on an ammoniac edge, there was a wrongness about it. Out here, though, it's different.

"You're awake." A pair of brown, sandy feet appears in my field of vision. It's Opal, carrying the cooking pot from last night. "I was just washing this in the river. I wondered if you were up yet."

"I want to keep traveling with you and the others," I say, startling myself with how fast my words come out. "Do you think I could do that?"

Opal is smiling at me.

"Of course. We'd be glad to have you." The dog is waggling against her shins and she sits down on the sand and runs her hands over him. "I'm the only young person in this group. We've been hoping to find other young people who would join us, but haven't had much luck. We'd be honored if you would continue on with us."

There's a warm, expansive sensation in my chest. Elation fills me as I move about my morning chores. Once the sun hits the water I wade out of sight and rinse my dress in the swirling brown current, and wring it out. I scrub my skin with sand, massage my scalp and run my fingers through my hair. The heat has come on, soft and bright, and the dampness of my dress, once pulled back over my head, feels good against my skin.

I push my bike through the brush back up towards the road, the others ahead of me. I've filled my water containers and Charlotte has given me a sack of a grain I don't recognize, as well as some salt folded into a square of cloth. The dog is in the pannier, jostling lightly, his eyes half closed with drowsiness. At the cracked highway we set off together pedaling west, the others in a clump and me stringing along behind at a slight distance.

We've been biking past sunset for a few hours, in the dark with the stars wheeling over us, when we turn off the highway onto a rough dirt road. Left to my own devices I would've stopped sooner, found a hidden campsite in a dry wash in the last of the light. But I'm not on my own anymore. I'm with this group now, and their goal today was to get farther and so I kept pedaling, even though I was exhausted and hungry.

My fatigue turns to wonder, now, as we pass through a broken wooden gate and make our way towards a high red cliff—it's a sort of smooth, mounded rock I haven't yet encountered on my journey. We dismount and the others gather kindling for a big fire in the red dirt. The cooling air smells of sage.

As I lift the dog from the pannier and set him on the ground, he zips around, exploring this shadowy world. I fear for him, out here, being so small. I've never had a small being to care for, and I worry that if he were to die in an accident then I would have to die too, because he's become such a part of me that it would make no sense to live on without him.

At dinner I stand in the shadows, shoveling hot stew into my mouth just beyond the warmth of the fire, watching as the group talks amongst themselves. Then there's a hand on my back, and I almost startle out of my skin. It's Opal.

"Jesus Christ!" I say, choking a little.

"Are you getting on ok?" she asks. Her cheeks are rosy, and her hair falls away from her face in wisps. I notice for the first time that her two front teeth are crooked. It's charming, it makes her seem more like... herself.

"Yes, yes," I say. "I just don't know you all or your customs, really. I don't want to do or say the wrong thing."

"You don't have to worry so much about that," she says. Her hand is still on my back, the tips of her fingers pressing into my skin. It's the strangest sensation. I try and think of what to say that would make her keep her hand there a little longer. "I found a camp spot I want to show you," she continues. "In case you want to set up camp there too."

I nod. I would agree to anything Opal said right now. She leads me to a strange landscape of smooth red boulders, as high as houses, among which there are flat patches of sand. In one of these hidden nooks is her bedroll; several folded blankets on the sand, some lumpy clothing as a pillow.

"There's room for you here," she says. The recent memory of her hand on my back radiates through me like heat. I unstuff my sleeping bag alongside her things. I fill the dog's water dish and he drinks and then settles himself on the sand with a deer bone he dredged up somewhere.

The weariness of the day is descending on me, my head is foggy. I know I'll fall asleep with my sleeping bag open and gather it around me in the wee hours when the chill comes. I'm lying on my sleeping bag, thinking about this, the sound of the dog's quiet gnawings nearby (he'll work the bone until that cold time and then crawl into the sleeping bag, with me), when I feel Opal's hand on my back again.

Am I dreaming? I don't move, don't speak, just let the sensation enter my drowsiness and mingle with my half-sleep. Her fingers trace my spine lightly, walk their way up to my neck and then dance in circles back down again, to my lower back. I stop breathing, unwilling to let the sensation of my own breath distract me from even a nanosecond of this. Her hand stills on the nape of my neck and plays with my loose hair there, sending shivers through my scalp. I can't remember the last time I was touched like this. I can't remember the last time I was touched at all.

"Are you sleeping?" Opal's face is down near mine, she's lying on the sand next to me and I can smell her breath—like salt and lemon-lime soda.

"No." I feel as though I've been drugged. I open my eyes and look at her soft, sweet face in the light of the half moon. I wonder what it would feel like to hold her face in my hands. The thought makes me dizzy. My hand grazes the smooth skin of her upper arm and she shivers and moves closer to me. I cup her face in my hands and run my thumbs over her cheekbones. She closes her eyes and I kiss her mouth, taste her breath and the stew from earlier. This is not Georgia. That thought is terrible, but also wonderful.

We breathe into each other. I wrap my arms around her, pull her into me. My hands fumble with her robes and finally find their way to bare skin, hotter than fire. I grab handfuls of her, squeeze them hard, rock her hips. She's melting. When she moans I can feel it in my mouth. Her breath is coming quick now, she's dropped down into herself. I move my fingers so softly, barely graze her skin, and she cries out, as though in pain. I cover her mouth with my hand. *Shhh.* My desire quickens but I will myself to go slow. The hours turn liquid and we are suspended in the place outside of time. *Do you want this?* I hear her breath catch as she nods *yes*.

She is soft against me afterward, tangled up in me, the stars are wheeling above us, the cold is coming on so it must be very late. After a time she is asleep, lying in my arms. I feel as though I'm in my body but also… I am still in her body, riding the waves of the sensation that she feels. I am the curve of her ass under my own hands, I am the arch of her lower back. I love this, leaving my own body to live, for a while, in the body of another person.

My thoughts and the pleasure pulsing through me, the wonder of this woman in my arms, keep me up until just a few hours before dawn and when I wake in the morning I'm groggy, but I feel high, the happiest I've been in ages. The day passes in a stupor, the edges of my vision soft—helping the others re-pack the trailers with supplies, gathering water from a nearby spring, making myself eat a little but feeling no hunger. Always Opal is there, moving in and out of the frame, her skin glowing, fixing me with an ethereal half-smile.

We make our way back to the highway, continue west. At dusk we camp in an oak forest, next to a stream among the golden fallen leaves. We've climbed out of the desert into the foothills of the mountains. The group hopes to get over and back down, into what the others say is another broad valley on the other side, before full winter comes. In these mountains are herbs to be gathered, plants with names that I do not know. The group gathers as it moves, plans its route to hit certain areas in certain seasons.

I am trying to listen to them talk about herbs as we eat our dinner around the fire, with its fresh nettles gathered from the forest, but I'm distracted, thinking about how long I'll stay with this group, whether I should follow them up into the mountains. Should I be looking for my mother right now? Trying to find the prison where she is, if she is in a prison, like Lisle said? And I'm thinking about Opal, about the salt of her collarbone and the way she'd felt in my arms.

After dinner I find Opal at the creek, scrubbing a pot out with sand and I squat next to her and rinse my own pot. The water is icy, it comes from snowmelt in the high mountains we're about to cross, and my fingers ache by the time I'm finished.

"I need to tell you something," I say, and she pauses, looks over at me with those glowing brown eyes.

"What is it? You love traveling with us, you're going to stay forever?"

"Opal." I set down my pot and wrap my hands in the skirt of my dress to warm them. "I'm trying to find my mother. She disappeared when I was nine, in the city. I haven't seen her since, and I always wondered where she was. Recently a friend gave me a note she wrote me years ago, saying to meet her in Nevada when I was grown. And then Lisle said that she's in prison, and that there's going to be a prison fire. I don't know which thing is true, and where I should be looking for her. And even if she is in prison, I don't know where the prisons are, or how I would free her. But I am looking for her, so I might not be able to stay with you forever." I press the palms of my hands into my eyes. I refuse to cry right now.

Opal looks at me thoughtfully.

"There's a prison in the valley on the other side of these mountains," she says. "It's a big one. We never go within a day's journey of it—the likelihood of being picked up by the rangers is too high—but if you stay with us until we enter that valley I can point you in the direction of it, and you can make your way there. If you have something of high value to trade with the guards you might be able to free her, but if she's not there, or if you catch the guards at a bad time, you'll just be imprisoned yourself, and you may never get out again."

"Those sound like terrible odds," I say. We sit in silence for a few moments, watch the gloaming come on in the oak forest around us.

"They are terrible odds," says Opal. "But I understand. I would've done anything to save my mother before we left. Anything. Sometimes life after she's gone feels meaningless, and I wish I would've died with her."

"Do these people you're traveling with feel like family, now?"

"No," she says. "I don't love them. It's not the same."

"Then why stay with them?"

"Survival." There's something new in her eyes—an urgency. Or maybe it's always been there. It's full dark now and we sit for a while in silence. "You go ahead and set up camp without me," she says after a time. "I want to stay here and think for a bit."

I find a clearing among the trees for camp. The little dog follows, dances happily in the leaves. He doesn't know this conflicted heaviness I carry, he only knows that we're together, well fed, we have a home for the night, and we're about to sleep.

Maybe last night with Opal was a dream, a drug whose high I'm just now coming down from. The things I've wanted most in life have always been like this—a handful of sand, seemingly solid at first and then slipping through my fingers and away.

"Things are pretty good, actually," I say to the dog, as I kick acorns out of the way and spread the sleeping bag on the ground. "I have people to travel with, food. I have you." He tries to climb onto the bag before I've laid it all out and I laugh and shoo him off but he persists, burrowing into the sleeping bag and getting it all tangled.

It's colder here, partway up the mountain, much more than the low desert we've been traveling through and I'm grateful to scooch down into the warm and let my stiff body unwind, the dog pressed against me like a hot water bottle, his nose in my armpit, our breaths mingling. I'm exhausted and sleep comes rushing in, not even my too-busy brain can hold it back tonight.

"You look so beautiful in the starlight, when you're asleep." The words come into my dreams. The forest itself is speaking to me, the bare oak trees. Then the tickle of a spider that's gotten into my sleeping bag, a huge one! And I thrash myself awake and instead of a spider it's Opal's face I see, she's set up her bedroll next to mine and she's leaning over me, one hand resting on my stomach, inside my sleeping bag.

"Shh," she says. "It's ok." The good feeling hits me like a narcotic and I lie down, close my eyes. If I'm still dreaming I don't want this dream to end. Opal's mouth is on mine, her lips so warm and soft. "I'm so happy you're here," she mumbles. "I'm so happy you're with us." Her hand is on my thigh now where my dress has ridden up. I wrap my arms around her and pull her against me. The whole world is here, in this woman. The entire universe.

In the morning I'm fuzzy with sleeplessness again, floating on my own little cloud. "Everything is beautiful and nothing hurts." That's what Georgia used to say, when we were on the rooftop together watching the sun set neon pink over the city. It's the only time I saw Georgia unbothered, her troubles lifted away, like a being who'd only just come to earth and knew nothing yet of its complications, or as though she was about to leave it, unfettered in the very last moment before death.

Today we ride our bikes on the narrow, winding highway up into the mountains, where the air thins and grows colder. The others layer on more robes. I have my wool sweater, which isn't enough for the evenings and

Charlotte notices, gifts me a brightly woven shawl to put over everything. I imagine I'm quite the sight—hair wild from the wind, cheeks burnished red, long faded flowered dress, bulky wool sweater and this bright shawl, draped over me like a blanket.

In the evening we sit around the fire scraping burnt grain from our pots and we sleep, exhausted, in the dirt. As we ride we stop to fix our bikes, and we don't bathe unless we cross a stream in the warmest part of the day and then we splash icy water on our tired bodies, gasping and laughing, and then shiver into our salty clothes again.

We gather herbs, lay them to dry on flat woven mats in the sun, bundle them into cloth sacks. I experience all of this from a place of untouchable bliss—Opal is here with me, lying next to me in the dark each night. She's reaching her arm around me when we sit next to the fire. I'm pressing my mouth into the top of her hair and breathing deeply the smell of her. The drugs are in my blood, drip, drip, drip. What does the future hold? It doesn't matter.

One afternoon we've stopped to gather a fuzzy, broad-leafed plant on the hillside. There was a cold wind this morning but now the day has warmed and I've taken off my shawl and spread it on a granite boulder in the sun.

In this moment, focused on filling my basket with these tender plants while the sun warms my face as it makes its way through the empty sky, I forget myself—I forget the city, I forget the person I was there. I am the mountain now. I am the autumn wind that moves through the plants. I realize I'm crying, and I wipe my face with the hem of my dress. This is possibly the most connected, and the least alone, I've ever felt.

"I understand why you all live like this," I say to Charlotte, who is working next to me. "This mountain—I feel like it loves me. Is that weird? I never felt this way, in the city. But the city felt like all there was when I was in it. So many people, that's all they know. They're born there and they die there. It's been that way for a hundred years."

Charlotte sweeps her hand out, over the rocky hillside, the empty sky, the baking valley below.

"A hundred years is nothing to the earth," she says. "Just a blip.

Civilizations come and go like a mushroom that pops up after a rain and then rots away. The earth is the mycelium below the soil. The earth has patience. The earth waits."

"So it has to end, then? All of those buildings, the infrastructure, the I don't know, language? The generations of people who raised their families there? It's all for nothing? It just collapses? And in such an ugly way?"

"It has to collapse," says Charlotte. "There's no other way." She goes back to harvesting, rooting around in the grass with her sun-weathered hands, dropping leaves into her basket. "Linear time is a construct that was created in cities, because linear time has a beginning and end, and cities do too. Out here, time moves in circles. This mountain, this sun"—she looks up at the sky—"These will always be here. And you're here now too." She smiles at me. "You've come back."

That second night after leaving the city, riding my bike in the dark, the cool air had finally started to clear—I'd never experienced air that smelled like that, and yet there was a familiarity I couldn't shake. Now I'm here, squatting in the sun with my basket, forgetting myself. The city slipping away like a stressful dream. Maybe this knowing was within me all along, like a seed.

That night Opal and I are snuggled together in our campsite, in the tall pines on the ridge of the mountain. The others say that this ridge is the highest we'll go and that the road will follow it for another handful of days and then we'll drop down, towards the valley on the other side. I'm thinking about the prison in that valley, where my mother might be. And I'm thinking about my life here, with Opal.

"Why do the others allow me to stay?" I ask Opal. Her head is on my chest and the dog is on the other side of me, his burrito-like body pressed against my ribs. I was asleep by the time Opal lay down next to me, unzipped my sleeping bag and crawled into my arms. She's been coming to bed late—while I get sleepy after dinner and a fire she likes to stay up for a while sitting out under the stars alone. She needs time to process, she says. To come back to herself. "I mean I know why you want me to stay," I add.

"Because I love you," says Opal. She squeezes me. We've been saying this to each other the last few days. What is love? I don't know. Have I ever known? It feels good to say though, so why not. More accurate would be to say *you are my heart's home.* I want to love the way squirrels love, curled in a nest together against the cold. Or the way the dog and I love each other—unquestioning loyalty.

"The others are glad you're here," says Opal, after a moment.

"But why? I don't contribute much. I don't know anything about herbs. I eat your food, use your bike repair supplies. I help when I can but it seems like I'm more of a drain than anything."

I can feel Opal shrug.

"It gets lonely for all of us. The group is small. It's nice having another person along."

"And you never had luck finding other people to join before?"

"We've tried to recruit..." Opal trails off. "Sometimes people don't stay." Before I can respond she squeezes me again, harder this time. "I know you want to find your mother, but I hope you stay with us instead of going to the prison and putting yourself in danger. I really, really hope you stay." I turn and wrap myself all the way around her, press as though to absorb her into my own body.

"I love you," I say, by way of an answer.

The next morning we're packing up camp, wearing all our layers, hands stinging from the cold, frost glittering on the grass that will eventually be banished by the midday sun, when I see Vernon touch Opal. Vernon is the first person in the group that I talked to, the older man who offered me water on the road. Opal is packing bundles into her bike trailer when he approaches her, rests his hand on her lower back as he speaks to her, and then slides that hand down to her ass. I'm stuffing my sleeping bag away in the trees just behind them, I don't think he knows I'm there.

I freeze, not sure what I should do. Opal frowns and pushes Vernon's hand away, gathers her shawl more tightly around her. He says something and she shakes her head, focuses on the ropes that cinch the trailer shut, and ignores him. Eventually he walks away.

Opal and I are sitting on a smooth stone in the sun eating our lunch later that day when I bring up what I saw. Her face darkens.

"I don't know why he does that," she says. "I've told him so many times not to touch me, that I don't want him."

"How long has this been going on?"

"Since the beginning," she says quietly.

"But he's Charlotte's partner," I say, louder than I probably should. "We have to get him to stop!"

Opal frowns. "I don't know," she says, sounding defeated. "I don't think he will. I think that this is just the way he is."

I'm stumped. I don't know what to say. We finish our lunch in silence and all afternoon I ride a bit behind the others, lost in my own thoughts.

That night in camp I hold Opal after making love and whisper into her ear.

"What if we ran away," I say. "Just the two of us. We could leave this group. We both have bicycles, and you know all about herbs. You can teach me what you know, and we can gather plants together and trade them for what we need. We can look for my mother together. We can settle in Nevada. Have you been there? We can grow a garden. We can trade our herbs for sheep and goats. We can get chickens. We can build a whole life together."

Opal doesn't respond. I feel a warm dampness on my chest and realize that she's crying. She shakes her head, almost imperceptibly.

"I can't, Bets. I can't leave them. They're everything that I have. I owe them my life. Without this group, where would I be?"

"But Vernon!" I say. "He wants something from you. We could run away. And we can find others. We don't have be alone."

"You don't know that." She's sobbing now, her voice choked. "You don't know how dangerous it is out there. You don't know! If I leave the group that's it. I'm as good as dead."

I do know how it is out there, I think. But I don't say this. I hold her, let her cry until the front of my dress is wet through. Eventually she's exhausted, and we both sleep.

A few nights later it's the full moon and I'm lying in my sleeping bag, unable to sleep. The forest is cast in silver, the dog is twitching with dreams. The fire in camp has died down, just the soft red glow of coals visible through the trees. The night is quiet, everyone in bed except Opal, who I know has wandered off to be with herself before sleep.

Maybe it's the full moon, but there's a sense of urgency inside me that I can't push away. Opal and I need to leave this group, and we need to go now. If we don't leave right away, something terrible is going to happen. I don't know what, but I can't shake the thought.

Extracting myself from the sleeping bag without waking the dog, I slip on my shoes, wrap my shawl around me and make my way through the flat, open pine forest, looking for where Opal might've gone. I've been wandering for a while when I see another campfire, flickering through the trees. I come upon a cluster of flat granite boulders, overlooking the dark abyss of the valley. The fire is in the sand, in a ring of stones. I make my way towards it, puzzled. Did Opal build this fire? Is this what she's been doing, every night?

There's the sound of small movements, muffled cries. I stop at the edge of the trees, staying in the shadows. There in the moonlight on one of the boulders is a scene so strange it takes me a full minute to comprehend it all.

Skin. Limbs. That's Opal. On her back. She's naked. But she's not lying on a blanket. She's lying on a man—one of the other older men, Cecil, who keeps to himself, who is mostly silent, who repairs the bike trailers delicately with huge, rough hands. Opal is lying on her back on Cecil with her legs in the air. It takes me a minute to work this out because Vernon is on top of Opal, obscuring most of her body—I recognize his thin, greasy hair, scraggling down his back. Vernon is inside of her. They're sweating in spite of the cold, bathed in firelight. I'm frozen in the shadows, shocked, uncomprehending.

"Breed me!" hisses Opal, suddenly. "Fill me up. Breed me!"

I cannot believe what I am seeing. No part of me can believe it. Is she here of her own volition? Does she want this? Whatever this is? I will my legs to turn, will myself to walk away from the scene, but I cannot. Then it's over and she's rolling off of Cecil onto the blanket, whimpering softly. Vernon stands, pulls a pot off the fire, wets a cloth with steaming water from the pot and begins wiping her down, gently.

"We better clean you up," he says. "Before you go to Bets."

"I know," says Opal. She's sprawled on her back, accepting the bath, languid, her face soft with pleasure. "We need her."

"You haven't given us a child yet," says Cecil. I realize that before this point, I hadn't known what his voice sounded like. "We're depending on you."

"I will," says Opal. "And if not me, Bets. She loves me, she's going to stay. And in time she'll love you too."

"I'm not so sure of that," says Vernon.

"Trust me," says Opal. "Give me time."

My legs have become unstuck. They're carrying me back to camp. My arms are lifting the dog out of my sleeping bag. He shakes himself awake, confused. My trembling hands are stuffing everything into my panniers, placing the dog on top. I have to move fast. Faster. The panniers clip onto my bike, I push my bike to the road. My feet are turning the pedals as I glide down the moonlit asphalt, away from camp. Is that someone calling my name? I can't be sure.

Hours later I'm still high on the mountain, pedaling, with no memory of the time that's passed. There were two intersections, and I chose my direction randomly at each one. The rest is black.

Am I still going the direction I need to go? And where is that, exactly? I pull my bike off the road and into the trees, having flashbacks to those first days out of the city, when I was so alone and unsure. I'm shaking as I spread out my sleeping bag again. The dog accepts our new situation, crawls inside with me. I am too tired to feel.

CHAPTER 13

When I wake in the morning it's cold. Frost glitters on the outside of my sleeping bag. I'm curled on my side in a ball, almost but not quite warm. Winter. It's almost winter. I've got to get off this mountain. Then I remember last night. The firelight.

I start to laugh. My laugh shatters the stillness of the morning, reverberates out over this high, rocky world. I laugh, and laugh, and laugh.

"What the fuck!" I say to the dog, who has wriggled out of the bag and shaken himself awake in the cold sunlight. "What the actual fuck!" Thirst, hunger, an empty stomach. And my laughter. I keep thinking the laughter will turn to crying, but it doesn't. "What in the literal fuck!" I imagine that the trees are laughing with me. They're in on the joke. They knew this would happen all along.

"You're afraid of being abandoned? So lonely you think you might die? Well have we got a situation for you…"

Eventually all the laughter is gone and I'm spent, and I lie there empty, staring at the pine needle ground as the day warms. My mouth is dry. There's hunger, far away. I rise in a stupor and gather twigs for a little fire. When the gruel is ready I can't taste it. The dog climbs into my lap to be petted but I feel nothing.

The bumpy asphalt carries me through the forest, seems to go anywhere but down. When exactly did Charlotte say that this road would drop down into the valley? And am I even still on the right road?

In the afternoon I admit to myself that the road is, in fact, climbing, and the one thing I remember the group saying was that we'd already reached our highest point, that our route wouldn't take us any higher. I must've taken a wrong turn at one of the junctions last night. But which junction? I haven't had any views all day—I've just been in this forest. I haven't been able to see the valley below to orient myself, see how I might get down.

Fuck.

I've got to stop biking in a daze like this. I stop and stand on the road, catching my breath. I need to focus, or I could get myself in serious trouble. What if something on my bike breaks? How much food do I have left? There's water at least—there are streams everywhere. But winter is here. I need to get down off this mountain.

As if in response, heavy dark clouds begin to gather on the horizon, and pile up on themselves as they move towards the ridge. Something in the air changes. I lift the dog from the bike and dump the panniers' contents onto the ground. I still have some grain, salt, lard, and I know I can gather more nettles at least. A few handfuls of dried javelina, broken down almost to dust.

"I am SO fucked," I say out loud to the darkening sky. I sit on the asphalt. The dog climbs into my lap looking for warmth and I hold him against me, kiss the top of his head. A breeze shakes the pine trees, bringing with it petrichor—the smell the first raindrops make when they hit the ground. No no no! Scrambling, I reassemble my bike and push it off the road, under the cover of the trees, just as the rain starts to spot the dry asphalt. Then a rushing sound as the clouds unleash.

The downpour is lighter in the forest but I'm still getting wet, everything is getting wet. I fumble for my tarp and string the ridgeline between two trees, stake the corners taut and close to the ground. By the time I scooch underneath it my sweater is damp but everything in my panniers is still dry, thank god, and I pull off the sweater as the dog and I burrow into the sleeping bag, all our things arranged around us, just enough room for everything inside the drip line. We'll stay dry as long as the wind doesn't pick up, start blowing into the open ends of the tarp.

The storm doesn't end after one hour, or two hours. The clouds settle in, dump their contents slow and steady on this high mountain ridge. There isn't a breath of wind, though, and for that I'm thankful. My vigilance on the drip line seems unwarranted and eventually I drift off in my warm cocoon, letting the afternoon melt into evening, and then night.

The cold wakes me—it's the hour before dawn, the coldest hour of the night, and the first thing I realize, as sleep leaves me, is that I'm wet. My sleeping bag is soaked, flat, stuck to my clothes, which are stuck to my skin. I touch the underside of the tarp—it's sopping with condensation. The fabric sagged in the night, touched my sleeping bag and all night the condensation has been running off, onto my sleeping bag.

Inside my bag is a small pocket of warmth, the core of which is the dog, curled up like the center of a cinnamon roll, and me around him. I push the tarp off my bag and scoot to the side so it's not touching me anymore. I burrow into my bag again but I'm too tense with cold to sleep. Time passes anyway, images and feelings dancing their way across the backs of my closed eyelids.

Opal. Georgia. The city. I remember stormy nights with Mother in the sedan—rain drumming on the roof of the car, the condensation from our breath dripping down the windows. Even though we only had a car to sleep in, it was a palace compared to what I have now. And we had each other.

Alone. I am alone again. Whatever roads I follow, they always carry me here. Is aloneness embodiment's most essential state, and our shifting relationships only temporary respite? Or am I just really unlucky. It's a question I'm not sure I'll find the answer to, in this life. I curl up tighter in my sleeping bag, letting the physical and emotional discomfort wash over me. I am in pain, therefore I exist.

The morning dawns clear. Bands of sun work their way among the trunks of the trees. I uncurl my stiff body, stretching it. The heat from my body has partially dried my sleeping bag. Soon the day will warm, freeing me from this miserable camp.

I have a plan today. Sort of? I think? I'm not sure where this road goes, and if I turned around I'm not confident that I'd be able to retrace my route back to where I split off from the group, to find the road that they were on, the correct road to get me down off this mountain.

What I do know is that the road I'm on right now is climbing—which means that if I continue to follow it up I'll likely reach somewhere with a vantage point. Then I can look down on the valley below and try and orient myself. Maybe, once I have a view of the mountain, I'll be able to see where this road goes. Or where other roads are. This road was built for a reason, right? It has to lead somewhere.

The sun dries my clothes as I ride my bike. My stomach is full of breakfast gruel, the dog is fed too and jostling softly in the pannier as we make our way. The cold and fear of the night slough off of me like drying mud, my joints loosen in the gentle day. I try not to think of how lost I am and how little food I have. I try and lean into this moment where, on the micro level, nothing is wrong, my strong legs turning the pedals of my bike, pulling the asphalt beneath me.

The road crests a rise—still wooded though, still no view—and I can see that it drops down, and then curves out of sight below. Ok, maybe we'll descend now. Maybe we'll get off this goddam mountain. I coast downhill, picking up speed, letting the wind ruffle my hair, letting my tired legs rest. How good it feels to just be carried like this!

There's a downed tree hidden behind a curve in the road and I don't see it soon enough. I try to brake but it's a huge tree, broken branches everywhere, and I'm going too fast. I can't even make sense of what happens next except there's a terrible grinding noise, I'm going over the handlebars, I'm bouncing, sharp pain in my body and then everything is still.

My first thought is the dog. I pull myself up—there's some blood on the fabric of my dress. My bike is tangled in twisted wood, the handlebars bent backwards. The pannier with the dog in it is facing up, it didn't get smashed under the bike, thank god.

As soon as I open it, the dog jumps out, looks around wide-eyed, startled, and shakes himself vigorously. He's ok. I'm weeping with relief. How stupid I was being. Why would I go so fast like that? On this janky ass road? I almost killed my best, and only, friend.

I'm sitting on the ground now, openly sobbing, my chest heaving, a tender pain starting to make itself known there, a stabbing burning each time I take a breath. The dog stands next to me, curious. I'm blubbering incoherently at him. He is everything in the world that I have, and he's so small, and it's my responsibility to keep him alive out here in this big, dangerous land. Snot is running down my face, and I lift the blood-stained skirt of my dress to wipe it away. That's when I see the cut on my leg—a sharp-ended branch must've dragged its way across my thigh.

The cut is rough looking and messy, but not too deep, and the blood is already starting to clot. When I stand the leg feels tender, and a little fresh blood oozes out. I run my hands over the rest of my body—I'm bruised, and maybe a broken rib? But otherwise ok. Lucky. I got lucky!

My bike is mangled though, one of the rims bent, the wheel rubbing against the frame. And walking is painful. And in addition, now that I'm around the bend I can see that the road does not continue to descend—it climbs, back up onto the ridge.

The ridge though! The clear open ridge! I can see it ahead of me, cast in soft yellow light. The road goes up there, and there should be a view! The view I wanted. There is that, at least. Better get there before the stiffness settles in, before my rib becomes all the way painful and pushing a bike is too much.

As I make my way gingerly up the hill the dog trots along beside me, the slowness of my bent bike matching the slow painful movements of my body. The road tops out in a rocky clearing and I can see the valley, spread out in the light below. The road ends here. There's a small house, a sort of one-room shack, up high in the air on stilts, with a long turning staircase leading up to it. I stand for a time watching the shack, waiting for movement, but there is none. No sounds either, just the stillness of this peaceful clearing.

I lean the bike against one of the metal supports, pull off my panniers and begin to mount the stairs. One, two, three, four flights. I grip the guardrail to support myself, wince at the pain in my leg and chest. With each turn of the staircase the mountain recedes below me and I can see farther, I can see the ridges leading away from this one, I can see more of the valley far below. The dog is right behind me, heaving himself up each metal step.

After six flights the staircase ends and there's just plywood above my head, nowhere else to go. I press the plywood up—it sticks and then comes free, revealing a square opening in the floor of the shack. I pop my head inside—I see a row of wooden benches, a metal table, some shelves, a small cot. A woodstove.

Each of the four walls is made up of huge windows. I lift the dog up, set him inside, and then climb in after him. It's nicer inside the shack than out—the walls block the wind, and the huge windows gather the warmth of the sun. Shelter. My god, shelter. Something inside of me releases, some tense little ball unfurls.

I drop my panniers on the floor. I should take inventory of this shack, see what is useful here, but I'm overcome with an unnamable exhaustion. I carefully lower myself onto the cot, curl up into a ball, and shut my eyes.

When I wake it's afternoon and the light is heavy. I fight the urge to close my eyes and fall back asleep, to sleep for a hundred years. The dog is sitting right in front of my face, staring at me.

"You're right, dog," I say. "I should get up and put things in order." I roll onto my back, and wince in pain. I'm thirsty. Did I put any water out for the dog? I fish a bottle from one of my panniers and fill the jar lid that serves as his water dish, setting it in the corner.

Anticipation percolates through me as I open a wooden cabinet above the metal table. It's the same anticipation I felt in the city, opening up abandoned apartments with Georgia. The time before mine was a period of unimaginable abundance of goods. Always I am mining that time, salvaging its leftovers, cobbling them together to make my own, spare life. What holdover treasures will I discover here?

The first thing I see is a pack of matches and a lighter and a roll of toilet paper, half used up. This, already, is a bonanza. I've been lighting fires with my flint and the dry inner bark of pine trees—I learned to make fires with the flint in the city, using paper trash as kindling, and Opal's group taught me about the tree bark. This lighter and matches will make things so much faster. That'll be nice. Until they run out, and then it's back to the flint. And toilet paper! I can't remember the last time I had toilet paper. In the city, toilet paper was for rich people. We used trash paper dampened with water, or water squeezed from a cheap plastic bottle to make a bidet. Since leaving the city I've used moss, grasses folded over into a bunch, smooth stones.

There's a deck of cards, a handful of dirty dice, a few pencils and some scrap paper. A small red zippered pouch with a white cross on it—a first-aid kit. These often don't hold much that's truly useful—some safety pins, gauze, things like that—but you never really know. Lastly, there's a note written on a scrap of paper—*Lottie*—*Moonlight at the end of the world, with you, falling in love among the stars. Yours, Carnelian.* I run my fingers over the words, place the note carefully back in the cabinet. Other people's sadnesses, years gone.

There's a long wooden storage box under the metal table and I lift the lid. Plastic bags. Packages! Seemingly intact. This box must be mouse-proof. I rifle through them—a Ziploc of broken noodles. A cardboard box of instant mashed potatoes. Some cans, their labels gone. Likely too old to eat without risking getting sick. And then some thick plastic packages that are still sealed—freeze-dried meals. Faded and old, but not yet expired. These are gold. They last decades. This is a major score!

"We're eating good tonight!" I say to the dog, who is busy sniffing every corner. He lifts his leg and lets a stream of urine run down the table support. "Hey now!" I say. "This is inside. You can't do that." He looks at me, uncomprehending.

In the bottom of the metal bin is a notebook, and I flip it open—it's full of entries, the earliest dated fifteen years ago. Fifteen years! Apparently this place operated as something called a fire lookout tower—a place to watch for wildfires. Back when there was still state infrastructure beyond the cities.

Someone lived up here and looked out these big windows and watched for smoke, and recorded their observations every day. And if they saw a fire they contacted some sort of authority, and those people would send out helicopters to fight the fire. Helicopters way out here! I can't imagine the infrastructure that used to exist, to move fuel all this way. Just the work it would take to clean the fallen trees off all these roads must have been staggering.

Elsewhere in the shack I find a metal lantern, lacking fuel, an enamel plate and cup, a couple of forks. On the windowsill is a pair of binoculars, a plant identification book, a book on local birds. A plastic tote on the floor holds an old rolled sleeping bag that smells pleasantly of mildew, and a couple of paperback westerns. There's a large blue water container that's empty.

A wave of dizziness reminds me that I'm actually quite hungry. At the table I rip open one of the freeze-dried meals. The plastic is brittle and breaks apart in my hands. I empty the contents into my pot with some water from one of my bottles and set it to boil on my small can woodstove. I've been gathering twigs in the morning and carrying them with me, in case I end up camping in a spot without trees and need to cook dinner, and I'm happy to have those twigs now, so I don't have to climb down all those steps.

While the water heats I close my eyes, allowing myself to enjoy the absolute stillness of this space. This safety is an illusion, I know. For true safety I'd need a source of water, some way to get more food, and ideally other people. But now that my bike is broken…

"We're just gonna chill here for a bit and rest," I say to the dog, who is napping in a sunbeam on the worn wooden floor. "And then we'll figure out what's next."

I think the meal was meant to be lasagna? Or some approximation of lasagna. Now it tastes rancid and the textures are all wrong, but the dog and I eat it anyway. The drowsiness that follows is a force that cannot be stopped and I lie down on the cot with the dog, the mildewed sleeping bag pulled over us, as well as my own sleeping bag. I imagine that I can sense that other time in the cabin's sleeping bag, that previous world. Lottie and Carnelian, smelling of flowers and pine pitch and salt. Falling in love at the end of the world.

When I wake it's dark, and cold. The dog is whining at me. He has to take a shit, most likely. Well, that's considerate of him to want to do it outside. The moon is still fairly large and the table and woodstove are cast in silver. I try to move... and I can't. I'm pinned to the cot. With pain. Tensing my abdomen to sit up causes a stab in my ribcage as though there's a sword running through it. "Fuck!" I say, aloud. "God fucking dammit!"

The dog lifts his ears and looks at me before whining again. Slowly, slowly I roll to my side, push myself into a sitting position using my arms. It's excruciating, but not impossible. My leg is sore but walking carefully is tolerable—however lifting anything, including the wooden hatch on the floor that leads to the staircase, creates another sword of pain in my chest.

I'm crying by the time I set the dog on the stairs beside me. I look at the dog. Maybe I can send him down by himself? But he's so small, and there are predators... openly sobbing, I make my way down the stairs after him, gripping the guardrail. By the time I reach the ground I feel as though I'm going to throw up. Not that though! Vomiting would be horrifically painful and would waste food. I want to laugh, but that would hurt too.

The dog noses around in the shadows, rounds his back, produces one tiny, perfect turd. My bike is there, leaning against the steel supports of the tower, glinting in the moonlight. I touch the metal, so cold it's almost frosty. I'm cold too. I'm starting to shiver, and that hurts. The dog is already bounding his way back up the staircase. I turn to follow him. I'll deal with my bike tomorrow.

The dawn comes long and red, the cold bite of nighttime banished by the slow warm of the morning. I woke when it was still dark and lay for hours in the sleeping bag, watching the night fade, the dog curled against my belly. When I am still the pain is still, but every time I move it hollers at me again. Now I close my eyes, feel the morning sun on my face. I've got to figure out what to do.

With great effort I get myself upright and make my way to the table to heat some water for breakfast. Putting weight on my leg feels worse today, and in a strange way. I lift my skirt and press my cool palm to the skin around the gash, which has scabbed over.

The skin is hot to the touch. And red. And swollen—sort of hard. Wait. Did I clean this yesterday? Did I even fucking clean this? I holler in the tower, letting my voice carry out over the bright, vacant world. The dog glances up at me, startled. How could I have forgotten to clean the cut on my leg? How? For all I know, it's got fucking sticks in there. I was so excited to find some stupid fucking matches and freeze-dried meals that I forgot to clean a fucking gash on my leg?

"No no no no no," I say to the tower, to the sky, to the whole uncaring universe that spirals around itself into cold, infinite space. I sit at the table and break sticks, unthinking, stuffing them into my stove. I pour water into my pot, shake the empty bottle—that's the last of my water—and light the sticks without comprehension. I unfocus my gaze at the blank windows and the blue sky beyond, waiting for the panic to pass.

The water boils over, scalding my hand. Brings me back into my body. Yesterday I ate a flake from the box of instant mashed potatoes—it tasted like nothing, as though the plant matter had been replaced by dust, the way bones in rock are replaced with minerals to make fossils. Oh well, I'm eating the potatoes anyway. I dump the contents of the box into the water, remove the pot from the heat and set it aside. I put my head on the cool metal table, close my eyes. Think. I've got to think.

I've never been much for wound care. Back in the city, organizing with Georgia and the others, that was never my role. I was good at breaking into buildings, stealing boxes of food from the backs of trucks that were unloading, dumpstering, making connections to get the resources we couldn't scavenge or steal.

Georgia was the one in the group with some basic medical knowledge. If someone stepped on something sharp or twisted their ankle jumping down from a chain-link fence, she was there. Hospitals were great places to get disappeared, so people like Georgia were crucial. It wasn't always possible to help every problem—like with Malachite and his abscessed tooth, and how impossible it was to find antibiotics—but Georgia, and others like her, did what they could.

Now, spooning tasteless potato mush into my mouth in this isolated fire tower far from the last vestiges of a dying empire, I wish that I had taken the time to learn basic wound care from Georgia. What an idiot I was!

I drop some potatoes on the floor for the dog and he horks them down and then licks the wood clean. I've got to get more water. What would kill me first, dehydration or my infected wound? I want to laugh. Where was the last water I passed? A little seep on the side of the road, yesterday. It made a clear pool in the grass.

How many miles back was that? My bike is too broken to ride, I'd be travelling on foot. And I'm in so much pain I can barely move. Maybe once my ribs have recovered some I can walk to that water source—in a few days? But right now I can't travel that far. I need to find something closer.

Shutting my eyes, I visualize the mountain. Where has the water been on this ridge, so far? It bubbles up from underground, streams and springs likely replenished by snowmelt. When traveling with Opal's group, we found it by watching for different kinds of plant life—there'd be dry slopes of yellow grasses and stiff, woody brush and then, in a fold in the mountain, a riot of green—we'd make our way to this drainage and follow it downhill, or uphill, sometimes splitting into two groups to go both ways, until we heard, or smelled water. It just rained a ton—I think back to my night under the tarp—so that should help things.

I eyeball the blue, plastic five-gallon water container that sits in the corner of the tower. I should take that thing with me on my search for water. Empty, it'll be light enough, but how will I even lift it once it's full, with my injured ribs?

"One thing at a time," I say out loud. In the cabinet I find the first-aid kit and rifle through it, not expecting much. There's some ancient band-aids, their glue likely useless, a roll of gauze, some sterile wipes. And then, good god—an amber colored pill bottle!

It rattles in my hand. It has pills inside! The label says doxycycline. A fucking antibiotic! I cannot believe my luck. I upend the bottle. The dozen or so pills in my palm are brown and oblong… and have I-2 etched into them. *These are not antibiotics. They're ibuprofen.* I take a deep breath and tip the pills back into the bottle, setting four aside. These will be helpful for the pain, at least. They'll make my water-gathering trip a bit easier.

It takes me a while to get down the stairs—my body has grown stiffer as the day has progressed—but by the time I'm walking along the ridge away from the tower, following a faint jeep trail overgrown with weeds that heads more or less in a westerly direction, the ibuprofen has kicked in and the pain feels a little farther away, isn't so sharp as to make me want to throw up my mashed potatoes.

The dog is trotting beside me, happy to be walking in the sunshine. My leg has begun to throb and I try to ignore it, repeating the mantra *one thing at a time* to myself and taking breaks whenever I need them, sitting on the water jug and staring out over the valley below.

I don't know how fast I'm walking or how much time has passed, exactly, but it's afternoon when the jeep trail ends and a single footpath continues on, along the rocky ridge. The footpath drops down into a cluster of trees and I see a promising sight—a depression filled with green grass. I dig with my fingers in the grass—the earth is dark and moist here, but there is no standing water. Damn. Below the depression is a cleft in the trees, dropping down, filled with rocks and boulders and green plants. Some of the rocks are wet. I should follow this drainage.

The going is slow, though—with my jug and my injured legs and my ribs. Each small drop down from a large boulder, dragging the banging water jug after me, makes me dizzy with pain and hunger now, too, and it takes me time to steady myself for the next obstacle.

I peek between the boulders as I make my way, looking for a pool of water. I find damp sand and more green plants, which is promising, so I keep going. The pain slows my pace to a crawl as the afternoon lengthens. I try not to let panic cloud my decision making as I push on, down the boulder-choked ravine.

The ibuprofen has long since worn off and the last of the light is fading when I smell minerals and feel the air change on my skin. I find the pool in the lee of a large granite boulder, clear water about elbow deep in the middle, dancing with water bugs. In this moment the rest of my worries drop away and the pain and panic-induced fog clears. In this moment I have solved the greatest, and most basic of life's puzzles and I want for nothing. I am happy in the purest sense.

I fill a water bottle and guzzle the entire thing. Now for the hunger. I pull a freeze-dried meal from my backpack and laboriously crunch up and swallow a few handfuls of the contents, which taste like salt and not much else, followed by another bottle of cold, perfect water. The dog drinks his fill and gets part of my meal, too, and then settles down in the warm sand, ready for bed.

Through the trees I can see the molten orange of the sunset and I allow a moment of perfect contentment to pass before I ask myself what exactly I mean to do now. The cold is coming and I'm already chilled, the heat of the day escaping into the atmosphere. I brought my sleeping bag with me and I decide to sleep here, next to the water, and figure out what my next steps will be in the morning, when the sun returns.

Animals will want to use this watering hole in the night, most likely, and I don't want to spook or be spooked by them, so I walk a bit into the trees until I find a flat, dry patch of ground. I'm more than exhausted, my broken body aching in new ways from trying to compensate for its injuries while I hiked down this ravine, and it feels blissful to escape into the warm depths of my sleeping bag, the dog warm against me, and cinch the hood closed over my face, leaving just my nose sticking out.

My sleep is full of nightmares and I wake multiple times in the night, unsure, at first, where I am, some part of my body uncomfortable or in pain. I roll over with difficulty and drift off only to wake again, in a new kind of pain.

I'm relieved when the first of the light begins to bleed into the sky and I lie there, eyes open, listening to the sounds of the forest. Aching and almost—but not quite—warm enough, I wait impatiently for the sun. Dawn finds me sitting on the sand next to the pool, shivering slightly, using one of my water bottles to fill the five-gallon jug.

Soon most of the pool is inside the jug, water bugs and all, and I am contemplating how to get the beastly heavy thing back up the ravine, to the ridge. Lifting it is out of the question—just one half-hearted try and my ribs are screaming at me—but maybe I can drag it?

The dog sits a little bit away in a patch of sun and watches without judgement as I use my knife to trim the hem of my dress in one long, spiraling strip. The fabric twists easily into a small rope that is not, I decide, strong enough to pull five gallons of water, and I reluctantly return half the jug to the pool.

Although I am disappointed, this turn of events pleases the water bugs greatly. One end of the rope ties to the handle of the water jug, and the other end I wrap around a thick stick, which will be easier to hold than the rope itself. I take a few tentative steps up the slope, my feet digging into the deep pine needles. The jug tugs me back, and then a bright pain blooms as my core engages, moving my broken rib, plus the dull throbbing pain in my leg. Fuck. There's no way I can pull this jug uphill.

My head turns to static again and I sit on the sun-warmed ground and try to gather myself. I mustn't panic. This situation is very bad, but panicking will make it worse. I must not make things worse. The dog pads over to me and climbs in my lap, curls into a donut and shuts his eyes. He's not worried. He trusts in my ability to figure things out. Oh that I was as clever and powerful as my dog thinks I am! I shoo the dog off and ease myself up again, slowly so as not to jostle my ribs and stare at the water jug, willing myself to solve this puzzle. I can't carry the jug. I can't drag the jug. What can I do?

The water sloshes as I pour the rest of it back into the pool. I chug a liter and fill the two bottles in my backpack. These two liters are all I can carry, but at least it's more water than I had yesterday.

The ravine looks completely different on the climb up and I recognize almost nothing. I chastise myself for not noting more landmarks, but my experience on the way down was clouded heavily by thirst, exhaustion and pain. Still, next time I should be more careful.

When I'm halfway to the top I sit for a long moment and let the pain subside, want to sit forever but make myself stand again. Hunger is making me dizzy—the freeze-dried meal I ate last night was the only food I brought, and I've already burned through the bit I saved and ate for breakfast.

My imagination conjures dumpsters full of stale bread, sheet cakes stolen off the backs of trucks, greasy street food and other abundances of the city. I see Georgia, her soft fingers on my scalp as she braids my hair in the first light on the rooftop, whispering to me about her dreams the night before. Would I have been better off if I'd just stayed? Yes. For a little while. And then?

"That world is behind me," I say aloud as I brush the pine needles off my dress and pick up the blue jug again. That world is lost. And in its place I've gained something I didn't even know I'd been missing; these mountains. The arid valleys. I mean to try and find my mother and I mean to make my home here, figure out what to eat and how to live and where the people are.

Or maybe just die trying.

A few minutes later I cross an animal trail, well used and clear as day, that exits the ravine and contours along the slope, through the forest. Above me I can see blue sky where the ravine tops out at the ridge, and this trail seems to make its way just below.

It's risky, reckless even, but a part of me wants to leave my original route and follow this trail. It'll be faster than making my way up the boulders, and less painful. I stand for a moment, considering. If the trail starts going somewhere I don't like, I reason with myself, I can just turn around and follow it back to the ravine. Or even cut straight up, to the ridge. From the ridge I can orient myself using my view of the valley below. I won't get lost.

This isn't entirely true. The pain fugue I was in yesterday really did affect my memory of the way here. But I'm at the point in this situation where I have to take risks. I just have to.

The trail cuts through oak forest that is lovely in the late morning light, the leaves on the trees golden, the path crunching underfoot. I wonder what sorts of animals come this way. Deer? Coyotes? I wish once more that I had a gun. But then again, where would I get bullets after I ran out? Better to figure out how to live my life without a gun.

The trail is climbing ever so slightly as I walk it, up towards the ridge. This is great. With luck it'll dump me back on the overgrown jeep trail, which I can follow to the fire tower. And I will have avoided much of the rocky climb out of the ravine!

The path tops out not at the jeep trail but in a flat, open pine forest and continues on, through the trees. The jeep trail is around here somewhere, I tell myself, as I continue to follow the path. I don't let worry creep in. As long as I'm on this trail, I'm not lost. Although I will have wasted a lot of time, I can always follow it back to the ravine.

There's something in the distance, in the open forest. It's gray and running parallel to the ground. A piece of an abandoned structure? Machinery? No, I see as the trail takes me closer, it's a simple fence, made from two rows of metal poles. The fence runs off in the distance and then turns sharply—a few more turns make a large enclosure. The trail ends at this fence, where one of the poles is broken at a joint and bent down, to knee level.

There's a metal sign on the fence. Legible as if it was just put up yesterday. *No camping within a quarter mile of the wildlife guzzler.*

What's a wildlife guzzler? I lift myself and the blue jug gingerly over the broken part of the fence, the torn hem of my dress catching on the metal and then freeing itself. On the far end of the enclosure is what looks like a corrugated metal roof, laid flat on the ground and tilted slightly downhill at one end.

My heart races, almost but not quite comprehending what I'm looking at. I walk around the roof in a big circle, but see nothing else manmade—there's just the forest floor, and this big piece of metal laid down flat on it. Then I spot a bit of concrete nearby. It's a rectangular tub, the size of a bathtub but deeper, sunk down into the earth. And it's full. Of green, scummy water.

That water is more precious to me, in this moment, than if I'd found a concrete tub of diamonds. I ease myself painfully down and dip my hand into the water—once the algae is pushed to the side it's actually quite clear, if tinted a bit yellow. Rainwater and snow must gather on that big sheet of metal and pour into an underground pool, which feeds this tank.

I can't believe my luck. Here is water in quantity, that I don't have to carry up a mountain. I can't be that far from the fire tower, which currently functions as my home. The dog sniffs the water and then paces its edge, chasing a water strider that dances on the surface.

"Dog! We're going to be ok!"—then, more quietly under my breath—"maybe."

I extract one of my water bottles from my backpack and begin filling the blue jug. And that's when I notice something else—all around the edge of the tank is a small green plant with lined oval leaves. In fact it's everywhere in this enclosure, growing in little clusters that poke up through the pine needles.

Something about the plant jogs my memory. I close my eyes, trying to recall. And then I see Opal, and the other members of her group, stooped over on the roadside, plucking the leaves when we've stopped midday to take a break in the sun. Opal called it plantain.

She told me about when they'd stopped in a village and a woman had brought her son to the evening fire—he'd cut his foot chopping wood and it had gotten infected. I was in such a lovesick haze then, it's difficult to recall details, but didn't Opal say this was the plant that Charlotte had used to treat the boy? She'd chewed it up into a paste, added hot water from a kettle on the fire, folded it in cloth to make a poultice and then pressed it to the boy's wound. Maybe it wasn't plantain, but some other simple green plant. I can't remember. Damnit! I gather the leaves anyway, a great quantity of them, and stuff them into my backpack. I might as well try these and see what happens.

In the end, I am not far from the tower at all. The clearing in which the tower sits is just through the trees. I am flush with endorphins after finding the water, and those endorphins allow me to move the water jug, which I once again fill halfway, to the base of the tower, using my homemade rope to drag it across the flat pine needle ground. I'm not sure how much this strenuous effort, or indeed the whole of the last two days' effort, has set back the healing of my ribs, but I can't be bothered with that now.

Leaving the jug at ground level, I drag myself up the flights of stairs in a stupor with just the two liters in my backpack. The dog is tired too and he hefts himself up slowly behind me. The relief I feel when I pop open the trap door and lift the dog and myself up into our current home is almost indescribable.

I make myself boil a bit of grain, which I share with the dog, and then I lift up my dress and fix my attention on the wound in my leg. I mean to treat it with a poultice made from the plantain, but first I'll need to open up the wound again, to clean out anything that might be in there. This is going to hurt. I swallow two more of my precious ibuprofen.

The pain is intense. Nausea rocks me as I scrub the crusted wound with a bit of gauze and some water that I boiled and let cool. The inside of the gash is gnarly—hot, parts of it white, and it smells a little bad, which I find very alarming. A square of fabric, cut from my dress and boiled clean in my pot, makes the material for the poultice. I spit chewed plantain into the fabric, fold it closed and dip this in the hot water.

The poultice scalds my skin but I hold it onto the wound anyway. My homemade rope, unwound back into a long strip of cloth, gets wrapped around the poultice to hold it to my offending leg, and then I lower myself gingerly onto the cot, where the dog is already curled up, and pull my sleeping bag over us both. The light outside is fading and I am beyond exhausted, but I have done all the things, all the things that it is possible for me to do in this one wild moment and now, at last, I can rest.

I wake shivering, the tower still dark, the stars winking in the huge glass windows. I fell asleep when there was still light and now I don't know what time it is. I think back to when I had a phone to tell me what time it was, when I kept track of days. Now "time" is something I feel, rather than name; the warmth of the midday sun, the sleepy afternoons and this, the bottomless, middle part of the night. Seasons are more important than days: this is fall, creeping towards winter. The climate is different here than in the city and yet already, I have come to know it.

What will it be like down in the valley? I wonder. *What will it be like in Nevada, and when will I reach it? Will my clothing be sufficient for winter there and if not, how will I get more?*

And then there is the problem of right now. Why am I shivering? It's not any colder tonight. I'm under both sleeping bags. My head feels strange. Should I make a fire in the woodstove? For that I'd have to venture down the stairs, to gather wood.

My body is pinned to the cot with fatigue. As though my limbs are sandbags. And if I made a fire, would the smoke from the woodstove draw attention to this tower? This whole mountain seems deserted, but what if it's not? I'll wait until a fire is absolutely necessary before I risk it. How long am I going to be here?

The room swims as I dig the rest of my layers from the bike panniers. I take a sip of water but it tastes foul. The water was fine yesterday. Is it my fever, making the water taste bad? I put on my sweater plus the large woven shawl and climb back under the sleeping bags. Still, I can't get warm. There's a little light now, the stars are fading. Slowly I draw myself back out of the sleeping bag and unwrap the cloth from my leg. The wound is still angry and red.

In a haze I break a few twigs for my little cookstove (I'm going to need more twigs soon) and heat an inch of water. I add this to some more chewed up plantain and re-apply the fresh poultice. Exhausted by this effort, I sink back onto the cot. The dog is happy with our hot little cocoon and doesn't notice my shivering, can't feel the aching that zings all over my body. Eventually sleep carries me away again, or some delirious approximation of sleep.

I've got to find my mother. I'm in the house in my dreams again, wandering its rooms, which go backward through time. My mother is here, somewhere, and I'm searching for her. I open a closed door and find a space with a folding table, a feast spread out on the table—there's roadkill venison, wild greens dressed with corn oil and salt, stale bread that's been toasted on the fire. It's the feast I made for Georgia last year, for her birthday.

I sit at the table and look at the roast meat, watch it cool. In the dream I know that Georgia will never arrive. I can't eat, and I can't get up from the table and leave. I'll sit here for hours, the longing its own kind of food, this desire feeding some hungry part of me that can never be full.

Then the light is on my face, the dog is whining and pawing at me. I open my eyes, look out the big windows at the blinding day. When I pull myself up my chest pain mingles with leg pain, then with all-over body aches and hot heavy head. I feel sick to my stomach. Opening the trap door with slow careful effort, I pause to lay my forehead on the cool wood, then lower the dog down to the top step. *Please be careful, don't get eaten.* Did I say that out loud?

As I watch him disappear, jostling his way down the metal stairs, time stops. What did the dream mean? Is Georgia somewhere out there? Will I ever see her again? Where is the prison where my mother might be? A small sound and the dog is there, waggling his tail up at me. I lift him back into the tower, crying out at the pain in my chest. He takes a long drink from his water dish as I drop the last of yesterday's cooked grain on the ground for him.

Now I'm back on the cot, a fresh poultice on my leg but no memory of changing it. The dog rests on the sun-warmed floor of the tower, his little legs crossed, watching the trap door, which is latched shut. I'm still so cold although I know, intellectually, that it's not cold in the tower—the afternoons are warm, almost hot in the full sun, and the tower gathers heat like a greenhouse. It's hard to get comfortable but eventually sleep takes me again.

In the afternoon the pain won't let me sleep anymore. My thoughts keep returning to those old wounds, deep gashes that no poultice of gathered herbs can ever heal. I need some sort of distraction, anything to keep me from running in circles on those old sad tracks in my mind. I pull the fire-tower logbook onto my cot and open it to the first page, that earliest entry I saw when I first discovered the tower.

Fifteen years ago is more recent than I would have thought, but I've lived my whole life in the city, and only knew what was happening there, my one small world. Way out here, in this fire tower, someone was living their life while I was a child in the park, doing workbooks and eating cold cricket gruel, waiting for my mother to return in the evenings. As I searched dumpsters for food scraps the person in the fire tower split wood for winter and logged what they did and saw each day.

At the beginning of the logbook there is just one person, Carnelian. He's paid by the forest service in food rations and occasional other supplies; currency has long since lost its value in this part of the world. He writes his story in the first few entries in the notebook; he's from a village in the low desert that was devastated by famine the year before he arrived here, when the summer monsoon rains never came and the dry riverbeds never flooded and so the crops couldn't grow.

The forest service still functioned insomuch that it was in the cities' best interest that the countryside not be engulfed in massive wildfires that would then darken the sky with smoke and spread to the cities, and so they still staffed the fire towers, although sometimes Carnelian wouldn't be able to reach anyone on the radio for weeks, and his rations would dwindle, and he'd wonder if this one final link to some larger infrastructure had been cut now too, and then a man in a sweat-stained forest service uniform would arrive on horseback, reeking of liquor, and unload canvas sacks of grain.

After these colorful first few pages there follows a handful of dry entries in the logbook mostly about weather and Carnelian's garden, and later his goats and chickens. I skip ahead through these until the entries grow interesting again, when Lottie arrives.

Lottie appeared in the middle of winter one year when there was a foot of snow on the ground, Carnelian had fallen off in his fire-watching duties because the risk was low when there was snowpack. He hadn't heard from anyone on the radio in almost a month and he'd been keeping careful track of how much grain was left in his sacks, worrying again. One day he decided to do his watch per usual and was looking west when he saw her, struggling up the snowy mountainside, a ragged backpack on her back.

He rushed out and found her frostbitten and slightly hypothermic, brought her into the tower and fed her hot broth. She told him that she'd left her village in the mountains to the south when disease had taken her mother, sisters, and her sisters' children. Her father had died years ago in a farming accident. She was crossing the valley and had gotten spooked by the prison rangers, had climbed up into these mountains, hoping to make it over them, but then the snow had come and travel on foot had become difficult, and she'd seen the smoke from his fire.

Once Lottie recovered she decided to stay, and she helped him in his duties. He was grateful for the company and they shared his food rations, and they bucked downed trees and split the wood into stove lengths. They snared grouse and squirrels and tended the goats and chickens, and when spring came they gathered nettles and planted the garden. The forest service man on his horse came more infrequently, and then four months passed without his hat appearing even once.

There was new talk on the radio now; it was prison rangers, communicating with each other as they searched for prisoners who had escaped from the prison in the valley below. The prison had become more permeable, Lottie and Carnelian learned, as technology failed and resources from the cities dwindled. A prisoner or two escaped almost every week. And yet, there wasn't enough munitions or manpower to do more than a half-assed job of hunting them down. The prison guards were underpaid and also itching to get free themselves.

The first prisoners arrived at the fire tower soon after the talk of escapees on the radio; it was two teenagers, one of them pregnant, and an older woman. They'd been attempting to get over the mountains and had seen the smoke from the tower's woodstove, the same way Lottie had. One of them had killed a javelina, and they roasted it in a pit in the ground next to the tower, after which they all had a feast.

The group stayed for a week so the pregnant one could rest, and the older one diagnosed and patched a hole in the roof of the tower that had been leaking in the rains. When they finally set out again Lottie and Carnelian were sad to see them go, and they tower felt empty at night without the three extra bedrolls on the floor.

They told Lottie and Carnelian that they were going to Nevada, and they implored the two of them to go too. There was clean water there from springs, they said, and wild burros whose milk you could drink, and the soil was good for growing things.

But Lottie and Carnelian had already, in moving to the fire tower, traveled farther from their homes than they would have liked, and they couldn't imagine going any further. After the first three, there was a steady trickle of prisoners. Some needed medical help, some were simply tired, or cold. They asked for food or they shared their food—stolen, scavenged, hunted, traded for—and this extra food helped Lottie and Carnelian. Some of the prisoners had no idea where to go, and waited around, hoping for a group to join. Many of them were headed to Nevada. None of them were going back to the cities.

I fold shut the logbook and ease myself into a standing position. The pain is noisy today, full of bass and staccato, a background symphony I can't tune out. I wonder if my mother could've been one of those escapees, headed to Nevada. Maybe she stayed in this fire tower years ago, looked out these very same windows, dreaming of a safe place where she could go?

"Nevada," I say the word aloud, to the empty fire tower. The dog looks up at me, from his spot in a sunbeam on the floor. There are only a handful of twigs left from the bundle I brought back from my journey to find water, and I break them and stuff them into my cookstove.

A quick inventory of my stores shows that I have a few pounds of millet left, plus some handfuls of dry meat, lard, salt, dried nettles and a couple of freeze-dried meals from the tower. My small pot rumbles as it comes to a boil, startling me out of my reverie. I feel as though I'm intoxicated, and not in a good way, although there are moments of a strange sort of euphoria.

In these moments I remember being back in the city with Georgia. Walking the empty streets late at night, the summer air warm on our skin.

Waking at first light on the roof of the warehouse, curled in her arms on several layers of flattened cardboard. The sunrise through all the layers of city haze—I could think about that light for hours.

I use some of the boiled water to make a new poultice from the now-wilted plantain before adding millet to the pot. I wonder how much time has to pass before I know for sure if the poultice is helping. How long before I am forced to come up with a plan b. Except, there is no plan b. I can't ride my broken bike, I sure as hell can't walk all the way down the mountain with this injury.

There's the smell of burning millet and I remove the pot from the stove. Then I'm back in bed, shivering, pulling the sleeping bags tighter around me. It's dark. Did I feed the dog? I must have. He seems content, wedged against me absorbing my fever. Beyond the windows are the cold, glittering stars. *Dear universe*, I say. *Please help me.*

My sleeping bag is suffocating me. I'm clawing at it, but I can't get it off. My fingers aren't nimble enough for the zipper. I'm trapped! I take great gasping breaths, trying to get air. At last the zipper comes unstuck and I open the bag, exposing myself to the freshest, coldest, goodest air. Air I could eat with a spoon, that's how hungry I am for it.

My face is wet, my greasy hair stuck to my forehead. My whole body is slick. I smell beyond foul. Not the stink of working hard without a shower for weeks in the sun but the putrid, ammoniac smell of illness. I didn't notice this smell before. I was too far away. Now I am here again. The cabin is tidy and bright with morning sunshine. The dog, who wiggles up and licks the stench from my face, is impossibly soft and sweet.

My fever has broken.

The wound, when I check it, is no longer angry. The skin around it is cool. By god, what if the infection is gone? I let out one long, slow breath. I replace the poultice, figuring that I should keep the wound dressed for now. I'll have to gather more plantain. My ribs still pain me but I'm learning to work around that—how to sit up, how to move around to do the things I need to do.

I follow the dog down the stairs and piss on the dirt ground, fill my water bottles from the blue jug that rests in the weeds next to my broken bike, venture into the woods for more twigs for my cookstove. My energy dips again once back in the fire tower and I eat some millet gruel and shake out my sleeping bags, hanging them on the stairway railing in the sun. On second thought I strip off my dress too and hang it next to the bags. I lie out naked on the cot. I reach for the logbook.

I pick up where I left off, reading the alternating entries by Lottie and Carnelian. The last prisoners recorded in the logbook are a woman and a young child—they were unrelated, but had found each other in the workhouses, and the woman had been caring for the child. These two stayed for weeks and ended up telling Lottie and Carnelian a great deal about the prison and its workings—the woman had worked in administration, and had overseen the acceptance of raw materials into the prison, and the transfer of goods out of it.

Her name was Sarah, and she said that the prison existed primarily to produce tech, assembled from various components that were sourced overseas. Lottie and Carnelian were surprised by this, as they'd thought that all international trade had ended years ago. Sarah said that this was almost entirely true, but that a good chunk of the government's remaining resources were used to source these few tech components that were made overseas—they weren't components for any tech still commonly in use—that tech was breaking, and becoming obsolete, and none of it was being replaced—these components were for a separate tech project, the details of which were a mystery to her.

"Why this fancy other tech thing?" asked Lottie.

"I don't know," said Sarah.

"And is the project complete yet?" Lottie asked.

Sarah shook her head.

"Conditions in the prison have been deteriorating for a while, delays in shipments of goods, there have been lots of complications."

Eventually Sarah and the young child left the fire tower and set out west to Nevada, the same direction the others had gone. There were no more prisoners after that. Lottie and Carnelian ate through most of what they'd put aside until they were subsisting off what they could harvest from their goats, chickens and gardens, and then winter came and the chickens stopped laying and the garden was buried under a blanket of snow.

Hunger began to color their days. They still had their emergency rations in the wooden box under the table, but they were hesitant to break into those. The radio had gone completely silent, and this seemed a sign that the forest service man with his sacks of grain was never, ever going to return.

One cold, clear morning Carnelian packed a backpack with supplies—they'd decided that he would set out on his own, to Nevada, to find out what was there, and that he would then return to fetch Lottie, hopefully within a month. Lottie could snare squirrels to supplement the milk she could get from the goats and the root vegetables they'd put away from their garden—it was enough food for one person to eke by, but not for two.

Setting out into the world was incredibly dangerous, and Carnelian figured, why should they both risk it? They roasted a chicken and ate it together slowly that last morning, never discussing what to do if the unthinkable happened—if Carnelian never returned. They both knew that he would. Fortune had been on their side thus far, and they knew that their love would bring them back together again.

Then there are only entries in the logbook from Lottie. How many potatoes from their garden were left, packed in sawdust in the small root cellar they'd dug with help from the prisoners. An animal got one of the chickens in the night, and then another; Lottie found a chaos of scattered feathers in the coop. She logged the snow, when it fell, and the warmer days that melted it in the clearing below the tower.

Suddenly there were notes of another sort; Lottie seemed to be ill. No, not ill, I realize with a start. Lottie was pregnant. If she knew she was pregnant when Carnelian left, she didn't say. She simply documented the progress once he was gone. Her cravings for sour foods, her nausea in the mornings.

A month passed, and then two, and Carnelian did not return. Spring softened the mountain and Lottie began venturing farther from the tower each day in an attempt to find people, another family on the mountain maybe, with whom she could trade goat's milk for grain. One day she excitedly wrote that she had found an old woman living in a squat log cabin on a hillside in the shaded forest a half day's walk away.

This hardy woman who had lived her whole life on the mountain had put away a ton of root vegetables, and was a trapper as well, and she traded furs with the farmers in the valley below and so she also had grain. She didn't need Lottie's meager goat milk but she took pity on her and gave her a large sack of millet and told her to visit often and that when the time came, she would help deliver the baby.

If Lottie was heartbroken that Carnelian hadn't returned, she didn't say. There were longer gaps between entries as Lottie spent more time at the old woman's cabin, then the flush of summer came and Lottie moved her goats and chickens over there, and set up her cot in a corner next to the old woman's hearth, to be close during the last part of the pregnancy.

The entries become shorter still as Lottie returned to the tower only occasionally, to check on things—to fetch garden supplies, to mend the trap door after a bear attempted to break in. The last entry is from July, more than a decade ago.

Startled two deer in the clearing when I arrived, eating volunteers from the old garden. I've been making my own bow—it's not perfect, but hopefully good enough to shoot straight. It would be a godsend to have venison to put away before this baby comes.

All the remaining pages in the logbook are blank. I flip through them several times, searching for something, any sign as to what happened to Lottie and the baby, but there is nothing. Not a single mark.

I return the logbook to the metal table and lean back on the cot, closing my eyes. There's a sadness in the tower, now, that wasn't here before. My throat gets tight and then I'm crying, mourning Lottie and Carnelian's lost love and then my own losses since leaving the city, leaking out of my eyeballs in a flood I can't control. It feels good, to feel all these feelings, Lottie's and my own.

After crying, I'm hungry. The half-burnt millet, scraped from the bottom of my pot, tastes pretty good. Then I venture out with the dog to gather more plantain from the wildlife guzzler. The ache in my leg is all but gone, my rib pain is sharp but manageable and it feels incredible to absorb the warmth of the afternoon sun. I take the blue jug with me and fill it at the guzzler, kneel next to the concrete trough harvesting the ribbed clusters of plantain. I'm lost in a contented reverie, the tips of my fingers stained green, when I hear the dog bark.

"What is it?" There's nothing in the woods. And then a narrow shape, making its way in the dappled light. "Hush!" I say to the dog. It's a small person. A boy, I can see as he enters the clearing around the guzzler. Dressed in buckskin, as well as clothing salvaged from a previous time, faded and stained the same color as the buckskin. The boy says nothing, just stands and stares at me. In his hand is a bow. I remember Lottie's bow, that she was making in the last logbook entry.

"Hello," I say.

"Do you live in the tower?" says the boy.

"Right now I suppose I do," I respond. The boy is silent. A few long moments pass between us. I feel as though I am being inspected; my worn sneakers, my faded floral dress with its torn hem, my oversized wool sweater, the oily tangle of my hair, the streaks of dirt and sunburn on my face.

"The animals come here for water," says the boy, finally. "It's a good place to hunt."

"I can see that," I say, nodding at the bow. "I get my water here too." More staring. "Are you hunting right now?"

"What's that?" says the boy, ignoring my question. He's pointing at the dog.

"It's a little dog," I say. "He's from the city." The dog and boy eye each other warily. "He's my friend."

"I'm hunting bear," says the boy. "The bear won't come if that dog is here."

"We'll be out of your way soon," I say. "I just came to fill my jug, and harvest some of this plantain." I hold up the leaves for the boy to see.

The boy says a word I don't recognize.

"Is that what you call it?" I say. "Where is your family?"

The boy doesn't answer.

"I mean to get a bear," he repeats.

I tuck the plantain I've harvested into the pocket of my dress and screw the cap back onto the blue jug.

"If you need help with the bear, or if you want to say hi, you can come visit me in the tower anytime, ok?"

The boy nods slightly and continues to stand motionless, like a sapling. He watches as I use my homemade rope to awkwardly drag the blue jug through the woods, back towards the dusty road. In the tower I break some twigs and cook a fresh pot of millet, elated. I spoke to another human being! I add a spoonful of rendered fat to the millet to celebrate, drop a little on the floor for the dog.

In the morning I'm sitting in the sun on the metal staircase of the tower, letting the light untangle the remnants of my dreams when I see the boy walking through the woods, just past the edge of the clearing.

"Hello!" I call. "Did you get a bear?"

He pauses. We stare at each other for a while again, then he turns and starts to walk away.

"Wait!" I call out. I scramble down the stairs, my shawl gathered awkwardly around me. When I reach the bottom he's standing at the edge of the clearing, waiting for me where the trees begin. "Did you get a bear?" I ask again.

He nods.

"Well," I say, "Do you need some help?"

"I've done it myself before," he says.

"Will you show me how to do it, then? I'd like to learn."

He is silent and then nods again before turning and disappearing into the forest, in the direction of the wildlife guzzler. I scramble to get a few things together—some water, my knife, some cloth sacks—and then the dog and I pad across the clearing, into the woods. There was frost last night—there is frost most nights, now—and the shaded forest is still cold. I find the boy a bit downhill from the guzzler, kneeling over a large black mass. The bear rests in broken brush, a few arrows sticking out of its middle.

The boy's hand is on the bear's side. There's a stench—the smell of an animal that scavenges dead things. I touch the dark, coarse fur. The animal is still warm, a room that has only just been vacated.

"I shot him in the lungs," says the boy.

"Is that where you're supposed to shoot them?" I ask. "I don't know much about bears. I'm from the city."

"You said that." The boy touches the bear's middle, where the arrows protrude. "The bear dies quick when you shoot him in the lungs. He doesn't suffer much or have time to get angry." He pulls a short knife from a sheath on his leather belt. "I've never been to the city. I've only ever been on this mountain."

"A bear is a lot of food, huh?" The boy looks up at me incredulously, astonished at my ignorance.

"You have to get a bear," says the boy. "It's got a lot of fat, is the reason. Everything else in the mountains is lean. Without a bear you'll starve."

"What about potatoes and grain?" I ask, thinking of Lottie's entries in the logbook. "Doesn't your family have a garden? Or trade with people in the valley?"

"Help me roll this bear onto his back?" he asks. Together we heave the bear belly-side up, and the boy pulls a length of twine from a sack and uses it to tie the bear's uphill feet to a tree. He cuts carefully into the skin around the bear's genitals, working to get the knife through the thick hide.

"You have to cut away the anus and tie a string around it," he says. "Then no urine or feces will come out and get on the meat."

"That makes sense." I watch as the boy does this and then continues the cut, up the abdomen towards the bear's chest. The bear's hefty outfit unzips neatly with the boy's careful work, revealing a clean white membrane underneath. The boy is grunting with effort, and once he reaches the sternum he stops, wipes his knife on the grass to clean it, and then takes out a small stone and sharpens the blade.

"This white stuff holds the guts," he says, nodding at the membrane over the belly. "You have to cut into it real careful." He pauses, and then looks at me. "You want to do it?" He hands the small bloody knife to me. I make a small cut in the membrane down near the genitals and place the first two fingers of my left hand, facing upwards, inside this cut. I curl those fingers and use them to guide the tip of my knife, held in my right hand.

It's hot inside the cavity, and there's a raw, salty smell that is not unpleasant. This is just like processing roadkill deer. A loop of intestines slips out of my incision, and I work carefully around it.

"I punctured the intestines by accident once," says the boy. "Stench was so bad I threw up. We still ate the bear though."

We? I think. I'm sweating with concentration, but I make it up to the bear's breastbone without either puncturing its bowels and making a huge mess or stabbing myself in the finger. The boy pulls open the incision and the rest of the intestines slip out. He reaches into the bear and gently eases out the stomach and the liver, all of which he cuts free with his knife and settles onto a clean patch of grass. He pauses to brush a strand of dark hair out of his dirty face. His arms are bloody up to the elbow. The blood is already drying on my own hands, which are sprinkled with strands of the bear's coarse, dark hair. The dog rests nearby, watching us.

"You have to get the guts out quick," says the boy, "or they'll spoil the meat. That's because they're hot." The cavity of the bear is steaming, and I help the boy tip it, spilling the blood that's pooled inside onto the ground. I call the dog over and he goes to work, lapping up a rivulet of blood from the dirt. The boy watches and smiles. "This bear would be a lot of food for such a little dog."

"Yeah," I say. "He can't do that much to help clean up, but he'll do his best." After a few minutes the dog is full and he returns to his patch of sun and settles down.

III

The boy takes the knife from me and dives back into the bear. Soon the entire mass of viscera is out, lying red and warm on the fresh grass. We begin to skin the bear, separating the fur suit from the rest of its body. After a time the boy holds out his bloody hands, shows me a long thin strip of meat. "The backstrap. We can eat it for lunch."

Is it lunchtime already? I look at the sky. The sun is way up there. The boy is already gathering wood, breaking sticks for kindling, making a spark with a piece of flint. By and by he produces a bit of wire, wraps it around the meat and props it over the small fire.

The backstrap is incredible. It tastes like an entire summer condensed in a bit of warm animal flesh. Afterward I can feel new life coursing through me, the kind of energy I'd forgotten I could have. The dog gets a little piece and gazes up at me afterward with wet, wistful eyes.

We return to our work as the sun slides down the sky, and I am reminded of how much shorter the days are getting now that winter is almost here.

"When do the bears go to sleep?" I ask. The boy pauses his knife and squints at the forest, lit with long bands of afternoon sun, as though the answer is written there.

"In a month maybe," he says.

"It's lucky you got one then," I say. The boy does not respond, just continues cutting the fascia from the hide with his knife. "Will this bear be enough to feed you until spring?" The boy frowns, says nothing, and after a moment I return to my own careful slicing, watching with satisfaction as the sticky underside of the hide comes clean. "Where did you learn to hunt bears?" I ask, trying a different approach.

"Grandma taught me everything." The boy grunts in frustration and then withdraws his knife, wipes the blood off on the grass, pulls his sharpening stone from a pocket and takes a few swipes at the blade. "This hide will dull your knife quick."

"Is Grandma... still alive?" I ask. The boy ignores me and continues where he left off. I refocus on my own work. I'm at the spine now, as far as I can go. With the boy's help I roll the bear over, so that we can skin the other side.

"Grandma died in the spring," says the boy, so quiet I almost don't hear him.

"I'm sorry to hear that," I say. "Are you on the mountain alone, then?"

"I guess so," says the boy. "I didn't want to leave Grandma. And there's nowhere else to go, besides." I don't know what to say and for a while we don't speak, the only sound the wind moving in the tops of the tall pine trees. There's blood crusted to my sweater and the skirt of my dress, smears of blood on my arms and face.

The day is cooling by the time we fold the hide up, wet side together, and set about dismantling the bear carcass. I'm working my knife into the connective tissue of one of the joints to separate it when the boy stands and surveys our work.

"Be right back," he says. A half hour later he reappears pulling a wooden sled that looks homemade. The forest floor is smooth with flat pine needles so the sled moves fairly easily. We fumble the heavy bear quarters into cloth sacks and heave them onto this sled, as well as the sack containing the guts, and lay the hide on top.

It was a small bear and still, the sled is so heavy it takes great effort for us to pull it. My rib pains me with each step forward, but I try not to show it. We leave behind the feet, stomach and intestines, for the other creatures of the mountain.

"Where are we headed?" I ask the boy, as we drag our burden through the dimming woods.

"Grandma's place," he says, after a moment. The dog trots along behind, hoping for more bear scraps. I try to take note of our route, so that I can find my way home later.

There's a small log cabin sitting low in the trees, and a clearing with a garden, enclosed in a fence of leaning boards and twisted wire. Or, what once was a garden—it's a tangle of weeds now, the gate swinging open. In the trees beyond the cabin there's a sort of camp—a lean-to of peeled logs chinked with earth, a fire pit, a counter of rough boards that looks to be an outdoor kitchen.

"Is this where you live?" We come to a halt next to the lean-to, both of us sweating and catching our breath.

"Yeah," says the boy. He dips into the lean-to and emerges with a fistful of string. There's a long pole tied between two trees and he tosses the string over the pole, catches the other end. "We'll hang up the pieces of the bear here." By the time the light is all the way gone we have everything hung. The boy disappears, and I hear the door of the cabin bang shut. Then he's back with a fresh square of cloth, to wrap a hunk of meat that he's cut off one of the quarters.

"You take this," he says. "For you and the dog to eat at the tower."

"Thank you," I say. "And can I come back tomorrow? To help you put this all up?"

"Yeah," he says, and for the first time he looks me straight in the face, and almost smiles.

When I pop out on the road I'm a little east of where I'd planned to be, but overall I do a pretty good job finding my way back. In the tower the dog and I drink water and I roast a few meat pieces over the flames of my little wood cookstove for us. Then we round that out with an expired freeze-dried meal which almost, but not quite, rehydrates when I add boiling water.

I am ravenous from all the day's work, and it's hard not to just eat all of my remaining food right now. The cot feels glorious when I finally stretch out onto it, the knots in my back unkinking. The dog is there, pressed against my side, warm and smelling of the forest. The desperate loneliness is farther away tonight, and sleep is gentle and deep when it comes.

Bear meat all sliced and hung in the smokehouse. Stew made from bear heart, in a banged-up pot from previous times propped in the coals of the fire outside the boy's shelter. As I watch the stew simmer I ask myself, *What will we do when there are no more factory pots left, and the last cotton T-shirt is worn beyond repair?* I find nettles growing wild in the garden next to the cabin and add them to the stew. The boy produces a few shriveled potatoes and we drop those in there as well.

Late afternoon we've all but finished processing the bear, and my ribs and leg are demanding that I rest. I say goodbye to the boy, promise I'll be back in the morning to help with the rest of the work. Walking past the log cabin I pause. I know I shouldn't go in there, but I can't help myself. I grasp the handle on the heavy wooden door, push it slowly open.

The inside of the cabin is dim, cool air, and a stale smell, dust and mildew and rot. As my eyes adjust I see a long board table cluttered with baskets and wooden bowls, a squat woodstove, a bed rumpled with wool blankets. A window, dim with dust and dirt, looks out at the garden. On the walls are hooks piled with clothing. Next to the bed is a shelf full of books—books! I shouldn't pry, but books!

The first few I pull off are mildewed, their ends bloated from getting wet and then drying again. I can't make out their contents in the low light. The rotten meat smell is stronger here. Maybe some dead mice? I glance at the rumpled bed. There's a tangle of white hair on the pillow.

Oh.

"You shouldn't be in here." It's the boy. He's standing in the doorway, silhouetted in the fading light.

"Is this... your grandma?"

"You shouldn't be in here," he says but his voice is smaller, more strained.

I place the book back on the shelf and turn to the boy.

"Is this why you live outside, in that shelter that you built?"

The boy makes a small noise, and I realize that he's crying.

"I didn't know what to do after she died." He wipes a hand across his face, leaves a smear of dirt. "Anyway, I came to find you just now because I wanted to show you something."

I follow the boy out of the cabin and into a stand of oak trees, where a wooden cross made from two sticks bound with twine stands in a small clearing littered with golden leaves.

"My mother," says the boy, quietly. He's still wiping tears from his face. "She died having me. I visit her here, and talk to her. It's something grandma taught me to do."

"Lottie," I whisper. The boy and I stand side by side in the bands of evening light that cut through the trees. "What will you do this winter? You can't spend it here, all by yourself."

"This is all I know," he says. I shake my head, then kneel down in the pine needles and take his hands firmly in mine.

"Listen. Can I tell you about a place we can go? It's called Nevada."

CHAPTER 14

GEORGIA

I buried grandma in the backyard, under the lilac bush.

The hole, dug carefully in the dark, took three days to finish. I was manic, so I didn't mind staying up all night. It felt as though my blood was boiling so it was nice to have something physical to do. Moving grandma from the house to the newly dug hole was easier than I thought it would be, as she'd grown so frail and had shrunk down to just a shrimp of a person, a tiny shape inside her long pink nightgown.

Her physical form wasn't how I remembered it at all, strong and round in the middle from a lifetime of hard work and good living, and it felt as though in that way she'd left me twice—abruptly when she died and before that, inch by inch over the past year.

To prepare her body, I wrapped grandma in her bedsheets and then her favorite quilt—the quilt was sewn by her mother from scraps of fabric from my grandmother and her siblings' childhood clothing, and I thought that made it a proper burial shroud because all that was gone now—my grandma, her siblings, her parents, the whole world they knew and all the ties that bound them.

On the third night I shoveled dirt over this bundle of grandma and quilt until the hole was filled, and then I stomped it smooth with my boots, which seemed barbaric. Now it's just me, alone in this house.

As long as I stay in this house I can pretend that my grandma is still alive, and that I am still caring for her. Once her death is known, the weekly boxes of food—her pension from a lifetime of labor at the city clerk's office—will stop arriving, and the city will take the house away, and I'll have nothing.

I stay here because there's nowhere else to go. Grandma left me very little money, not enough to pay even a month of the rents in this city. And besides that, the city has gotten much more dangerous as of late. There's a sort of hopelessness in the air, an atmospheric pressure of defeat. A hulking storm that's gathered, black clouds about to break.

The city is dying. Will I die with it?

Each morning I ask myself this, drinking dandelion root tea and watching the street come alive through the lace curtains on my grandma's living room window. I don't leave the house much anymore. Over the years my friends have died, been disappeared, or left the city of their own accord. And then the last time I came back, Bets was gone. Bets. The only one who's never abandoned me.

I always felt that things were trending this way for me, that one day I would be completely alone here, the last one left. So why, then, do I stay? I like to think that I could just leave the city, save myself before it's too late, and start a new life somewhere else. But I worry that my heart is too broken, that it's been crushed too many times to weather the journey. How much loss can one human being endure? Is there anything even left of me to lose?

Most days it feels like no. Most days it feels like there's an empty black socket where my heart should be, like I should find some fentanyl and go quiet, follow grandma to whatever peaceful, formless void exists beyond this world. I don't get the fentanyl, though. I look out at the crowded street and get lost in memories—the rock bottoms and the laughter. There was so much laughter. The ecstatic laughter of pure freedom, back when it felt like freedom could still be a thing.

Bets. I wish I knew where Bets was. I have a feeling that she's doing just fine, that she's found some new world beyond the city and that she's thriving there. But maybe I just like to imagine this. Maybe I couldn't stand it any other way.

I don't think about Philip. I never did let my time with him bleed into my life here, in the city—the world I shared with him was separate. I was a different person when I was with him. I wasn't Georgia of the city—sunburnt, chapped hands ripping plywood free, sorting through junk in an abandoned elementary school, looking for books or other contraband.

With Philip I wasn't in the city, I wasn't even on this earth. I was in a dream. On a ship in the ocean, crashing on waves. Sometimes it was a musical, and there were songs—good songs and I was singing, and I tried to remember these songs, but when I returned to the city and sat at the piano in grandma's living room I could only recall their disjointed parts.

The first time I met Philip was last year at a bar, a private bar for rich people, a secret bar down some busted concrete steps in a back alley in the industrial part of town. I scrubbed the dirt off in grandma's bathroom while she slept, gave myself a pedicure, shaved everything, put on a satin slip dress and did my hair up. Lip stain and blush. Eyeliner made from charcoal.

The bouncer at the bar was my friend. I stole wallets from the men at the bar but I didn't actually *take* any of the cards. In the women's restroom, in the stall with the door closed, I pulled everything out of the wallet and photographed the cards with my phone and then reassembled the wallet and slipped it back in the man's jacket pocket.

When done correctly, the man never noticed that the wallet had been gone at all. Or he thought he'd just misplaced it, because he hadn't been able to find it and then there it was! Right where he'd thought it would be.

Those photos went straight to James, the bouncer, and then I deleted them off my phone. The cards wouldn't be charged for weeks, sometimes months—the men would have no idea where the numbers had been stolen. And James paid me in cash.

Then one day I met Philip. He grabbed my wrist as I was slipping my hand into the suit jacket draped over the back of his booth.

"Looking for something?" he asked.

"Sorry," I said. "I thought this was my jacket."

"It doesn't matter," he said. He had heavy eyebrows, sad eyes, and was clean shaven, which I always found repulsive. "I've seen you before.

Have a drink with me?" I didn't feel like I could say no, so I slid into the booth beside him. There was a young woman with him—thin, arms stacked with gold bracelets. Slumped against the wall of the booth, eyes half closed, she smiled at me.

"Your beauty is ethereal," she said.

"You should come to my place sometime," said Philip. "It's outside the city. It's quiet. Have you ever been outside the city?"

"No," I said.

"Yes, come join us," said the woman. "It's wonderful out there. There's an owl, and the sun… the sun is different."

Philip was writing his number on a drink napkin. He pressed it into my hand and I walked quickly from the bar.

"Where are you going?" hissed James as I passed, climbing the concrete steps into the street. It was raining, and the drops darkened the hem of my satin dress where it showed beneath my jacket.

"Out of here," I said.

I never went back to the bar.

Whatever made me decide to call that number is still a mystery to me. Two weeks had passed and it was a cloudless, hazy morning, on the rooftop where Bets and I often slept. We'd eaten our breakfast and then she'd left me, upset about something—she'd wanted to talk to me, but I'd woken up feeling so far away, like I sometimes got, a million miles away, and I couldn't come back into myself. I'd felt this way yesterday too, and the more Bets tried to pull at me the further away I went. Truth was, I wanted to leave entirely. Crawl out of my skin or at the very least, run away from the city. But where could I go?

Philip's compound was two hours east, past the checkpoints. It was a giant house perched on the rim of a canyon, surrounded by ponderosas. I gasped when we left the haze behind us, when the smell of sewer was replaced with the smell of warm pine sap. The wind from the jeep window beat my hair until it was tangled. The sun was, in fact, different.

There was a cement walkway leading from the parking area to the front door of the house.

"Stay on the walkway," said Philip, as he unloaded our bags from the jeep—I had just one small, dusty backpack. "Don't disturb the topsoil. I didn't want any neighbors, is why I built on the edge of this canyon. It's fine, as long as we don't kick anything up."

The whole front of the house was windows. Facing the windows were long couches, and tropical plants in heavy pots, some of them with bright flowers. The young woman I'd seen with Philip was on one of these couches, lying back watching a raven ride wind gusts above the canyon.

"I want to feel how she feels," I said to Philip, dropping my backpack on the tiled floor.

Though I could take some guesses at what he gave me, I'm really not sure, and to be honest I didn't care at the time. I just knew that it was sublime to sink into that couch, to drink cold water cleaner than anything I could find in the city and then clink the sweaty glass down on the tile floor, to lie back and watch the wind whip the ponderosas along the canyon rim.

Philip knelt on the tile between my legs, pushed my knees apart gently, lifted my dress, put my cock in his mouth. I melted further into the couch, the feeling in my cock melding with the sound of the wind against the house until I came in his mouth. He moved on to the other girl, did the same to her.

She was like me. All the girls he brought there were like me. He didn't fuck us, there was only this, and then he would lie on his back on the cool tile and grasp one of my ankles in his hand, fondling the ankle bone with his thumb—and he would talk at us. For hours, while we drifted in space with the wind.

He told us about the singularity. In the singularity, a human brain and all its synapses are mapped so thoroughly that they can then be recreated in a computer, and that uploaded brain experiences a synthetic consciousness. The person's brain can then have experiences in a virtual world, and never die.

"That's stupid," said the other young woman, whose name was Margot. "You men just want to live forever. You can't recreate consciousness."

"It's not stupid," said Philip, unbothered. "We've been working on this for a long time. It's beautiful. Can you imagine it? You won't be tethered to a fallible body anymore, and there won't be any pain. Don't you want to live forever?"

"Absolutely not," said Margot. "What you're describing is, I believe, what happens after we die. And I can't wait to get there."

Philip ignored her.

"We have the technology. Or rather, we did have the technology. There's been some hiccups, sourcing things. Supply chain troubles and all that. But we're throwing everything we have at it. And I believe we'll get there before it's too late."

"What do you mean, too late?" I asked. I felt like the whole conversation was taking place inside a dream.

"The physical world has so many limitations," said Philip. "Our current human civilization depends on constant growth. The momentum is what keeps it upright. But progress is slowing. Once progress stops, which will likely be soon, the whole thing will collapse. The bulk of people on earth will die. The handfuls of people left will be thrown backwards thousands of years. So, this physical world cannot be relied on. It has a ceiling, and humans have been pressing themselves against that ceiling for a while now."

He extended his other arm and stroked the long leaf of one of the plants. "We're like a fig tree that's outgrown its pot. But there's no bigger pot to go to. The singularity will transcend all of this, these stubborn physical limitations. Not only that but all our brains, once uploaded, will be connected to each other. There won't be any loneliness. And there will no longer be any need for suffering. Suffering only exists to allow us to adapt and evolve to our shifting physical environment. We'll be free of all that."

"Again, that sounds like what happens after death," said Margot.

"But all the bits and pieces to make the computers," I said, "those are from the physical world. You can hardly find anything in the city anymore. How do you plan to get such specialized computer parts? And replace them after they break?"

Philip was silent for a time, his head turned to the big windows. A storm was moving in over the canyon but it seemed stuck at the opposite rim, curdling in space, while the sky on our side stayed clear.

"We're trying," he said. "We're so close."

At first I would just spend a night at Philip's place, and then two, and eventually I stayed for a week at a time, eating the canned fish and oranges from his pantry and losing entire days on that couch, or next to the pool, or in his bed, drifting in and out of a dream while listening to the small sounds of the girl sleeping next to me. I never told Bets where I went.

Every time I was in the city and I got that urge to crawl out of my skin I would call Philip, and his driver would pick me up in a plain black car, and I'd drop my dusty backpack on his tile floor and he'd give me drugs.

It's not that I wanted to hurt Bets by not telling her where I went or how long I'd be gone, it's just that, in those moments, I found myself mute—I wouldn't be able tell you what I was feeling if you put a gun to my head. At Philip's I could exit my brain entirely. And he was harmless. Annoying and kind of dumb, but harmless.

One night at Philip's we were lying out on loungers next to the pool, watching the stars, and I couldn't stop thinking about Bets. *I shouldn't be here*, I thought. *I should stop hurting her like this. I should figure out how to be a different person.* Then I thought, what if there was something I could do, to make it right? To make this escape I'd found less selfish? What if there was something I could give Bets?

"Philip," I said, in the warm darkness.

"Hmm?" he replied, half asleep.

"I'm looking for information," I said. "For a friend of mine. I need a favor from you. I'm trying to find her mother. She disappeared a long time ago."

A few days later there was a phone call, and Philip told me what he had learned.

When I returned to the city after that, Bets was gone.

I never went back to Philip's.

After grandma died, I started saving some of the food from the weekly boxes provided by the city. I have a pretty good stash now. As I look out the window at the noisy street I think about how I could venture out, and trade some of this food for other supplies I need, maybe even a spot on one of the trucks headed out of the city, to the prisons.

People smuggle themselves west this way, pretending to be prisoners. It's a terrible journey, in the back of a truck stuffed with other humans, no windows, and there's always the risk that the truck won't stop, won't let you off en route—that the driver will take you straight to the prison with everyone else, and that way collect a nice fee on both ends. And even if you do get dropped off, there's no guarantee you'll get dropped off somewhere you actually want to be.

I remember the note that Grandma gave me, when I last returned to the city.

Once you're grown, come to Nevada where the wild burros are. We can make a life there.

And below that, in Bets' handwriting:

Talk to Beryl. Love, Bets.

When I went to Beryl, he explained the note. Now I wonder if I should, in fact, go west on one of the prisoner trucks, let chance determine where I end up. Could I ever find Bets? Bets is a needle in a haystack. Bets is gone forever. For all I know, Bets is dead.

No.

Dominic sells fry bread at the stand on the corner and I've been using him for years to find goods on the black market. One morning I leave grandma's house for the warm stink of the street and make my way there, every sound and movement startling—I've grown too accustomed to the stuffy quiet of indoors. By the time I reach the fry bread stand I am trying not to panic.

Dominic is pleased to see me, in that way where every goodbye could be a person's last, and each reunion is a sort of miracle. I tell him about the food I have stored away, and what I'm looking for. Currency used to be the way to go for these things, but these days food means more than money.

His face darkens when I mention the prisoner trucks.

"The journey is very dangerous," he says. "I can get you onto a truck, but I can't guarantee what happens after that." He's looking at me in a funny way, and then I realize that look is concern. It's been so long since someone's looked at me like that.

I shift uncomfortably. I'm wearing an old dress of my grandmother's. One by one, I've been pulling them from her closet, wearing each until it reeks of despondent loneliness and then burning it in the backyard, holding it by a corner of the fabric and watching it go up in flames, smoke rising to mingle with the smog of the city.

Today's dress is made of a loose material, patchwork yellow and white, and I realize that I probably should've already burned it by now, that the white parts are stained, the hem ragged and muddy from digging grandma's grave.

Over the dress is the canvas work jacket I've worn for years, found on the tenth floor of an abandoned apartment building, in a room that contained a dirty twin mattress, one trash bag of clothing and a few children's toys. The jacket keeps me warm in winter as long as I layer sweaters underneath but it, too, has seen better days. As for my hair, last month I discovered a handful of silver in the black, like weeds coming up in a garden of dark flowers, and then I stopped looking in the mirror entirely.

Dominic sighs. "I can get you a spot on a truck. Tomorrow. And then I'm going away for a while." He pauses, looks down the street teeming with cars and bicycles as though at something beyond, something only he can see. "Maybe for good." He looks back at me. "I wish you all the best, Georgia."

"Thank you," I say. We look at each other for a time. There are no words for this part, for the uncertainty of leaving one's entire life, even when that life has been slowly emptied of everyone and everything that gives it meaning. I'm learning these days that in the course of one's life, there are many deaths. And these deaths, though terrible, are doors—plate-glass doors you have to crash through with the full weight of your body, but doors nonetheless. And we have to keep going through these doors, if we want to live.

CHAPTER 15

BETS

There's a rattling sound in the clearing below the fire tower and I look up from attempting to pack everything I want to take into my small backpack to see the boy pulling a cart. He hollers up at me and I clamber down the stairs for a closer look—the cart is made from the wheels of my bicycle, scraps of wood, two metal poles and what appears to be a piece of an old car hood.

"You made us a cart!" I say, delighted. "Where did you get the materials?"

"Grandma's scrap pile," says the boy. "We used to find stuff all over these mountains and haul it back to the cabin."

"This will help us so much," I say. "We can bring more food, and water."

"Are you sure we should go?" says the boy, squinting up at me. "We could stay up here for the winter. Try and get another bear before they den up."

"No," I say. "I don't want to be up here on this lonely mountain forever, just barely surviving, until my luck runs out. And I don't want that fate for you, either."

Into the cart goes our cloth sack of dried bear meat, our metal tin of rendered bear fat, some dried berries that the boy gathered in the summer, and my contributions of my remaining grain plus all the nettles from the boy's grandma's garden, which I dried on the metal steps of the fire tower.

We also pack the blue plastic jug, filled with water from the wildlife guzzler, as well as everything I was carrying on my bike. The boy's items are wrapped in buckskin and tied with cord. He has knives, a carved wooden spoon and bowl, flint for starting fires, his bow and arrows, and a few other odds and ends. Over all of this we spread the bear hide, which the boy will sleep wrapped in at night, and which will also serve as a place for the dog to ride when he gets tired of walking.

The weight of the cart makes it cumbersome, especially downhill, and we take turns pulling it—or rather, attempting to control it—and the backs of both our legs are soon bruised where it bumps against us.

It was hard say goodbye to the fire tower, so warm and safe and lit with such nice yellow light, but I know that my nice hidey-hole will eventually become a cave of slow starvation when winter sets in for real, so I shut the trap door and descended the metal stairs, dog plodding behind me, and did not allow myself to look back.

The boy knows all the roads on this mountain and where they go, and this is a godsend. Our first objective is the valley below, and the boy says we should reach it by tomorrow. Sundown finds us in a brilliant forest of golden oak leaves, lower and warmer, already, than the ridge with the fire tower, and we set up camp in a quiet spot just off the road. After chewing some dried bear meat dipped in fat I unstuff my sleeping bag on the clean leaves and fall asleep happy and content, and even a little excited about the newness of the journey that lies ahead.

///

Sweat drips into my eyes, blurring my vision. My brain feels slurry with heat. I press my cool hands to my face, enjoy a moment of total darkness. The boy and I are crouched in an arroyo in the broken shade of a leafless palo verde tree, hiding from the heat of the day. We've got our shoes off and our feet—our poor feet!—are propped on the sand, getting some air.

We both have the most terrible blisters. They started soon after we reached the valley and transitioned from cool ponderosa and oak forest to baking low elevation Sonoran desert, with its asphalt that ripples in the heat and saguaro cacti that seem to be gesturing at each other, like people in a play who were frozen in time.

Since so many of the trees and plants here evolved without leaves in order to preserve moisture (the boy explained this to me as we walked, as well as everything else he knows about this desert) there is little shade, and it exists mostly in the form of the low dirt walls of dry washes.

Now, curled uncomfortably in this arroyo, our bodies wedged as best we can get them into the sliver of shade, and having to shift continuously as this shade moves with the sun, we resolve to change our travel strategy, and walk only at night.

The highway we're following is wide, and empty, and in pretty good condition, so we shouldn't have much trouble following it in the dark. And according to my *RVer's Guide to the American West,* if we stay on this highway it will, eventually, lead us to Nevada.

Falling in and out of a fitful sleep in the arroyo, curled in the dirt, the afternoon fades into evening and the air finally begins to cool. At dusk we rouse ourselves, somehow more tired than before we took this rest, and repack the cart. The blue water jug is alarmingly light, and I slosh what's inside—maybe a gallon left? We've got to find more water soon.

Once repacked, the dog hops up onto the cart and we're off. We're limping at first, moving slow down the road in the thick golden dregs of the day, but after a time our blisters warm up and don't hurt so bad. I experience a moment of near euphoria—my dress is crusted to my body with salt, my skin is red from the sun and my legs are stiff and achy from so much walking, but it's cooler now, the horizon glows indigo while the stars wink on one by one and presently a soft breeze blows, the air grazing my skin under my dress like a lover's touch.

I start to sing—it's a tune of Georgia's and I can't remember all the words, but singing it reminds me of her, and that feels nice. I wish she was here, right now, on this dark road under a billion warm glittering stars. I think that she would like this.

The boy looks over at me.

"This is the farthest I've ever been from the mountain," he says.

"Are you having fun?" I ask. He nods.

"It's like the stories grandma used to tell, about crossing the desert. When she was young."

The moon is rising—it's a half moon and it lends us its silver light. Ahead of us looms something dark, a tall thing blacker than the night around it, and we pause in the empty road and try to make sense of it.

"Should we hide?" whispers the boy.

"No," I respond, after a moment. I pick up the cart and move towards the tall thing, which cuts the desert in two. Once we're right at it we can see that it's a wall made of rippled metal, rising high above our heads, originating far away and then terminating right here, at our feet.

Everywhere are signs of human and animal traffic—footprints, trash, bones, all glowing white in the moonlight. Bending over, I tug at a bit of fabric that sticks from the dirt. It's a little girl's T-shirt, full of holes. It's so faded you can't tell what color it used to be. I place my hand on the wall. It's warm, still radiating the heat of the day.

"This used to be the edge of the United States," I say.

"There isn't a United States anymore?" says the boy.

"No. Whatever's left is just in the cities." We both stand, looking at the wall. The only sound is the soft wind, moving through the yellow grass. After a time I pick up the cart's handles and we continue on, down the road.

We see the headlights during our second night of walking in the dark. Normally, headlights in the distance would cause me to turn off the road and get myself hidden as fast as I can; but we're out of water, have been out of water since the afternoon save for a few ounces I set aside for the dog, and the danger of our imminent dehydration outweighs the risk of whoever might be in this vehicle.

We can't make out the man at first, only his flashlight, which he points in our eyes. He's stopped the truck right in the middle of the road and it rumbles, a sound that reminds me of a world I'd begun to forget. There's a voice from the cab of the truck—there's two of them.

"You got your documents?" says the man with the flashlight. His voice is soft, but the power behind it is not. The dog had barked once when the truck was pulling to a stop and I'd hushed him—he's in my arms now, hidden under my shawl, the warmth of his small body a comfort to me.

"We don't have any documents," I say.

"What village are you from?" asks the man.

"You got any water?" interrupts the boy. The man swings the beam of his flashlight onto the boy, takes in the deerskin pants and tangled hair. In the lights of the truck I can see that the man is slight, and that he wears some sort of uniform. They're rangers from the prison. Fuck.

"Frankie can you get some water for this kid," the man calls to his colleague in the truck. The truck shakes as Frankie steps out—a big man, he rifles around in the truck bed and lumbers into the flashlight beam, hands us each a plastic bottle of water. I drink the entire thing, one moment of pure transcendental bliss, no thoughts.

"Where are you two from, then?"

"The mountain," says the boy. "We're from the mountain." The man moves the flashlight beam back to me, takes in my dirty sneakers, the ragged hem of my dress, the shawl with my arms crossed under it, my hair wild from the wind. He moves the beam to our cart, sees the bear pelt.

"You two kill that bear?" Neither of us speaks, and after a time the man gestures to the truck. "We'll have to take you in," he says. "We'll put your things in back."

"In to where?" I ask, but the man doesn't respond, and I know the answer besides.

The back seat of the truck is warm and comfortable, and the night passes smoothly beyond the windowglass. The dog is asleep in my arms. We didn't die of dehydration while walking in the desert—that's good. That's very good. But now, what?

We'll go to the prison. Will my mother be there? Was this what I wanted all along, to be taken to the prison in this valley in hopes of finding her? Was I only pretending to myself that I was headed to Nevada? I knew the danger of the rangers in this valley and I convinced the boy to come with me anyway. And the dog—what will become of the dog? My thoughts are like birds, flying in ever-tightening circles.

In the front seat the men talk, the low murmur of their voices blending with the whirring of the truck's wheels on pavement. We're driving away from Nevada. Erasing days of walking. No. This is all wrong. If only I could get out of this truck somehow. Could we kill these men? Steal their water? Take the truck? I glance at the boy. He stares ahead, as if watching something in the far distance.

No. They have guns. We can't.

"What village are you two really from, then?" Frankie's voice. I must've drifted off. I startle awake to see the man twisted around in his seat, his broad face half-lit in the dash lights of the truck. The boy is staring down at his hands. "You gonna answer me?"

"We're not from a village," says the boy. "We're from the mountain like I said."

"Who else was living up there with you?" continues Frankie.

"We're already taking them in," says the other man. He's driving slow, watching for potholes in the road, the yellow line ticking in and out of the circle of the headlights. "We don't have to interrogate them. They're tired, let them rest."

"Come on Nelian," says Frankie. "We haven't picked up anyone in weeks. There might be more people up there. I know you're new to patrols, and I'm telling you, you have to be aggressive about it. That's the only way to reach the quotas."

Nelian. The name bounces around in my panicked skull like a ping pong ball. *Nelian.*

"It was just me on the mountain," says the boy. "My grandma died in the spring. Then Bets showed up a while ago. Now it's the two of us."

"Where's your parents, then?" says Frankie. He's watching us again, his mouth downturned.

"My mom died having me," says the boy. "I don't have a dad."

"Huh," says Frankie. He turns around in his seat, looks at the road.

"You think the boy is for real?" he says to Nelian. "You think he was surviving up there all by himself?"

Nelian shrugs. His face is a mask.

Carnelian. That's the name of the boy's father, who disappeared. Is Nelian short for Carnelian? No. That would be crazy. Why would he leave Lottie, just to go work for the prison? It doesn't make any sense. Maybe Nelian isn't short for anything. Probably just a coincidence.

"Where were you two trying to get to, when we picked you up?" It's Frankie again. "The direction you were walking, there's no villages for a long ways. No water either."

"We didn't really have a plan," I say. "We were just trying to get to Nevada." The dog stirs under my shawl and I stroke his head softly until he settles down again. I am grateful for the darkness in the back of the cab.

Frankie snorts. "I've heard about Nevada. People talk about it like it's Big Rock Candy Mountain. But I tell you what, there's no place out there that's safe. None. I've been doing patrols for years, and I have seen some crazy shit. The only safe place in this world right now is in a workhouse. You get fed every day, you have a place to sleep that's protected. Sometimes I think I'd be better off in a workhouse than out on patrol. The desert is a dangerous place."

We're pulling off the pavement, onto a rutted dirt road. The headlights show a clearing in the cactus and a circle of stones for a fire ring.

"This is camp for the night," says Frankie. "This road is pretty messed up and we've got a half-day's drive left to get to the prison. Nelian and I will sleep out here, we'll lock you two in the truck. Don't want you running off into the desert trying to get yourselves killed again."

The rangers build a fire and spread blankets on the ground. We are let out to pee, handed a packet of crackers and a bottle of water each, and then the doors click shut as we are locked inside. I'm so anxious that I eat the crackers without tasting them, can hardly appreciate their novelty.

My last cracker goes to the dog, then I pour some of my water into my cupped palm for him. Our hunger at least somewhat satisfied, I curl in the passenger seat with my shawl over the two of us while the boy stretches out on the seat in back. The moon has set and the stars burn like fire overhead. Just hours ago I was as free as those stars. Now I want to scratch at the windows until my fingers are bloody. I know that I won't sleep.

I witness the whole night, the twirling stars, watch the black fade to grey, watch the mountains backlit with gold. Nelian and Frankie are up, making coffee at the fire. They're arguing about something.

"I just think we should drive these kids back to where we found them," says Nelian.

"Nah man," says Frankie. "We're already way behind quota. And anyway, we're saving these kids' lives."

"Is it really so bad if we don't make quota? You said yourself this valley is emptying out. We haven't seen anyone for weeks."

"I need this!" shouts Frankie. "Just a few more months and I'm done with this patrol. I'll be eligible for transfer. I can go south, to the prisons on the coast. I'll be free of this busted-ass desert. But not if I don't make quota. God dammit man. You are not fucking this up for me." He swigs the last of his coffee emphatically and slams the metal cup down on the hood of the truck. He gathers up his bedroll and walks it around the truck, to the bed.

There's a gunshot. The boy and I both startle in our seats. My ears ring. Heavy silence. Then the dog begins to bark.

The driver's door swings open. It's Nelian. He glances at the dog in my lap, raises his eyebrows but says nothing. He lifts himself into the driver's seat, turns the key. His hand is shaking as he shifts the truck into drive. As we pull out of the clearing I glance in the side mirror and see Frankie, lying face down in the dirt. We hit a rut in the road and Frankie's metal coffee cup slides off the truck's hood and clatters onto the ground.

The sun is coming up, pushing yellow light across the valley. We're driving the other direction on the highway, now. The correct direction. Towards Nevada.

///

"Why did you save us?"

We've been on the road for hours, eating up pavement as the sun swings ever higher in the sky. It's a question I've been forming and reforming in my brain, working up the guts to speak it out loud. Earlier we stopped for a pee break and Nelian gave us more water as well as sealed packets of what seemed to be chili—beans and soy meant and a sauce resembling tomatoes.

We ate the food squatting in the shade thrown by the truck. I dropped a few spoonfuls on the hot asphalt for the dog. Now the boy is asleep in the backseat, his mouth slack, his body jostling a little each time we hit a pothole. Nelian stares ahead at the road, doesn't answer my question.

"Are you the boy's father?" I ask, quietly. Nelian glances at me, looks back at the road. "Why didn't you come back?" At this, Nelian's face collapses a bit.

"I did come back," he says. "I got picked up by the prison patrols just a week after leaving the fire tower. I spent two years in prison before I was able to escape. When I finally made it back to the fire tower, Lottie wasn't there." His eyes dart to the rearview mirror, checking that the boy is still asleep.

"I read the logbook and looked for the old woman's cabin. There wasn't anyone around the day I found the cabin but I saw baby clothes and baby things. Then I found Lottie's grave." His eyes are wet. He rubs a hand over his face. "That's when I knew that Lottie was dead, and that it was my fault. Lottie had died because I had gone."

He's silent for a while. We both watch the road, the hot empty desert.

"The thought of actually seeing the child was horrifying," he continues. "This living reminder of what I had done. I got out of there as fast as I could. But I didn't want to go to Nevada anymore, not without Lottie. I felt that there was no place left in the world for me. The prison has a rewards system for escapees who turn themselves back in—you can become a guard, and then a ranger. It seemed like the easiest way to disappear forever, to consign myself to the sort of miserable life that I deserved."

The truck is quiet after Nelian finishes speaking. The desert is flat, awash in light, cacti stretch their arms in the sun.

"What about Frankie? How will you explain his disappearance?"

Nelian shrugs. "I'll think of something." And then, "The desert is a dangerous place."

At dusk we stop to camp in a cluster of rocks in a dirt clearing not far from the road, where a fire ring overlooks a barren canyon. A dry riverbed snakes in the canyon, its banks choked with brush.

"Are you driving us all the way to Nevada?" the boy asks, as Nelian heats dinner for us on the fire. The dog is poking around in the rocks, his tail wagging, not a care in the world.

"I'll get you within a few days' walk of the border," says Nelian. "You'll be on your own after that. But you'll be out of range of the prison patrols, at least. And I'll give you as much water and food as I can." The boy sits a little bit back from the fire and spoons hot chili from his wooden bowl.

I watch him watch Nelian the way a rabbit watches a coyote. I want to tell the boy that my father was absent for most of my life, too. That I also live in the world where fathers are mostly fictions, characters in story books.

After a few hours of driving the next morning we're pulling off, onto the shoulder. All around us is scrubby desert, bisected by this blacktop that unfurls towards the horizon, the whole world radiating the still soft heat of the sun.

Nelian lifts our cart from the truck bed, opens the spigot on the large water tank in the back of the truck and fills our blue jug. Then he pulls an armload of packaged meals from a metal box and dumps them into the cart, stands for a moment contemplating the middle distance and then grabs another armload, dumping those into the cart too.

We spread the bear hide over everything, put the dog on the bear hide and then stand in the bright road, looking at one another. Or rather, Nelian looks at us while the boy looks down at the blacktop.

"Hold on," says Nelian. He disappears into the truck cab, reappears a few minutes later with a scrap of paper. "I drew you a map of the tinajas ahead," he says. "Depressions in the rock that hold water after rains." I fold the paper carefully, slip it into the pocket of my dress. "Things should get easier from here on out," he says. "You're less likely to run into trouble."

"You don't know that," says the boy, quietly.

Nelian opens his mouth to speak and then shuts it again. The boy keeps his eyes fixed on the ground. Nelian walks around to the front of the truck, hauls open the door. The engine rumbles to life and the truck pulls away.

The boy doesn't move. The sound of the truck grows fainter in the distance, and then it's gone.

"We should get walking," I say, my hand over my eyes to shade my face. "It's gonna be hot soon. Maybe we can get a little ways and then find some shade to siesta." The boy stays motionless, his eyes down. "Hey," I say. "Did you hear me?"

The boy screams, the sound like an angry, injured animal and runs off the road and out into the open desert. I watch him sprint towards some distant bluffs, his legs pumping fast. The he turns and wheels around, back towards the road. He stops and bends over, struggles to lift a large stone from the dirt. He screams and throws it at a nearby saguaro. There's a hollow sound. The boy hefts another small boulder and throws that one too, assaulting the saguaro's thick trunk.

He screams again, pulls a long stick from the dirt and bashes it against the saguaro until the stick breaks into pieces. When I reach him he's breathing heavy and ragged, tears streaking the dirt on his face. I wrap my arms around him and pull him to me, feel his heaving sobs. My mind cycles through all the things I could say. *Don't cry. Your father loves you. He did the best he could. He didn't want to leave you. At least you had your grandma. And you have me now.*

"Just feel it," I say, instead. I'm on my knees, rocking back and forth while the boy cries into my shoulder. "Just feel it. Feel it as hard as you can."

The rest of the day the boy and I don't say much, just walk the road at a steady pace, our legs fresh and our blisters quiet after our two days of rest. We walk through the heat of afternoon, stopping only to eat and water ourselves and the dog. The boy's grief is palpable, a thick fog that presses down on us. I am here with the boy, in his fog. I don't try and beat the fog away. Camp is in an arroyo a bit off the road, its sands swept clean by the last flood, where we are more or less hidden. We don't build a fire, just eat sun-warmed packets of chili in the gloaming and then lie down under the stars, each of us lost in the worlds of our separate thoughts.

I'm thinking about my mother as I drift off, this woman whose fate I've imagined a thousand different ways. In my imagination now she's out here in this desert, searching for me. I picture her wandering the road we just walked, calling my name. She's wearing clothing the color of sand. Her hair is long and silver, it reaches her waist. There's a pack basket on her back, full of cornmeal and dried fruit gathered from abandoned orchards.

She knows where the secret water in the desert is, the places where the animals have been drinking since before time began. She knows this desert as well as she knows herself. And she's walking the road, searching for me. Calling my name.

I can't sleep.

I dig through one of my panniers until I find the RVer's guide, whose pages I can just make out in the moonlight. I sharpen my pencil, flip through the book until I find some white space, and begin to write.

CHAPTER 16

JANE

The sun is coming up. Another brilliant sunrise in this windswept desert. After ten years in a cold, dim prison, I feel that I will never tire of this clean, shocking light. Another morning in the driver's seat of this box truck, rumbling over the cracked asphalt headed north. I've been awake for two days now, driving. Stopping only to gather information on the road ahead—which stretches of highway are too broken, washed out, or flooded to take, what alternates I should use instead—and once to get gas.

Gas is scarce but so is food, and the back of the box truck is full of cricket gruel, potato flakes, soy meat. When researching this trip in prison with those who knew the area I was warned, again and again, to make a wide berth around Las Vegas, but I also knew I would have to go there in order to find fuel.

I was hardly in the outskirts of that sun-baked city with its burned-out skyscrapers glittering in the light when I was stopped by militia, but once I told them where I was coming from they said they might be able to find me a connection—they'd already heard of the prison break—and after waiting for hours, sweat-soaked napping on the hot pleather of the truck's bench seat, I was able to hire a guy who drove with me into the city late that night.

We pulled into a hushed warehouse with the headlights off and were greeted by a thin man with nervous red eyes who looked fifty but was probably twenty-five. I traded this man half the food in the back of the truck for enough gas, both in the tank and in jugs in the back, to get me the rest of the way to where I was going. I was beyond relieved to see the lights of Las Vegas receding in my rear view mirror a few hours later, and I told myself that if I could help it I'd never go into any of the cities again.

Now, as the sun climbs higher in the hot, cerulean sky, I think of the small settlements in the remote northern part of the state that I'm hoping to reach by nightfall, road conditions permitting. For two years in prison my cellmate was Myra, a woman from one of these settlements—she'd travelled from her village to Las Vegas in search of pharmaceuticals for her dying sister and had been stopped at a checkpoint, arrested for not having the proper documents and disappeared to the prison.

While we lay in our narrow beds after lights out, watching the single square of moonlight from the small high window move across the cell wall, Myra told me of abandoned mining towns tucked into wet folds in the arid mountains, where her people salvaged lumber from the collapsed barns to build cabins in the cottonwoods along streams that ran year-round. There were wild burros there, she said, descendants of burros who escaped the gold miners of the 1800s, and these animals, once corralled, provided meat and milk and helped transport goods.

Eventually I helped Myra escape the prison, and in return she promised me that if I ever got out I would be welcome in her village. I never heard from her after that last goodbye, the night of her departure, smuggled out by one of the guards, and I have no idea if she made it home or was instead sold to another prison, or worse. I don't even know if her village still exists, or what I'll find when I reach her mountain range, one of the hundreds of small ranges that rise like islands from the cracked valleys of this state. This hope is all I've got, but it's better than nothing.

As the morning wears on and the long thread of highway unspools before me I find myself thinking about Bets, as I do every day, as I have ever since I was taken from her that cold morning so long ago. I've often asked myself if, once out of the prison, I should try and make my way back to the city, to find her. But although my prison record has been erased, I could easily be disappeared again for some other reason, at the first checkpoint I encountered.

Entering the city would likely be the end for me. And then what could I do for Bets? Nothing. And yet I know that, in some ways, not wanting to return to the city to find her makes me a failure. Maybe I am a failure. Just a failure in a box truck, rumbling blindly north through Nevada.

Years ago when I learned about the settlements in northern Nevada I sent a note to her in the city—did she ever get it? If she did get the note is there a chance that she's out here too, in this desert?

By afternoon the day is worn, no longer fresh, the sky a dull white. I stop to take a piss and that's when I see it—a dark swath in the road, a crumbling void that formed when the asphalt collapsed into a sinkhole. Jesus fucking Christ.

I wasn't told about this obstacle during my last stop, at a roadside stand where a sun worn man with no front teeth sold braided bundles of dried corn, and I heaved a case of soy powder onto his table in exchange for information on the road ahead. Or maybe he did tell me, and I forgot? After two days awake, my brain's not working so good.

The hot asphalt next to the truck tips up at me and I sink to my knees, steady myself with my hands. I'm getting one of my dizzy spells. There's a terrible spinning in my guts and then I'm throwing up the cricket gruel I had for breakfast. Oh, dear. Not this, not right now. Not when I've still got so much driving ahead of me.

Can I pull off onto the shoulder here, and sleep for a few hours in the bench seat of the truck? There's a lot of danger in that. The back of the truck is still half full of cases of food. That food is all the resources I have, to trade for other goods, both on this drive and to make a new life when I reach Myra's village.

No doubt that some of these buildings and houses I've passed on my journey haven't been as abandoned as they've seemed, and that there are people watching me. Waiting for me to break down, run out of gas, get a flat tire. Or get stuck behind a sinkhole such as this one.

In the end I have no choice. My body is refusing to cooperate, and it's all I can do to start the truck again and steer it onto the shoulder before collapsing onto the sun-warmed seat. My vision is blurring and I shut my eyes and listen to the quiet sounds of the desert.

I have no idea how long it will take for this spell to pass, how long before I can drive again. Hopefully a few hours of sleep is all I need. In the meantime, if someone wants to rob me, they're welcome to have at it.

To comfort myself I think of Bets, back when we still had our apartment. Bets sleeping in her bed in her dim, wood-paneled bedroom, the heavy curtains drawn closed to block out the lights of the street below. I would sit on the edge of her bed after returning from my waitressing job and stroke her hair. She was an angel. She was the only pure thing left in this world.

CHAPTER 17

BETS

In the afternoon of our first day after leaving Nelian, the boy and I drag the cart off the road into the thin shade of an arroyo, eat a packet of chili and curl in the dirt to siesta until the day cools, but I cannot rest. I pull the map of tinajas from my pocket and study it carefully again. There are sketches of road intersections, a few rock features, some dry rivers. But how far between each thing, and what if some of these water sources are dry?

The map is just pencil marks on lined yellow notebook paper—these pencil marks are all that stand between us and death in the huge, hot, empty desert. Round and round my thoughts go, while I lie sweaty in this sliver of shade. I'm beginning to think we should've stayed on the mountain. Being on the mountain was lonely and dire, but not as lonely and dire as this. What if we never find any other people out here? How long will our food last?

By and by the sun drops lower and the air starts to cool and the boy and I haul the cart back to the road and continue on. The dog walks a bit, loping alongside us, before whining to be lifted onto the bearskin. The dog does not seem particularly concerned about our situation. Today, in this moment, he is alive. He has food and water and he has us. For him, this moment is the only thing that exists, and so he is happy.

The next day we stop at the first tinaja on our map, even though we aren't out of water yet. The pool takes a while to find, scrambling around in a rocky drainage that drops off in a series of ledges, but then it's there—cool dark water reflecting the sky. Full of water bugs, the sand around it littered with the tracks of animals. I use my pot to scoop the water into our jug until it's full again and we have a long rest in the shade of the cool rock, relishing this moment of relative abundance.

We don't reach the next tinaja until three days later, and by then we're pretty much all the way out of water, except for a liter I've set aside for the dog. I've decided that if I'm to die of thirst, I won't be taking the dog with me. I'll leave him with water, and maybe once I'm gone that water will buy him time to find more water for himself, using his special dog senses, and he'll have a chance at survival. The boy agrees, and so we have a special bottle we plan to keep always full, even when the blue jug is empty. Like it is this morning.

The boy and I went to sleep thirsty last night—we'd judged distance on the map wrong and thought that we would reach the tinaja before dark. We did not and so we're looking for it now, climbing a hillside of tumbled black rock as the heat creeps up with the rising sun.

The dog is below us next to the road, resting in the shade of the cart. He'll bark if anyone comes near, but we haven't seen a single person, or sign of people, since leaving Nelian, and I've stopped factoring the existence of other people into our daily planning.

Other people might come out of nowhere, with who-knows-what intentions? Great. At least I'll get to die of something other than dehydration. We crossed the border into Nevada a few days ago, there was a metal road sign, full of bullet holes—I looked at it and felt nothing, I was too tired and worried about water sources to care.

This tinaja is supposed to be on a shelf of rock partway up this rocky hill. Large, uneven boulders alternate with thick, thorny brush, so the going is slow. I'm thirsty and already too hot, and I'm trying not to panic. The thorns grab at my dress and shins and the boulders shift underfoot. When we finally reach what seems to be the shelf there's only a patch of damp mud, swarming with flies.

No.

We sit on the cool mud and I rest my head in my arms. The next tinaja, by my best guess, is at least a couple days' walk away. We won't last that long without water, hiking the road in this heat. So what now? But my brain is empty again. I have not a single idea.

There's a tinkle of volcanic rocks shifting as the boy gets up and moves around on the hillside. I keep my head in my arms. I wonder how long I can stay this way. Maybe forever.

The boy is calling me and I lift my head. My face is sticky with sweat from my arms. And tears? Where is the boy? How much time has passed? It's too hot on this mountain.

I use my hands to steady myself as I work my way uphill on the warm boulders. There's a ridge, a cool breeze blowing here, a view of the valley below, the highway a dark ribbon cutting the desert in half.

The boy is calling again. I follow his voice downhill, through some brush. The air changes and my heart jumps in my chest. I can feel it on the hair of my forearms.

The boy is standing in a shaded creek bed below me, waving his hands in the air. When I reach him I see that the creek bed is dry.

"Did you find water?" I ask, confused.

"In there," says the boy. He points to a low tangle of branches, impenetrable except for an opening close to the ground. "I saw all these trees growing in this one spot, then the animal tracks and bones scattered around. I couldn't get into the spot where the trees are growing, but then I saw this opening. I crawled in on my belly. There's a pool in there, in a little patch of grass! Listen, you can hear it!"

I listen. The faintest of trickles, soft music coming from within the overgrown cluster of branches. My breath releases, I feel myself sinking back into my body.

We camp in the shaded creek bed, the boy, the dog and I. We hide our cart in an arroyo next to the road and bring the blue jug up, plus our sleeping things and food. We eat, drink, rinse our faces and bodies, lie for hours watching the light move through the tree boughs, swatting flies.

"Hey," says the boy, quietly, from his bearskin. "We're in Nevada now. We should find people soon."

"I don't know," I say. "It looks… the same."

The boy sits up and points to animal tracks next to him in the creek bed.

"At least there are animals," he says. "Coyote." He traces his finger around some dog tracks. "Mountain lion. Javelina. And these—I'm not sure. Wild burro maybe. I've never seen them, but grandma told me about them."

"I've heard about the burros too," I say. "I've been wondering this whole time if they were real."

"Yeah," says the boy. "My grandma said that a long time ago miners brought them here, back when digging up metal was super important. Some of the burros became feral and they reproduced like crazy. There's supposed to be tons of them here now."

I let myself feel one single moment of hope and then slide back into a sort of blank contentment, lying on my sleeping bag watching the light move.

The next several days are good. The tinajas are tricky to find but we do find them. Our bodies are strong, our feet callused and sturdy. We're hungry but not too hungry. The road begins to climb into some mountains of bright granite, and the days cool. The plants are changing—from mesquite trees to oaks, bare dirt with prickly pear to yellow grass and catclaw. Still, we see no signs of people.

We run out of food ten days after leaving Nelian. We have water, at least for now, but we're hungry, and morale is the lowest it's been. At night in my sleeping bag I wonder how long it takes to die of hunger. Weeks?

I'm starting to wish that death would come sooner. Why draw it out with all this suffering? It's time to be mulched back into the earth. Maybe in my next life I'll be an oak tree. I'd like to live as slowly as an oak tree.

The next few days are a strange blur. As we walk I slip in and out of awareness, from this world into others, and back. Memories play in my head like movie reels. I have so many rich, colorful memories. What happens to our memories after we're dead? To our stories? What a shame, to lose all these beautiful stories.

But then, maybe they are never lost. If each moment is the only thing that exists then each moment lives forever, no? Lovely choreographies, unspooling eternally forwards and backwards in time. Woven together into a beautiful piece of cloth. The past is always there because it is irrevocably woven into the future, and vice versa.

This thought is comforting to me. I'm not alone on this road with the dog and the boy, waiting to die and be forgotten forever. I exist, I have existed, and therefore I will always exist. Here in this desert and also in the fire tower, and with Opal, and with Georgia in the city. With Beryl in the junkyard and way back, in the park with my mother, studying my school workbooks while she smoked cigarettes and tried to work out the puzzle of our future.

My mother. How stupid I was, to set out on this journey to try and find her. Those memories of her are the only thing that's real; any hope of tracking her down in this vast, arid wilderness is just delusion.

The next day we see the settlement, or rather the tall metal wall around it that glints in the midday sun. We're on a rise to the south and we stop, startled by this shining thing so out of place. We're back in the low desert and the air in front of the wall glimmers in the heat rising off the road. The dog sits up on the bearskin rug, perks his ears expectantly.

"What do you think that is?" says the boy. "People?"

"Probably," I say. I grab the boy's hand and pull him and the cart off the road, behind a boulder. We crouch there, observing the wall from a distance. We wait, but there is no movement.

"Maybe everyone's dead?" says the boy. "Or not at home?"

I frown.

"I don't like the looks of this place," I say. "I wish we had some way of knowing who lives here. You know, I've been thinking. What if instead of looking for other people, we try and find something like what we left behind in the mountains? A high elevation place, with animals to hunt and a water source? Maybe an abandoned cabin."

"We had that and you told me we should leave and come here, to Nevada," says the boy.

"I know," I say, putting my hands over my face. "And maybe I was wrong. Maybe I'm putting us in danger." It's hard for me to think straight today. Fear clouds everything, and I can't quite figure out the source of the fear—am I just hungry? If I had some food would this decision feel less overwhelming?

"Let's at least knock on the wall and ask if they have any food," says the boy, as if reading my thoughts.

I shake my head. "I don't know. We have water still, that's the most important thing. And maybe we'll find some food soon."

"Find some food where?" says the boy. "And we won't have water for much longer. And what if the next source is dried up?"

The boy is right. My fear doesn't matter. Again we're weak with need, floating in that liminal space between survival and death, and the choice has been made for us.

We pound on the hot metal wall with our fists. At first there is no response, just the echo of our pounding ringing across flatlands, towards the hills. But then there's some soft shuffling, a creaking noise and a panel in the metal wall slides open a foot.

A woman peers out at us. She's old, her face creased from the sun. Her head and shoulders are wrapped in a shawl of light, thin fabric. Her expression, as she gazes at us, is watery, thoughtful, not unkind.

"You've traveled a long way," she finally says.

"Do you have any water?" says the boy, before I can stop him. "Or food?"

The woman looks at him, then back at me.

"Our resources are limited here." The panel slides shut again, and I can hear her shuffling away. Standing this close to the wall, I can hear other things too: the braying of goats, the laughter of children. A wave of dizziness overcomes me and I lean against the metal to steady myself.

"We should go," I say to the boy, but I can't seem to gather myself to move.

The panel pops open and an arm extends, an earthen pot balanced on the palm.

"Oh my god," I say. The boy grabs the pot and drinks, and then passes it to me and I drink too. It's water, the best water we've tasted in weeks. The woman is watching us, her expression unreadable.

"We don't have anything else for you." She moves to slide the panel shut again.

"Do you know of any other villages?" I say, quickly. "How far to the next one, and if they might have food?"

"No," says the woman. "We keep mostly to ourselves. There are villages to the north, but I haven't been there."

"We won't make it much longer if we don't have food."

The panel slides partly shut.

"Wait! What about trade? We can trade you things!" The panel pauses. "A bear hide! A sleeping bag! We'll trade you anything." I'm grabbing things off the top of the cart, showing them to the woman. "A cookpot! A woodstove made out of a can!"

"What are those?" says the woman, interrupting me. I'm holding out the boy's moccasins—they're too broken, at this point, to be wearable, and he's been walking barefoot.

The panel slides all the way back open. An arm extends, and I place the ratty leather shoes in her hand. She turns them over, examining the holes worn into the soles, the stitching and what remains of the beadwork.

"This design…" she says. "Where did you get these?"

"My grandma made them," says the boy. "Up on the mountain." The woman looks at him. "Do you want them?"

"No, I don't want them," says the woman. The panel slams shut and there's a great, metallic wrenching. A huge door in the wall begins to crank open. The woman is standing in the dirt on the other side, wearing a tunic of light cloth, belted at the waist, her feet in dusty sandals. She motions inward.

"Come," she says. "We have food for you."

I let out the breath I didn't know I was holding. It's all I can do to steady myself, to walk through that door without falling over. The boy pulls the cart inside and the dog sits up on it, watching everything.

On the other side of the wall is a whole world, shining in the bright sunlight and glorious in its order. There are tidy rows of corn. Around the corn are small round houses, made of mud and what looks to be the wooden ribs of saguaros. People are sitting on mats in the shade of these houses, resting in the heaviness of the afternoon. The people look up as we pass—they're wearing light tunics like the woman's.

There is a peal of laughter and two small children, naked and with feet caked in dirt, chase each other across the clearing. Goats bray from a pen. Clusters of mesquite trees create dappled shade, and doves call from their branches. It's cooler in this village than out in the open desert, and the air feels almost damp. I soon find out why—our guide leads us to a wide, deep pool among the mesquite trees.

"It's our spring," she says. "The water is good here."

I close my eyes to stop myself from crying.

The woman says her name is Nickeline. She looks thoughtfully at my sun-faded flowered dress with the ragged hem, the boy's stained deerskin pants. I become aware, for the first time in many days, of how filthy I am—dress crusted with salt, skin patchy with chafe, arms red from the sun. Face streaked with dirt. Hair so greasy I'm not sure it's possible to detangle it at this point.

The woman is staring at my feet. I look down and see my white sneakers gone grey and scuffed, the holes on the sides and across the left toe box from all our days of walking, which I've sewn shut, punching holes in the fabric with my knife and lacing strips of fabric through, only for them to tear open again.

The woman steps forward, puts her hand on my arm. "This will be a good place for you to rest." Now the tears are coming for real, and I don't try to stop them. Another woman appears, and hands us each a clay pot of some sort of porridge, a mixture of grain and seeds. I sit on the ground and drink mine quickly, still crying, drop some on the ground for the dog.

Afterwards there is a metal tub, salvaged from abandoned cattle pastures, filled with cool spring water. A bar of rough soap, for myself and my dress. I rub the dress against itself, wring and beat it on the sides of the tub. I even wash the dog, lifting him against his will into the clear water saying, "I'm sorry! I'm sorry!" and scrubbing him with the soap, rinsing him and then releasing him onto the ground, where he shakes himself vigorously and then immediately rolls in the dust.

Clean rendered tallow for after my bath, rubbed into every part of my sun-cooked, aching body. A tunic that smells of the wind that rises in the desert at sunset. My wet dress draped on the branches of a mesquite tree.

The boy gets clean too, and then we are led to one of the small mud houses, where a low doorway opens into a cool, dim room in which two woven mats are spread on the floor. It's evening, and a weariness hangs about my body like a kind of fog.

Nickeline seems to understand, and she hands us a clay pot of spring water and another with more porridge and leaves us alone. The boy spreads the bear hide on his mat and I unstuff my sleeping bag on mine, and lie down with the dog to watch the light move through the holes in the mud wall, eventually falling into the deepest and most exhausted sleep of my life.

The doves calling and the crowing of roosters wakes me at sunrise. My sneakers are missing from the doorway of the hut and at first I think *on no, they've stolen my shoes!* But then I see in their place is a pair of new sandals—soles made from the tread of an old car tire, leather straps. I gasp in delight, slip my feet into them. There's a smaller pair, too, for the boy. Outside the golden sun is angling its way over the walls of the village, illuminating each small hut in turn.

There's a noise and I startle. Nickeline is there, and she hands me a folded cloth. Inside I find warm tortillas and boiled chicken eggs.

"Thank you," I say, feeling like I might cry again. "I don't know how to thank you. It's just... What is this place?" I ask her as I eat one of the eggs. "How did you all come to be here?" The boy appears behind me, his hair messy with sleep, and I hand him the bundle of breakfast.

Nickeline smiles. "Many of us are the first people. The ones who were here before the cities. Not all the same tribes, but from different tribes—some from east, or to the south. We wanted to remember our traditional skills, so that we could live again the way we used to, before the roads, the power grids, factories. But not exactly like that. Because the plants have moved, the water has moved. It used to be cool in this valley in the winter, now it's hot all year. And many of us come from different traditions with different practices, and some skills have been lost forever. We take what we have and weave it together, try and make something new that's useful now, and we think of original things too."

I don't know what to say. I never could have imagined, when living in the city, that a people like this existed. I feel like I must be asleep. Soon I'll wake sweaty in an arroyo on the side of the road, the water jug almost empty—my real life.

"Why did you take us in?" asks the boy, in between bites of tortilla.

"Would you two like to help us with work on a new hut this morning?" Nickeline asks, ignoring his question.

Clay from a pit nearby is mixed with water and this is spread, in globs and handfuls, over some saguaro ribs, the ends of which are buried in the earth. The saguaros don't grow this far north, says Nickeline, but the villagers travel south in June to harvest the saguaro fruit, and they bring ribs back with them when they return.

It's messy work, spreading the mud on the saguaro ribs, but with so many of us it hardly feels like work at all, and before the sun is at its zenith the hut is covered. I rinse with a pot of spring water and drink another slurry of grains and seeds.

The village goes quiet in the midday heat. I leave the boy and the dog and find Nickeline sitting in the dirt outside her hut, spreading mesquite pods on a mat to dry. Her hands are as weathered as her face, the lines forked and branching like the arroyos that cut across the desert valley. She invites me inside, where the air smells of charred wood and animal skins, and hands me a cup of broth.

"Why did you accept us?" I ask her. "I'm sorry I have to ask, but I've met some people on the road who… wanted things from me that I didn't want to give. At the gate, it seemed like at first you didn't want to. What made you change your mind?"

Nickeline frowns as she ladles her own cup of broth.

"We have very limited resources here. We can't usually take people in, as much as we would like to. Even children. But the boy…" she sets her cup down on a low wooden table, wipes her hands on her tunic. "Those moccasins of his. The beadwork is one of our designs. Although it's been ages since I've seen that particular design."

"The boy's grandmother made those moccasins," I say.

"Yes," says Nickeline. I wait for her to say more but she only stands in the doorway quietly, looking out at the bright day.

"I'm looking for my mother," I blurt. "She disappeared when I was young, in the city. I thought I would find her here, in Nevada. I wonder if you've seen her?"

"Your mother?" says Nickeline, turning to me. "Tell me a bit about her."

I tell Nickeline what my mother looked like the last time I saw her, the way she smoked, how she did her hair. My friendship with Brittania, and the way my mother disappeared. Lisle's story about the prison, and how there would be a fire.

Nickeline doesn't speak for a time after I've finished talking, just watches me thoughtfully, her arms crossed over her chest.

"I'm not sure," she says, finally. She lifts a pot from the coals, sets it in the dirt. "I'm afraid I don't have any information that would be helpful for you." The fist of hope that's been growing in my chest deflates.

"And the other villages to the north," I say, "you've never visited them?"

"Like I said at the gate," says Nickeline, "we keep mostly to ourselves. I've heard stories of these villages, but I've never seen them with my own eyes. People try and survive in all different ways out here. Sometimes they make it. Other times they don't. For all I know, those villages have failed. I don't know."

I feel dizzy on the walk back to my hut. Once inside I curl up on the mat, pull my knees to my chest. Crying would make me feel better, I know, but I'm too empty. The dog finds me, plops down with a thump, his small warm back against my back. The afternoon is still, all life suspended in the heat. I close my eyes and wait for sleep to carry me away.

When I wake it's dark. The boy is on his mat on the bearskin, his arms flung above his head, mouth open in sleep. The dog twitches with dreams, small legs kicking the air. I want to sleep more, too, but I can't.

My mother isn't here, in this village. So, what now? Do I continue north, through the barren desert to the other, unknown villages? The risk would be immense. I can't put the boy through that again. And yet I can't leave him here alone either. What if Nickeline decides at some point that they don't have the resources to care for him? What if the village throws him out, back into the desert? I'm all that the boy has in this world. He needs me. I can't abandon him.

CHAPTER 18

It's afternoon and we've finished another hut. I crouch in the dappled shade of a mesquite tree, brushing the dried mud from my hands and wiping the sweat from my face. This hut was for a young couple, Jasper and Jet, who are expecting their first baby soon. We erected the hut next to the hut of Jet's parents. I watch as Jasper, whose arms are caked in mud up to the elbows, passes a crock of water to the boy, and then they laugh together.

The boy has been spending a lot of time with Jasper and Jet, helping as they get ready for the baby—working in their garden, softening goat hides, hanging meat in the smokehouse. He and Jasper even went javelina hunting.

They didn't see any javelina that day but they did climb high enough into the hills to find a stand of alligator junipers that were nice and straight where they competed for the light, and they gathered wood to make more arrows for their bows.

Now Jet appears, walking slowly, her tunic billowing behind her in the breeze. I watch as she gathers the boy in a hug, squeezing him against her belly. My mouth turns down in disgust and then I force my face into a more neutral expression. *Bets,* I whisper. *What is wrong with you.*

Jasper is calling my name. I extract myself from the soft shade of the mesquite tree and join them and the other villagers around the new hut.

"Bets," Jasper says. "We're so grateful for everything you've done for the boy. How you've cared for him and kept him safe. Without you he wouldn't be here with us today."

"I mean of course," I say, stupidly.

"He'll be happy and safe with us, and we'll be so glad to have him. Although we've only known him a short while, he's truly become part of our lives." The other villagers are all watching us. Jasper and Jet stare at me, expectantly.

"We're very glad to be in this village," I say, finally.

"They want me to move in with them," blurts the boy. "They have space now. I'm going to help with the baby, and with hunting."

"The boy is still a child," says Jet. "A child needs a family. We can be his family." She pulls the boy to her again, and the other villagers erupt in happy shouting. The boy is smiling at me, at Jet, at Jasper. The dog is barking and pawing at the boy's legs, excited by the hubbub.

"We'll have a feast tonight, to celebrate," says Jasper.

"Great," I say. I'm suddenly cold, even though I'm standing in the sun, and I wrap my arms around my body.

Melons, beans, corn, mesquite flour pancakes. Goat meat stew and saguaro wine. Everything spread on wooden tables in the shade. It's evening and the light is long and yellow, the heat of the day beginning to dissipate, and the air is filled with the sounds of laughter. I haven't seen a spread of food this decadent since I was a child at Brittania's house, eating salmon roe and cupcakes with rainbow sprinkles.

I fill a bowl, and then another. I eat until my stomach aches. As dark falls someone builds a bonfire, and I watch the sparks rise up against the black of night. The dog weaves around people's feet, searching for dropped food. Jasper scoops him up and he licks happily at the man's face. I leave the crowd and walk alone back to my hut, thinking I'll lie down but when I get there I can't rest. There's just one mat in this hut now, one mat and one modest pile of belongings.

How small a single life can feel. I walk in circles around my lonely mat a few times and then my feet carry me out of the hut, away from the center of the village, away from the light of the fire. They carry me towards the far end of the village, where the spring is. There's a mesquite forest there and I enter it, ducking deeper and deeper into the trees, thorny branches scratching me as I push my way through.

At last I reach the far wall, the known limits of this world, and I press my back against it, sink down onto the ground, pull my knees to my chest and rest my face on my knees. It's quiet here, I can no longer hear the sounds of happy laughter around the fire. There are only these mesquite trees, calm and still in the warm dark.

"Bets." I startle at the sound of my name. "Bets." The voice is soft and seems to come from the forest itself. There's a rustling and the darkness parts, revealing the warm orange glow of a fire. There's someone silhouetted there, holding back the hide that covers a doorway. It's a hut! I stand and brush myself off.

"I didn't know anyone lived back here," I say, apologetic.

"There's a chill coming on," says the stooped figure. "Why don't you come inside by the fire."

I duck through the doorway into a softly lit room, where a mat is spread on the dirt ground alongside the fire, whose smoke rises through a hole in center of the loosely woven roof. On the floor are piles of baskets, as well as mounds of basket making materials: cattail, willow, rushes, devil's claw. There's a large earthen pot and the person, who I can now see is an old woman with silver hair that hangs down around her face, dips a tin cup into the pot and hands it to me.

"Drink." The woman watches me while I take a sip—her eyes are small and watery in her heavily lined face. The tea is bitter, but not unpleasant. The woman nods and lowers herself onto the mat with a sigh. She picks up a partially finished basket, the ends of willow radiating out like bicycle spokes, and pats the mat beside her.

I sit down, close my eyes, feel the warmth of the fire on my face. The only sound is the soft rustling of the woman's hands as she works the willow of the basket. "Why are you sad," she says, after at time.

"I'm not sad," I say. "Do I seem sad? I'm happy. The boy has a family now. A home."

"Yes," she says. "The boy belongs here."

"What does it mean to belong?" I ask.

The woman frowns and continues working on the basket.

"When I was young, things were much harder," she says, finally. "There were too many babies, and not enough to eat. I had a sister, and she became pregnant. She was told that once the baby was born she would have to take it into the desert and leave it to die. So she left in the night. She told me she was going as far away as she could get, to the mountains. I never saw her again."

"That's awful," I say. The woman nods.

"When the boy arrived, and I heard about his moccasins… that was my sister's beadwork. His grandmother was my sister's child. My sister raised her child alone in the mountains, and then her child became an old woman who raised the boy, before she died. She taught him our ways. So he is one of us now. We're grateful to you for returning him to us."

I think of the boy's grandmother, just a shape under the blankets in her cabin, a splay of white hair on the pillow. The tables cluttered with baskets, the overgrown garden.

"I'm so glad," I say, "that the boy has somewhere to belong. And that's horrible, how the village couldn't support all the babies, when you were young."

"It lasted a long time," she says. "There have always been lots of babies here. A blessing and a curse. A few years ago a man, Jude, started coming around. He travels all over the area, he has a truck. He told us that there were families in the cities who couldn't conceive and that he could take the babies there and give them good homes. We sent the babies with him because we didn't have a choice—it was truly either that or leave them in the desert to die—but we never really knew what became of them.

"He would return every full moon, and at first he would tell us updates—what the families were like, what the children were learning. But then he stopped telling us anything at all. He would just arrive and take the children that we couldn't keep. It was awful.

"But then, last year, a woman came through. She was ill and wanted to rest here for a time. She said she'd escaped from the prisons and that she was from the city, that she'd lost her whole family. She was in the village when Jude came, and she learned about our problem with the babies. It turns out that in the city she'd helped people with abortions and birth control, and she knew all about the wild plants that could be used for that—knowledge that had been lost to us.

"She taught the women what she knew, took them into the mountains to gather the herbs. When Jude came next, we had no babies for him. Since then we've been able to keep all the babies that are born. Jude still comes monthly, and we turn him away. He's persistent, but we'll never send any children with him again."

"This woman who escaped from the prisons," I say. "What happened to her?"

"When her health improved she went on her way. She wanted to find the villages in the north. We warned her against the journey, but she was fearless. I don't know what became of her."

"What was her name?" I ask.

"Magda."

My heart sinks.

"But I don't know if that was her real name," the woman continues. "Many people who escape the prison use new names, as a way of cutting ties."

I'm quiet for a time, staring into the fire, watching the small flames move over the coals.

"How does a person know where they're supposed to be?" I ask.

The woman looks up from her basket. "You belong wherever there are people who claim you."

"What if you don't have anyone to claim you?" I say. "I'm looking for my mother. She's supposed to be somewhere in Nevada, but this is the first village we've found, and getting here was so dangerous. I don't know if I should keep looking for her."

The woman puts a hand on my shoulder. I can feel its heaviness and warmth.

"Your mother may be out there," she says, "somewhere in the desert. In this life we sometimes have parents, and sometimes we have children. And there are times when we have neither of these; in these times, the earth claims us. The earth always claims us."

I stand up from the mat. "Thank you for that."

Back at my hut I lie awake on my mat, unable to sleep. It's too quiet in here. By and by there's a small snuffling and the dog appears; the party must be over, no more dropped food to snatch off the ground. The dog noses his way into my armpit and settles himself there, his little snout on my shoulder, his body against my side.

Now I assume the aloneness will dissipate and sleep will come, but it doesn't. I sit up slowly so as not to wake the dog and pull the *RVer's Guide to the American West* from the small pile of belongings next to my mat. I extract the pencil from where I've tucked it in the book and flip through to a page with some white space. What I need to do right now is write.

CHAPTER 19

JANE

The sound of a drum rings out over the desert. It's a metal drum, an alarm drum, to signal the arrival of a great army in the distance, an army that's just crested the horizon. I'm standing on a rocky ridgeline, a pack basket on my back, and I've got to run. I've got to find Bets and run.

The drum grows louder until the sound fills my brain, bounces against the bones of my skull. My cheek is wet where it meets warm vinyl. I rub my face—sweat. I'm in a truck, lying on my side across the bench seat. It's so hot I can barely breathe.

The drumming again. Someone is banging on the door of the truck. My head swims. There is no air. I lurch for the handle of the door and shove it open. It swings wide with a rusty creak and cooler air rushes in. I gasp, filling my lungs.

"It's too hot for you to be in this truck." A woman's voice. She's wearing a tunic of sand-colored cloth, a shawl of the same fabric is draped around her face. She peers at me. "Do you need water?" I stumble from the truck, sink into the shaded dirt along its side. Footsteps recede and when the woman returns she pushes a clay pot into my hands. "Drink this."

I do—it's some sort of tepid tea, red like hibiscus. It's hard to swallow, hard to get my throat to work, but I manage. I crumple onto my side in the dirt and the woman places a cool, damp cloth over my eyes. I feel her fingers in my hair, stroking gently. "Our village is nearby. You should come there and rest for a time."

"I can't leave the truck," I say.

The villagers know of a dirt track that wends through the desert brush, bypassing the sinkhole. One of them drives the truck for me while I lie curled on the passenger seat, and then steers it back onto the road and the rest of the way to the village, pulling it expertly through the metal gate. I am led like a child to a small mud hut where a woven mat has been spread on the dirt floor. On the mat I am shaking, suddenly so cold. The woman smooths a blanket over me.

"You'll feel better after some rest," she says.

The day wanes. The woman brings me seed porridge with pine nuts in it and more hibiscus tea. The dark is soft and the night creatures call to each other. I sleep, and my dreams are full of threats. The army has crested the hill, pouring into the valley below. Where is Bets?

I startle awake and the soft night is there, cradling me in its warm palms. In the morning I feel clear-eyed. I lie on my woven mat and watch the light move through the holes in the mud wall, listen to the village wake around me.

After a lifetime in the city and then ten years in prison, I will never again take for granted this feeling of outside air on my skin, good air, air that smells of dust and the earth, not the stale of damp concrete corridors or the stink of trash fires.

I pull myself up slowly, rub the salt from my face. My urge is to get back on the road headed north but I know that I shouldn't go yet. I'm exhausted beyond words, and if I keep trying to push, my illness will just take me out again. I need to rest not just for a day or two, but possibly for a while. I don't know this village though, and it's a risk to stay here, especially with my truck full of food. That food is my only currency.

The woman in the sand-colored shawl brings me breakfast porridge. She tells me her name is Nickeline. I introduce myself as Magda—a lie, but I want to leave as little of a trail as I can as I make my way north on these broken roads.

After breakfast I follow Nickeline around, helping with chores where I can. We spend the afternoon sitting in the dirt alongside her hut,

Nickeline showing me how to weave mats. A few mothers have left their toddlers with us while they gather kindling outside the village.

"There are so many children in this village," I say. "You're so lucky. You have good water and soil? And it's not too hot to grow here?"

"We're very fortunate." Nickeline pauses in her work. "Although it's not without its challenges."

That night I sleep the sleep of death again, another sleep more rejuvenating than anything in recent memory. The morning, when it comes, is sublime. I lie on my woven mat, buzzing with gratitude for that sleep. I decide I am strong enough today to join the women who gather firewood in the arroyos.

Lunch is cold corn tortillas wrapped in cloth and boiled chicken eggs. One woman squats in the dirt and stacks sticks for a small fire, produces a kettle and boils tea for all of us. We drink it out of small clay cups. Carrying the firewood back to the metal gates is hard, and I'm the slowest in the group, but I manage. Back at the village, the children run to greet us—such happy, energetic children!

That night I wake in the dark with what feels like a fever. Maybe I shouldn't have helped carry all that wood. Every time I try to go against the grain of my illness, this is what ends up happening. I toss and turn and finally give up on rest, walk outside in the moonlight, look at the stars. My joints are stiff and my muscles ache. I close my eyes and lift my face to the night sky. *I don't begrudge you this,* I whisper. In the morning I wake exhausted, my mind cloudy.

"I think I'll lie down today," I say, standing in the doorway of Nickeline's hut. She's stirring a pot with a wooden spoon, and steam rises around her.

"Of course," she says. She seems distracted. "I'd been meaning to talk with you. I know you've been ill, and it's good that you're here, resting. In a week, after you've had some more rest, we should talk about you resuming your journey."

"Resuming my journey?" I repeat. Nickeline sets down her wooden spoon and looks up at me.

"We would love it if you stayed longer. Absolutely love it. The other women adore you, as do the children. But we have such limited resources"—she closes her eyes, her mouth tight—"we cannot take anyone new in. Not even one single person."

I return to my mat to rest and all morning my mind races, thoughts moving in and out with the fever. One week. One week is not enough. My hope was that with a month of rest, possibly two, I'd be able to store up enough reserves to continue north, but today I can barely get up off my mat, and in a week I might not be much improved.

In the afternoon I fall asleep and I'm back on the ridge, the sun beating down on me, watching the army in the distance advance. I take off my pack basket, swing it around and look inside. There are bundles of dried roots in there, neatly tied with string. I break off a piece, hold it up to my face, inhale its scent.

Voices wake me in the evening. Two people, passing by my hut. I catch bits of the conversation.

"They are well, the twins from this summer, and the little girl."

"But can you tell me more about how they are? Which region have the twins gone to?" It's Nickeline. I stand in the shadows of the doorway and peer into the darkness.

"I cannot tell you more," says a man. He seems almost angry. "You know this. After the exchange I cannot offer more details."

I slip from the hut and follow them, keeping to the shadows. They make their way to the spring.

"Do you have children for me?" he asks.

"Perhaps," she says, after a moment. "I'm hesitant, though, to send them with you. What if you're selling the children to the workhouses? Or to rich people to work as slaves, or worse? I have no proof that these children are going to good families, like you say. I know that there are many wealthy childless families in the cities that would be good homes for them. But I have no proof that the children are ending up there."

The man shrugs.

"You don't have to believe me. Instead of sending your extra babies with me, why not let them die?"

Nickeline sighs.

"At least then we would know for sure what became of them." The two sit in silence for a bit. "We have so many women pregnant this month," she says. "Soon, people will begin to go hungry. I don't know what's worse—that our people go hungry or that I send these children with you. Who am I to make these decisions? Sometimes I want to be the one, sent out into the desert to die." The silence returns. Eventually the man rises.

"Well," he says. "I'll return on the next full moon. And you'll have the children for me then?"

He lets himself out of the gate, and I hear the metal slide shut behind him. Nickeline lifts her skirt to her face and weeps softly into it.

The next day my energy feels decent enough in the morning so I take myself into the desert, bringing with me an empty pack basket that I borrow from the villagers. It's made of willow, just like the one in the dream, but a different shape, and the straps are deerskin. I climb into the hills, picking my way around the creosote and prickly pear and over the sun-baked boulders.

I'm beginning to feel a little ill by the time I find what I'm looking for and I dig it up, cut it free with my knife, drop it in the pack basket. There isn't much of it here. To find more I'd need to go into the mountains—it really likes to grow up higher, where the oaks and yellow grasses give way to open ponderosa forests.

I hurry back to the village before the dizziness overtakes me. I get down a little gruel and wilt onto the mat in my hut until late afternoon, when I can gather a bit of energy again. I find Nickeline making a pair of sandals in the shade of her hut.

"I think I can help you," I say, as I sink onto the ground beside her.

"What do you mean?" she asks.

"With the babies."

She pauses in her work, one strip of leather pushed partway through the slit in the rubber sole. Her hands are callused and tan, almost like leather themselves. I pull the bundled roots, crusted with soil, from my pack basket and present them to her.

"Make a strong decoction from these," I say. "Give it to the women who are pregnant. They'll lose their pregnancies. Then you won't have to send away the babies." She takes the roots from me, lifts them to her face and inhales, just like I did in the dream.

"We've been so lucky to have so many children in our village," she says, her eyes closed. "But it's a curse, too. So many things in life are like that. What we ask for, what we dream for… it becomes our burden." She brushes dirt from the bundle of roots. "How did you learn what you know?"

"A decade ago I worked in the city," I say. "Providing abortions. I was hoping to get an apartment for my daughter and I…" I trail off, and the woman looks at me with curiosity. "Anyway, there are a hundred ways to do it. This root is one of those ways. It'll make the mother ill—she'll throw up. But it won't kill her. No food, just this decoction, night and day. After a few days she'll pass the fetus."

"When we first found Jude, I thought he was a godsend," says Nickeline. "That he was really helping us. He told us stories of wealthy families who could not conceive, of places where all the children had died and families were so happy at a chance to receive a baby. But now he just comes and demands the children, he won't tell us anything. Sometimes, when we ask too many questions, he threatens us. But what other choice have I had?" She places her hands over her eyes, as if to cool them, and then drops her hands in her lap and looks up at me. "Will you teach us how to gather this herb?"

"I will," I say.

CHAPTER 20

BETS

I drop the watch on the mat in front of Jude.

"I want to trade this for a ride north."

He and Nickeline are seated in the dim of Nickeline's hut, drinking saguaro wine. It's the hottest time of day and the village is silent. Even the goats have ceased their braying in the heavy heat. Jude picks up the silver watch and turns it over, studying it.

"Where did you get this?" he asks.

"It doesn't matter," I say. "I want to go north. Can you take me?" Jude looks at me, then back at the watch. He runs his thumb across its front, presses it to his ear. Then he shakes his head, as if clearing a thought away.

"I can certainly drive you north. At least, as far as the roads will allow in my truck." He looks at me again, really studies my features this time. I force myself to stare back and he's the one to finally turn away, slipping the watch into his pocket. "I leave tonight."

All afternoon I am outside of myself. I spend the evening with the boy at Jet and Jasper's cabin, grinding mesquite pods, and eat dinner there; a kind of bean I haven't seen before, and tortillas. Afterward I pack a few things into my backpack—my knife, my sweater and shawl and the RVer's guide.

The dog is curled on my sleeping bag, asleep. I watch his small chest rise and fall. *Don't cry,* I say to myself, wiping the tears away with the back of my hand. I write a note on a page torn from the back of the RVer's guide.

I'm going north, to try and find my mother. There are more villages there, and she might be in one of them. The journey is dangerous, so I'm going alone. You and the dog are safe here. You both deserve to be safe. I love you both so much, and I want you to be safe. Please look after the dog for me.

"Bets? It's time." The dog pops his head up and lets out a low growl.

"Stay," I say to the dog, and I stuff my sleeping bag into my backpack, leave the note on my empty mat. The dog tries to follow but I hiss *stay!* and waggle my finger at him. Tears sting the corners of my eyes. The dog obeys, sits back down on the mat, watches me silently as I duck out of the hut.

My heart is breaking as I follow Jude through the dark, the huts of the village receding in the shadows behind us. My knife is in the pocket of my dress and I run my fingers over its wooden handle, soothing myself with the familiar shape.

Jude's truck is parked just inside the wall of the village. It's a huge truck, lifted, with jugs in the back for gasoline and water, metal boxes for food, tools, and emergency supplies.

The wheels of the metal gate cry out as we heave it open and then Jude pulls the truck out, its engine rumbling in the still night, and I heave the gate shut behind us. I haul myself up into the passenger seat of the truck and rest my backpack on my lap. There's a fist rising in my chest and I swallow, forcing it down.

I feel as though I'm floating high above the desert as we turn away from the village gates. The truck's headlights slice the dark, revealing patches of broken road. I stare out the window. *Don't think, don't feel. Just go.*

A few minutes later I come back to myself and realize we're driving south, not north.

"Wait," I say, confused. "Where are we going? Why are we driving south?" Jude doesn't answer, just stares ahead at the patch of road illuminated in the truck's headlights. "Jude," I say, my voice rising in alarm. "Jude. Why are we driving south?"

Again he doesn't answer, just stares ahead. "Jude!" I'm shouting at him now. He grimaces and reaches out his right hand, hitting me across the face and sending my head bouncing against the headrest.

"Shut up!" he shouts. "Shut the fuck up!"

The pain in my face is loud and bright. A hand to my nose comes away with blood on it.

"What the fuck?" I say to Jude.

"Where did you get that watch?" he barks.

"You hit me!" I say. "You fucking hit me!"

"Tell me where you got the watch," Jude is saying. "Did you steal it? Are you a thief? A thief from the city? You got a bounty on your head? Is that why you're way out here?"

I feel the balloon of my consciousness lift up, out of my body. I let it go, let it rise through the metal roof of the truck and out, into the dark night. The balloon of my consciousness looks down on the shining truck as it moves along the road, dodging potholes and jostling over cracks in the asphalt.

The balloon notices the bright stars, the hills in the distance, the crescent moon. I'm disappointed when the balloon begins to sink of its own accord. When it drops back into my body, I look at Jude, his jaw set in a scowl, his fists clenched on the steering wheel. I slide a hand into the pocket of my dress and finger the knife.

"I have to pee," I say.

"Bullshit," says Jude. "Tell me where you got the watch."

"It was given to me," I say. He looks over at me, takes in my ratty flowered dress, my tangled hair.

"Not possible," he says. "Now how about this. You tell me where you got the watch, or I kill you right now."

"Ok but can I pee first? I'm gonna piss all over the nice leather seats of this truck."

"Jesus Christ," says Jude. He stops the truck in the middle of the road. "Don't get out until I let you out." He exits the driver's door and walks around the front of the truck to my side. Quick as I can I sidle over to his side and am out that door, running across the road and into the desert. I'm fast but he's fast too, and we're both stumbling over rocks in the dark, and then he reaches out to grab me and I turn and slash his hand with my knife.

"You bitch!" he cries, and he grabs a handful of my dress with his other hand and wrenches me down, onto the ground. "You bitch!" he cries again as he punches me in the face. He's breathing heavy and there's blood dripping from his hand onto my dress. I try to pull myself up and he kicks me, hard, and then he yanks me up by my dress and pushes me in front of him, back toward the truck. I see my knife, glinting in his hand.

Back at the truck he shoves me inside and then rifles around in the bed, returns with a fistful of gauze. He wraps his hand, tears some medical tape with his teeth and tapes up the gauze. He lets out a long breath and starts the truck.

"I should just fucking kill you," he says, as he pulls back onto the road. I don't respond. I'm staring out the window, my face throbbing. My lip is split and it hurts to move my mouth. I rest my head against the cool glass and close my eyes.

"I stole the watch," I say. "From one of the Feldspar brothers. Months ago, in the city. After I killed him—I drove my knife into his neck. You can kill me now. I think I'm done. I'm done with all of this."

Jude pounds his fists against the steering wheel and I look over in alarm—he's grinning, his teeth shocking white in the dark of the cab.

"What?" I say. "Why are you happy?"

"Yes!" he's saying. "I can't fucking believe it! That watch is valuable, but *you* are the real prize."

"Oh come on," I say. "What does that even mean? Just fucking kill me already." He's shaking his head furiously.

"No way."

"Ok, where are we going then?" But he's still shaking his head, and I close my eyes again and rest my face against the cool window, too tired to care.

CHAPTER 21

"Can I ask you a question?" We're still driving, the night still an impenetrable blackness beyond the circle of the headlights. Jude glances at me.

"One question," he says.

"Does this have to do with my mother?"

"Your mother?" Jude furrows his brow.

"Yeah. Like, do you know where she is? Is that where we're going?"

Jude shakes his head. "That's enough questions."

"Hey," says Jude. "Wake up." I open my eyes. I must've fallen asleep and I'm startled to realize we're surrounded by buildings—we've left the desert for some sort of town. We're pulling into a parking garage. The garage is unlit, and as we drive along the rows the headlights illuminate abandoned cars, their windshields thick with dust.

We park in an empty space and in the side mirror I see Jude open one of the metal boxes in the truck bed, produce a handgun and put it in the waistband of his pants. "Get out," he says, after opening the passenger side door.

"Where are we?" I ask.

"This used to be a museum," says Jude.

"What is it now?"

"You run away and I'll shoot you," says Jude, by way of an answer.

"You can shoot me right now," I say.

Jude ignores this and pushes me towards the stairwell. He pulls a flashlight from his pocket and flicks it on.

"A flashlight?" I say, stunned. "How do you charge that thing?"

"No more fucking questions," snaps Jude. I follow him up two flights of stairs, and then we open a door onto a carpeted hallway. The smell of mold and decay hits me and my eyes water. The hallway leads to a large room where tall objects cast strange shadows in the beam of Jude's flashlight.

On one wall are the words *How to Survive*, spelled out in three-foot-tall letters. I walk towards one of the objects. It's a panel covered in colored squares. Up close I can see that each square is different—some are fuzzy, some are hard, some are sponge-like. *White spruce pulp and mycelium*, reads the text under a white square. *Wood fibers, plantain, bread*, is the text below a chunky brown square. *Concrete mixed with recycled diapers*, reads another. There's a square of fabric. *Brewed protein*, it says underneath.

I start to laugh. Jude stares at me, alarmed.

"Recycled diapers! They thought that if they mixed concrete with recycled diapers…"

"Hush!" says Jude. He beckons me into another darkened hallway. At the end is a room full of paintings, some of them as tall as I am—there are mountains lit with alpenglow, meadows full of wildflowers. I stand close to one of them, touch its surface. The paint is soft, and mildew creeps in from its edges. How old is this painting? Hundreds of years old? And now it's decaying, here in this abandoned museum.

"It's ok," I whisper. "We have the real thing now."

There's footsteps, someone making their way down the hallway towards us. I wheel around and Jude does too, and a tall man in a clean suit steps into the beam of Jude's flashlight. My first reaction is shock at how clean this man's clothes are. I've forgotten that there are places left that still have hot running water and chemical soap. Other than his freakish cleanliness, there is nothing remarkable about this man—straight posture, bald head, boring face. He could be anyone or no-one at all.

"The watch," he says to Jude.

"Who are you?" I ask.

The man ignores me.

"The watch," he says again.

Jude reaches into his pocket, produces the silver watch. The man takes Jude's flashlight and shines it on the watch, turns it over, studies the back. Then he looks at Jude, looks at me, then back at Jude. He takes a handgun from his pocket, points it at Jude's head, pulls the trigger.

There's an explosion and I jump. One of the paintings falls off the wall, clatters onto the ground behind me. Jude's body is on the ground too, blood beginning to pool around him. My ears are ringing, and I can't seem to slow my breathing.

"What…" I say.

The man's face is blank and his eyes are like marbles, lifeless.

"I wanted to thank you," he says, after a moment. "For killing my brother. And for saving this watch. For smuggling it out of the city, and protecting it. It's you I have to thank for everything, really."

"You're one of the Feldspar brothers?" I manage. The rushing in my head is a tsunami and I swim against it, try not to get pulled under.

"You saved the singularity," he says.

"I don't know what that is."

"The fucking singularity." He shakes the watch at me. He drops the watch onto the tiled floor and smashes the handgun onto its back. I flinch as metal pieces go skittering. He crouches and picks up the broken watch, plucks something small from its insides and holds it in his palm. He leaves the gun on the ground.

"The singularity is the only thing that matters," he says. He's speaking quietly, as though to himself. "Proteus stole this from us, years ago. I didn't think we'd ever find it again. At least, not before we ran out of time. But now I have it, thanks to you."

"Do you mean Proteus Feldspar?" I ask.

"My brother," says the man. "He wanted… he always hated us. He wanted control. He almost succeeded. You killing him was a lucky thing. It's a shame that you know so much. You're clever. You could be very useful, in the workhouses." He bends over, plucks the gun from the floor.

I wrack my brain for what to say. "Why do you want the singularity?"

"Who wouldn't want the singularity?" says the man. "All consciousness, joined together. No more illusion of separateness. And we can live forever like that. This," he gestures at the paintings on the wall of the dark gallery, "Is a stupid, useless way to live."

"You want this singularity because you're lonely?"

"Everyone is lonely. Embodiment is a curse. All my life I've tried to escape the pain of that curse. But there isn't any way. I'm on the outside. We all are. Togetherness is something that happens somewhere else, beyond the pedestrian drudgery of this realm. Togetherness is what happens in the singularity."

"I still don't understand what the singularity is, though."

He groans. "I'll show you." He tucks the gun into his waistband and produces a laptop from a black bag, opens it, slides the chip into a small device, sets the device next to the laptop.

The light from the laptop screen illuminates his face—the taut, smooth cheeks, the emptiness of his eyes. He clicks something on the screen and music starts to play, quiet at first as then louder, filling the room with sound.

Sail away, sail away, sail away
Sail away, sail away sail away

"What?" shouts the man. He jabs at the keypad on the laptop but the music doesn't stop.

From Bissau to Palau, in the shade of Avalon
From Fiji to Tyree and the isles of Ebony
From Peru to Cebu, hear the power of Babylon
From Bali to Cali, far beneath the Coral Sea

The man looks panicked.

"What is this music? Why can't I stop this? Where are the other files?"

Sail away, sail away, sail away

There's running footsteps in the hallway and then a woman is there, softly illuminated in the shadows. She's wearing a long cotton dress of patchwork yellow and white squares and a canvas chore jacket, and her heavy black hair cascades down her back in a single braid.

She has a long knife in her hand and before the man can react, crouched on the floor with the laptop she drives her knee into his back, pulls the gun from his waistband and sends it flying across the floor. The man cries out in surprise and his shouts blend with the music.

Sail away, sail away, sail away.

"Georgia?" I cry out.

Georgia is kneeling on him know, her hand wrapped around his neck, her knife to his throat.

"There was never any singularity," she shouts at the back of his head. "There will never be any singularity. There is only this earth. This life. This is all we've ever had. And I won't let you destroy that for the rest of us." And then there's red, shooting onto the dirty tile. And the man goes limp. And the song ends.

CHAPTER 22

I see the roofs of the village first, pale green tile above the bare winter trees. We dip down off the gravel road onto a rough dirt track, jostling as the truck navigates the deep ruts. We're in Jude's truck, and Georgia is driving. Next to me is the boy, asleep with his head back, lolling on the seat's headrest. The dog is on my lap, curled into a little ball, his nose tucked under his tail.

We roll to a stop in front of the first of the houses, a small square cabin, its boards mossy and warped. Outside the truck the air is rich and wet; we can hear the soft burbling of a stream running through the village. A woman is carrying a bundle of branches and when she sees us she shrieks and drops the wood on the ground.

"What is it, Margey?" says another woman, emerging from the doorway.

"It's just me," says Georgia, stepping from the truck. Margey shouts and runs to us, wraps her arms around Georgia and then looks at me, takes my hands in hers.

"You must be Bets," she says.

I say nothing. I am blank, my insides echoing like an abandoned grain silo. Bats make their homes in me, the wind blows through my open doors. Georgia shoots Margey a look and Margey gives my hands one last squeeze and then drops them, turns her attention to the boy. He's rubbing his eyes. The dog is wagging his tail and greeting everyone.

"Are we here?" says the boy, looking up at me. "One of the villages in the north? Is that what this is?"

He and Georgia both wait for me to answer, and when I don't speak Georgia says, "We are here. This is a good place. We're safe."

After Georgia killed the Feldspar brother she rifled around in Jude's pockets until she found his keys and we fled the museum, drove into the desert for hours with the truck's headlights off, only the moon for light, until we found a faint dirt track that led into some hills where we were hidden and we stopped to make camp.

"How did you find me?" I asked Georgia, as we lay on my sleeping bag under the warm stars.

"I didn't know I was finding you," said Georgia. "When I snuck out of the city, it was in a transport truck full of prisoners. In the desert the truck was attacked by a band of rebels, and they set us all free—they told me about their cause, and I decided to join them. We were hunting one of the Feldspar brothers at that museum. I had no idea that you would be there too."

She wrapped her arms around me, squeezed me so tight it was painful. She smelled of woodsmoke and hair grease and I started to cry, fear and relief leaking out of me in waves. She kissed the tears as they fell down my cheeks.

I woke in the morning with the previous days' events clamoring in my brain and watched as Georgia assembled a small breakfast fire.

"I'm making us some cricket gruel for breakfast," she said. "Just like old times." I laughed. We ate the cricket gruel together, sitting on my sleeping bag passing the spoon back and forth while the desert warmed around us. After eating we lay back down, just held each other for as long as we could, until the sun was full beating down on us and the heat became intolerable.

"We should get going," said Georgia, sitting up on the sleeping bag. She began to tidy up, shoving things back into my backpack. She held up *The RVer's Guide to the American West*. "What's this?" she said, flipping through the pages. "Is this what you were using as a map?" she laughed a little, skimming the chapters about RV parks and the top RV-accessible sites.

"This is so funny. That there used to be all these places just for people to vacation. With water even!" She paused on a page. "You were writing in here," she said. "Keeping a journal?"

"Yeah," I said sleepily. "In the beginning I wrote letters to you."

Georgia began to read aloud but I wasn't really listening—I had my eyes closed and I was remembering the way her body felt against mine when I woke in the night and lay awake, looking up at the stars.

"When I close my eyes," read Georgia, "I can see the map of the medical ward's corridors in my head—if I were to walk out this door, take a right, pass through another door, walk down a flight of stairs and take a left, there'd be a series of doors that led outside, to a side parking lot. I could've found a way through these locked doors years ago. I could've arranged a pickup with someone on the outside, so that there was a car waiting for me. I could've bribed the underpaid guards to wait an hour before sounding the alarm.... But this is not that sort of plan."

She skipped farther forward in the RVer's guide, started reading again. "As the morning wears on and the long thread of highway unspools before me I find myself thinking about Bets, as I do every day, as I have ever since I was taken from her that cold morning so long ago. I've often asked myself if, once out of the prison, I should try and make my way back to the city, to find her. But although my prison record has been erased, I could easily be disappeared again for some other reason, at the first checkpoint I encountered. Entering the city would likely be the end for me. And then what could I do for Bets? Nothing."

Georgia went quiet but kept reading, flipping back and forth through the guide. After a time she turned and looked at me.

"Bets," she said. "What is this? Were you writing a story?"

"What? No, I don't know what you mean."

"Bets," said Georgia.

"Georgia," I said, mimicking her.

"Bets, you have to have known."

"No," I said. There was a rushing in my head, soft at first and then growing louder.

"Bets. Your mother is dead. You know that."

The feeling of cold water, first in my guts and then spreading throughout my body. The warmth of the sun was gone. The planet was spinning below me and I was rising, into the cold blackness of space.

"No," I said again.

"She was shot in her car while waiting for you in the park," Georgia is saying. "You found her body when you returned that day. I asked… a friend about this, in the city. Someone who could get information. That's what he told me. That you were the first one to find the body. Your screams attracted the police. They took your mother's body and the car, and they tried to take you too, but you ran away and hid somewhere."

"I hid in the tunnels," I said. A crack had opened in the universe. Beyond the crack was only blackness. I was being pulled toward the crack by a great force. This was it, this was the end. The final and most complete thing. I remembered Jude's blood yesterday, pooling on the tiled floor of the museum. I remembered my mother's blood, soaking the headrest. The way her hands were limp in her lap, an open packet of cigarettes on the seat next to her. Her eyes looking at nothing. My screams, growing louder and louder.

"You should eat," says Georgia now, in this cabin in this village. She scoops cold amaranth from a pot into a bowl, places the bowl in front of me. The cabin is one room, its old logs chinked with moss.

There's a table and benches, tallow candles glowing in glass jars, a bed heaped with wool blankets. Georgia opens the iron door to the woodstove and feeds a stove length into its orange insides, latches it shut again. She ladles water into a tea kettle and sets the tea kettle on the stove.

On our way north in Jude's truck we stopped at Nickeline's village and visited the boy and dog. They were both so happy to see me—the boy cried, said that I'd abandoned him. The dog wouldn't stop wriggling his whole body. I told the boy where I was headed with Georgia and he begged to come along. Jet and Jasper agreed that he could go, if only just to visit, as long as it was safe.

"It's safe," said Georgia.

He's in another cabin tonight, being tended to by Margey. The dog is on the bed in the nest of blankets, only his little nose poking out.

"Is she ok?" the boy asked Georgia on the drive, when I wouldn't talk, wouldn't answer his questions.

"She will be," said Georgia. "I think."

Now I pick up a spoonful of amaranth and place it in my mouth. The tiny grains pop like bubbles in my teeth. I spit the amaranth out, back into my bowl.

Georgia is watching me, her brow furrowed.

"I think you should join us," she says. "Join the rebels. Remember when we used to organize, back in the city? It's like that, only... more hopeful. Because we're free now. We have all this." She waves her arm, taking in the contents of the cabin.

"I'm too tired," I say. I try to eat another spoonful of amaranth, spit it back into the bowl. "I think I'll just stay here. Is there a garden? I'd like to garden."

"Yes of course there's a garden," says Georgia. "And animals. Whatever you need." She's still watching me, her eyes full of questions.

That night I lie awake while Georgia and the dog sleep beside me, under our mountain of quilts. At some late hour Georgia stirs and pulls me close to her in the dark.

"I'm leaving in the morning," she whispers. "I have to get back to the others."

"I figured," I say, "that you would go. It's ok. I don't belong to you anymore."

"I never wanted you to belong to me," she says, mumbling with sleep.

"I know," I say. "But I did. Not anymore, though. I belong to myself now." I feel her breath on the back of my neck.

"I'm happy for you. And when you get tired of tending your goats or whatever," she says, and we both laugh, "you should join us. I'm serious." I don't respond and eventually I feel her breathing become even and deep and I roll away, stare up at the dark logs of the ceiling.

CHAPTER 23

It's early morning in the village and I can smell the smoke of woodfires, people warming their cabins after another frosty night; the winter was bitter but it's spring now, and already the chill is less, the yellow light on the ridges more hopeful. I push open the gate to the pen where Margey keeps her burros and talk to them softly. They produce the most milk in the morning so I like to milk them first thing, before the sun comes up, before my other chores.

"Shhh," I whisper to Pansy, the younger one, and run my hand along her back. After this I'll take the kitchen scraps to the chickens and ducks and gather their eggs. And then the garden, where I'm building a new fence, and the seedlings need tending—it's much more relaxed gardening here than in the city, less pressure to get it all done before the day gets too hot and the water scalds the plants.

As I milk the burros I think about the note from my mother that mentioned burros, the note that Beryl gave to me. Even though the note was fake—Georgia told me that Beryl wrote it to try and convince me to leave the city, so that I would survive—it still lives in a place in my brain that feels real, as real as the idea of my mother wandering this desert in sandals made of car tires, a pack basket full of herbs on her back. As real as the actual memories; our sedan, the cold corn tortilla sandwiches, her cigarette-yellowed fingers on the steering wheel.

One metal pail is full of milk so I set it aside, grab another and move to the second burro. The traders came through yesterday, with their handcarts of cloth and nails and salt, their big, muscular pack dogs. I shut the dog in my cabin so he wouldn't try and pick a fight with one of their dogs and traded some burro cheese for these new milking pails. Or rather they're old pails, but new to me. The traders had a note for me, from Georgia. They often do. Her notes are always the same—where she's been and how she still thinks I should join her. Join the resistance. Join the rebels.

Oh my god, I finally got to see the Pacific Ocean, said one of the notes that arrived this winter. *I wish you were with me. You would've loved it. It was massive, bigger than you can even begin to imagine. Reassuring, all that space that's never been truly known by people. A reminder of how small we are, like staring up at the milky way.*

After reading yesterday's note I folded it and tucked it into The RVer's guide with the others and went back to my chores. There's enough work here to keep me busy, but it's not the kind of work that crushes a person, keeps them awake at night.

The peace I've experienced these last months is more solid than any I have ever known. I feel quiet inside, still like one of the small tarns we find in these high mountain passes. I even sleep pretty good, although sometimes I wake in the dark for no reason.

Lately, I've been talking to my mother. I built a little shrine in the ponderosa forest, spread my shawl on the pine needles and arranged things there that reminded me of her; a bowl of cricket gruel, some bluebells I found growing on the mountainside, my little tin can woodstove.

After finishing with the burros I put the milk in the barn to cool, wipe my hands on the skirt of my dress (a new dress, salvaged, dug from the bottom of one of the trader's handcarts, green cotton with little yellow flowers) and head to this shrine. I sit on the ground alongside it, lean my back against the wide trunk of a ponderosa. The bark smells like warm vanilla, and I can see sunlight dancing on my closed eyelids.

I'm thinking about my mother's prison break. Not the prison break I wrote about in the RVer's guide, but the real one—because, you see, I didn't make that part up. It was a story she told me a hundred times. There were two years when I was small when she wasn't there—it was just me and my father in the apartment. He'd give me bread and soy meat and I'd do my best to stay out of his way when he was home, hiding in my bedroom with my propaganda workbooks.

Then, one winter, mother was back; thin and dirty and tired, but crying with happiness. She held me on her lap, a blanket wrapped around both of us, and told me the story of what had happened; she'd been months behind on our car insurance payment, and she'd been pulled over; the cop said that she was being taken to a workhouse just for a few weeks, to pay off the debt, but once there she discovered that they meant to keep her forever.

She made friends in the workhouse and together they orchestrated a massive prison break; she told me about memorizing the shapes of the keys and replicating them in the machine shop, about stuffing bread in the door latch, about swiping a nurse's uniform and making a dummy of herself from her clothes and inflated plastic bags. And finally, about stealing the delivery truck and driving it straight through the fence and continuing to drive until she was within a day's walk from the city, at which point she ditched the truck and finished the journey on foot, under cover of night.

"And that is how I got back to you," she said, after she finished the story.

"But won't they come get you now?" I was terrified and I burrowed deeper into her lap, pulling the blanket tight around us.

"No honey. We burned all the records. The whole record room. I had to jump out of a second-story window to do it. Look." She showed me the tear in the side of the nurse's uniform she was wearing, the dried blood on the shirt. "There's no longer any record of me ever having been in that prison at all."

Yesterday after the traders came, I was skimming the note from Georgia that they gave me when my eyes caught on the words *Nickeline's village*. The boy was there now, helping Jet and Jasper plant corn in the dry riverbeds that would flood when the summer monsoons came. I closed my eyes then opened them again, forced myself to read the whole note slowly.

I think they're headed for Nickeline's village. We could really use some support.

The wind moves through the tops of the ponderosas and maybe I'm imagining it, but I swear I can feel the trunk move against my back. I look at the shrine I built for my mother, the rusted, fire-blackened old soup can and the wilted fistful of bluebells and the cricket gruel, now speckled with ants.

This morning I want to tell my mother that it's ok. That she doesn't have to solve the problem of the future. That no matter how precarious things felt back then, curled in our sedan while cold drizzle gathered on the windshield, there was no way to truly lose. That just by being alive, we'd already won. That there's nothing else to be gained. In fact, through all of human history, that's the most anyone has been given—this fleeting, brutal life, with its unrelenting pain, and still the sun keeps rising—there's no contest, nowhere to go, no other place but this.

I will myself to reach back through time and comfort my mother with these thoughts. That last morning with me in the park, as she put the corn tortillas in my backpack-

We've won, I want to tell her. *We've already won.*

Margey is in her cabin chopping up the last of the cabbage, dug from the sawdust in the cellar where it overwintered, into hunks for kraut. There's a head of garlic too and she pulls a few cloves off, smashes them under her knife. The dog is at her feet following her every move with his eyes, waiting for her to accidentally knock something edible off the counter.

"You got salt from the traders then?" I say.

"Yeah," she says. "They're always so happy for duck eggs." I watch her chop, the light from the window gathering on the cutting board and eventually she pauses, looking up at me. "Are you ok?" she says. "You look a little pale."

"I'm going away for a while," I say. "I don't know for how long."

Margey frowns.

"Don't say you're going to join Georgia? That you're putting yourself in danger like that?"

"Will you look after the dog?"

"Well of course I will," says Margey. "But Bets…"

"Thank you," I say, as I back out of the cabin. I turn and run towards my own, remembering all the times I ran in the city, in what feels like a hundred years ago. I find my backpack under the bed and throw a few things inside, not even sure what I'll need. Who is headed towards Nickeline's village? What kind of support is Georgia asking for?

I think of my mother yanking on the driver-side door of the prison supply truck. I imagine her lifting herself onto the warm vinyl seat, the pleasure she must've felt at finding the keys in the ignition. I imagine her slamming the door shut, the truck rumbling to life as she turned the key. Staring down the fence in front of her, putting her foot on the gas pedal. I bet she didn't hesitate. Not even for a second.

ACKNOWLEDGEMENTS

I first conceived of this story in fall of 2020, while camped in my van at a remote hotspring in northern Nevada. Since then there have been many, many drafts, and dozens of wonderful friends and beta readers have been kind enough to give me feedback on those drafts. I am beyond grateful to all of those wonderful readers, whose wise insight helped shape the story into what it is today. I am also bursting with gratitude for my editor, April Kelly, my cover designer Alejandra Wilson (who also designed the cover for *Thru-Hiking Will Break Your Heart*), and Euan Monaghan, the book's interior designer.

ABOUT THE AUTHOR

Carrot Quinn is the author of *Thru-Hiking Will Break Your Heart* and *The Sunset Route*.

WAIT, DON'T GO YET!

If you enjoyed this book, please consider leaving a review on the book's Amazon page. The more reviews this book has, the more visible it will become in Amazon's algorithms. Thank you!

Printed in Great Britain
by Amazon